To all our erring sisters, past and present, for their difficult yet honorable decision; to my husband, Scott, for his unwavering love and support, which has sustained me. To Simon Duffy, for his diligence and persistence in the difficult task of editing the manuscript. A sincere and heartfelt thank you to Shane Cashion and Tradeworks Publishing, for taking a chance on me and Our Erring Sisters. Last, but not least, an earnest thank you to family and friends who encouraged me, inspired me, and celebrate with me.

Our Erring Sisters

By

Carol Henwood

November, 2004

The chirping of my cell phone startled me. I answered it and the words, "I've found your son and he would like to meet you," stopped me in my tracks.

Chapter One

"Go on upstairs Ella, your father is ready to talk to you. He is waiting in his room and is expecting you. This conversation between you two has to happen now."

Given a choice, I would have opted for a cold, soapy enema rather than facing him under these dire circumstances. Judge Henry Cane, my Daddy, had been a judge for the last twelve years, and had recently accepted an appointment by the governor to serve on the highest court in the state. My timing couldn't have been worse. Della Cane, my mother, was still reeling from the recent confirmation that I was indeed pregnant. My father had received the shattering news concerning my condition earlier in the day. Mama had suspected for a month or two that I might be pregnant, but could not bring herself to believe it was possible. She made an appointment for me to see a gynecologist in town; I objected and told her that nothing was wrong with me, my cycles were just irregular. Mama's worst fears were confirmed, and the gig was up.

"How could you have been so reckless and allow yourself to get pregnant?" Mama demanded to know. Mama and Daddy had never approved of Lucas, or of our going steady. "Going steady, what a ridiculous notion that is." Equally as ridiculous, she insisted, was the way I so proudly wore his letter jacket, which hung down to my knees, and his class ring which I wore on my ring finger of my left hand, secured by rubber bands wrapped several times around its girth to keep the oversized ring safely on my hand.

"Oh, Lucas is certainly polite enough and, yes, he is tall and handsome, but he is not the type of boy we think you should be dating," was the mantra I constantly heard.

"It is understandable Ella, how you could be infatuated with him, but a serious relationship? Never! He isn't from the right kind of family and we know nothing about his parents, except that they

Our Erring Sisters by Carol Henwood

are not from Desota, are divorced, and all three children live with the father. There can be no stability or a sense of family under those conditions."

Lucas and I were from separate worlds, and my parents had no intention of allowing me to become a part of his.

"I knew we should have forbidden you from seeing him months and months ago. If we had maybe we wouldn't be where we are today. But, here we are and you have to face the music and talk to your father to decide what is to be done about this dreadful mess," Mama sternly stated as she busied herself rearranging the items on my dressing table.

"I know I do," I pitifully offered, trying to postpone for another few minutes the dreaded confrontation with Daddy. "What is he going to say to me? Is he really angry and going to yell and get all red in the face and maybe have a heart attack, or what?" I nervously asked, like the young, frightened girl I was.

"How do you think he feels, Ella? He is dumfounded! As if the alarming fact that his 18-year-old daughter is pregnant isn't bad enough, there is the embarrassment and humiliation this news will cause our family if it gets out. Your father is heartbroken and sad, as am I, but he loves you very much and wants to do the best thing for you and for this family. Now stop stalling and go on upstairs, you have much to talk about." Mama turned and walked out of my bedroom, indicating the conversation was over. I stood up and walked over to my dressing table, looked at myself in the mirror and brushed my hair, as if it would make any difference. "My life's a mess, what difference does it make if my hair's a mess, too?" Studying my reflection in the mirror, I said out loud, "I don't look any different," contemplating some subtle change in my features. I was aware of the fact that I was considered to be a pretty girl, and I enjoyed the attention it garnered. I have large blue eyes and long eyelashes (my best feature), sandy blonde hair, and a little nose, slightly pug (my least favorite feature). I stood five feet five inches tall with a slender frame. None of those attributes could get me out of the fix I was in now. I half-way expected some obvious mark to appear on my face and reveal to the world that I was an

Our Erring Sisters by Carol Henwood

unmarried, pregnant teenage girl. Possibly a large letter P would materialize on my forehead, announcing my condition, much like Hawthorne's Hester Prynne from *The Scarlett Letter*, who was made to wear the letter A sewn onto her clothing, announcing her adultery to one and all. Stalling as long as I could without being summoned by my mother, I adjusted my blouse which was loose and covered my still small but growing tummy. "Okay," I said to the reflection in the mirror, "let's get this over with." Giving my blossoming belly a gentle pat, I started on the longest walk of my life. I knocked softly on the door, hoping there would be no answer and I could scurry away undetected, like an errant mouse. No such luck.

"Come in," Daddy said in his rich baritone voice, which didn't sound as strong to me as it usually did. He was a barrel-chested man, standing five feet ten inches tall, but appeared taller, possibly because of his personality, which was enormous. Strikingly handsome with tanned skin from hours on the golf course, and thick, wavy, silver hair combed straight back, he was the epitome of a Southern judge. Central casting in Hollywood couldn't have picked a more perfect man; he just looked the part. Hesitantly opening the door to his combination bedroom/study, I found him sitting on the sofa shuffling some papers, looking older than he did yesterday. Was that possible? Yesterday his life was going along just fine, as far as he knew, then Mama revealed the terrible news to him. Not wanting to make eye contact, I kept my eyes averted, looking anywhere but at him.

"Have a seat, Ella," he indicated patting a cushion on the large sofa where he was sitting. Daddy had the look of a man who was all alone in the world, a man who had just found out his youngest teenage daughter was pregnant, and he couldn't undo it. I was frightened to see him like this, and to know I was the cause of it. Always a confident and take charge man who was able to solve problems with ease, this was one problem that couldn't be fixed with a phone call. I tried to avoid looking at him, instead staring at my hands which were placed in my lap as if I was attending an afternoon tea party.

3

Our Erring Sisters by Carol Henwood

"Your mother has given me the shocking news that you are pregnant. I am astounded that you allowed this to happen, not to mention the fact that you engaged in intimate relations with this boy. Of course, we are not stupid and know these things can and do happen, but to other people, not to those who were raised properly and should know better. Well, Ella, what do you have to say about all of this? This is a devastating state of affairs for this family and we need to make some serious decisions right now."

The fact that my parents knew I was pregnant was bad enough, but the realization that they knew I had engaged in sex was worse. The images that must be flashing on and off in their minds had to be like a scene from a bad movie. Lucas and me in the front or back seat of a car with the windows fogged up, both of us in a state of partial undress, fumbling and contorting ourselves into a position where we could successfully get it done, which wasn't easy for Lucas who was way over six feet tall. My face grew red with embarrassment just pondering what they were imagining.

"Ella, look at me, now is not the time to be coy. Your mother says you are four months pregnant. Why in God's name didn't you tell us sooner? What in the hell were you thinking, that nobody would notice, that it would just go away? You know we never wanted you to date Lucas Slade exclusively. He is not the type of young man we think you should be seeing on a regular basis. But, you insisted on having things your way and continued down that path and here you are now. According to your mother, you haven't told Lucas about this. Is that true?" The former prosecutor was taking over as Daddy started his cross examination of me. Twisting and shifting around uncomfortably, I finally looked at him sheepishly. "No, I haven't told Lucas yet. I have been trying to figure out by myself what to do, and ......"

"You figure out what to do?" he bellowed louder than I think he had intended to, his anger surfacing. "Your disgraceful behavior and ill-considered decisions thus far have landed this family in an impossible predicament, Ella Louise. Spare me any of your valuable advice and well thought out solutions." It is often said that children would prefer to have a parent yell and scream at them

Our Erring Sisters by Carol Henwood

rather than say they are disappointed or saddened by a particular behavior. Not so in my case. At least disappointment and sadness are quiet emotions.

Regaining his composure, my father steeled himself and asked, "Do you want to marry this boy, Ella?" Not expecting the question, I was taken aback, hemming and hawing unable to put together a coherent sentence. I knew what I wanted to say and do, but could not muster up the courage to fight for my position. There were others to consider here, not just me, probably least of all me. The next utterance out of my mouth would chart the course of my life and affect the lives of two families, not to mention the unborn baby. The romantic idea I harbored of life with Lucas and our baby would have to be put aside for the harsh reality of what would be best for everyone. The fact that Lucas and I were in love was irrelevant. I believed he would have been more than willing to marry me, leave college, forfeit his basketball scholarship, if necessary, and get a job to support his family. But he would never have the option of making that choice. There is a misconception put forth by some experts that teenagers cannot experience true love. In fact, teenage love may be more pure, deep and powerful than that of those who are older and more experienced. No matter, we would not have the opportunity to prove that to anyone.

"Ella, do you want to marry this boy?"

"No, no, I can't. I'll do whatever you want me to Daddy, I got myself into this mess and I'll do whatever you say. Lucas doesn't suspect anything and I won't tell him," I said in a voice a little too loud. "He doesn't get to come home much because he doesn't have a car, and it's the middle of basketball season, too. I'll just tell him I want to break up since we never see each other anyway. He doesn't have to know," I added in a defeated voice.

Daddy stood up and rubbed his hands together, with a noticeable look of relief on his face. "That's the conclusion I was hoping you would come to. I have many friends, Ella, and I have made some calls and have been informed that there is a facility in Atlanta where unmarried, pregnant girls who want to keep their condition a secret go and live for the duration of their

Our Erring Sisters by Carol Henwood

pregnancies. It is not free, however. For those who have resources payment is expected. But, this is the road we must take and I have been assured this place is reputable and your identity will be protected. Privacy is of the utmost importance in this matter. No one need know about this, Ella. We can tell everyone that you are a counselor at a summer camp in North Carolina. It is a believable story. They do not have a space available until late June, so you will have to stay here at home until then, and try and keep out of view of the neighbors. Your brother does not know about this situation, and we want to keep it that way. We will tell him when we think the time is right."

Sighing, I thought how Tarleton, my younger brother, would react when he found out. It could be very difficult for him being in high school and having to answer questions concerning the whereabouts of his sister. We had always been close and this would be hard for him.

"Emily Anne already knows. Your mother shared her suspicions with her and she has been a comfort to Della." I had an inkling that my sister knew, although she had never confronted me about it, but then she was away at school, enjoying college life, and we didn't see other unless she came home for a weekend.

"It would kill your grandmother if she heard of this, so this business must not be discussed at all."

Mimi, my mother's mother, was the dearest, sweetest woman in the entire world. She had raised four children by herself, being widowed at twenty-nine years old. My father said she was the most amazing, Godly woman he'd ever met. Mimi must never know. I did not want to be the cause of any more sorrow in her life.

As Daddy was arranging my life for me and describing Emmeriah Parrish Home for Unwed Mothers in detail, as had been reported to him by one of his investigators, I sat motionless. I mentally removed myself from the surroundings and from the tedious and frightening commentary. I stared out the bedroom window, watching a large oak tree, its branches buffeted by a gusty wind, rhythmically pounding the window, not hearing a word that was spoken. Instead of listening, I recalled the memory of the last

Our Erring Sisters by Carol Henwood

time Lucas and I were together, holding hands as we sat on a park bench waiting for his ride back to school to come and pick him up. Prurient thoughts of Lucas filled my mind and made me want to be with him more than ever. I remembered every word we had spoken to each other that day, not realizing it would be the last time we would be together, or be happy. The afternoon had quickly turned dark and gray with a steady rain falling, matching the somber mood within the room and in my heart.

I stayed for what seemed like hours in my father's room, listening to, and mindlessly agreeing with him on the details of the next few months of my life. I knew my parents' intentions were good; they only wanted to do what they considered best for everyone involved, and my marrying Lucas Slade was not an option to them. So, I agreed to go into confinement in another town, have the baby alone with no family near, and give our child up for adoption, without ever telling Lucas about any of it. Everything would be neat, clean and hushed up. I was feeling sorry for myself and wallowing in self pity. I knew I had no right to protest or indulge in those useless emotions, since I had brought this upon myself. My insistence upon a marriage between Lucas and myself would have been met with obstacles, too many to overcome, my protestations dismissed. Therefore, I would do what was necessary, and a phone call to Lucas was the dreaded next step.

Chapter Two

June, 1966

The first time Lucas Slade asked me out was in the fall of my senior year in high school. I had become aware of him the summer before while we both spent mornings at the high school, he at basketball camp, and me at cheerleading practice. He had a girlfriend then and I was dating Clay Bishop who attended a rival high school. There was just something about Lucas that was captivating and kept my interest peaked. I had never talked to him at school, I only noticed him, because he was hard to miss. He stood six foot five inches tall, the epitome of tall, dark and handsome, always laughing, smiling and joking with his friends in the hall between classes. He appeared carefree and happy. He didn't know I existed, but I had him in my sights. By the time school started in the fall, I was not involved with Clay Bishop anymore, thank goodness. I'd had enough of boys who were in love with their cars, washing them, racing them and talking about them constantly, as well as the preppy boys from the private boys' school in town. They were uninteresting. Lucas was different from both groups. He no longer had a girlfriend either, so I thought maybe he would notice me and ask me out. He did. We started dating, and soon we were going steady. I was in love for the first time ever and I was as happy as I could be. My parents were anything but. They hoped Lucas was a temporary and minor distraction for me and I would discard him shortly. They were wrong.

After months of pondering the burning question as to whether or not I should have sex with Lucas, and I mean everything on the menu kind of sex, I finally made a decision. Tonight I was going to give myself fully, completely and willingly to him. I had already graduated from high school and tomorrow we parted ways to attend different colleges. Lucas was always patient, never pushy or insisting that I do the sexual things I'd only read about in the

Our Erring Sisters by Carol Henwood

occasional trashy paperbacks that my friends were passing around, or snippets of conversations overheard from some of the more experienced girls in school whose reputations always preceded them. I thought I was probably the only eighteen year old virgin in town, and I'd waited long enough. Eighteen was considered to be a grown woman, even though I didn't feel grown up in many ways. I only knew what my body was craving each time I was near Lucas and by God, it was time.

"Ella, I don't want you staying out late tonight. We have to get an early start for Athens tomorrow to get you checked into your dorm, find out your class schedule, and everything else that's got to be handled." Della Cane didn't want Ella going out on a date tonight with Lucas Slade at all. She was so worried that they were already having sex, and if they weren't yet, they would now.

"Mama, I've got to see Lucas tonight. We won't see each other for almost two months, with me being in Athens and him at Batesville State in Alabama, and especially since he doesn't have a car to come see me. It's our last chance," I sighed as I finished applying my favorite pink lipstick and spraying a little Youth Dew on my wrists and base of my neck.

"Thank God for small favors," Della said under her breath. "I see there is a new movie playing at the Desota, why don't you two go get something to eat, see an early movie and come on home after that? There will plenty of time for you to see each other in the fall," Della said, promoting a public place where they would have little opportunity to have physical contact, but she knew her plan was doomed, they would find a way regardless.

"On the marquee it says that *A Man for All Seasons* is playing, but I don't want to see that, and I doubt Lucas does either, but maybe. We'll see," I answered, knowing we were going to the drive-in and didn't care what was playing. It would be dark and just the two of us together in the car. But, if not there, we would go to our favorite parking place. I was excited and nervous at the same time, the anticipation of what was going to happen tonight made me giddy. I have a limited knowledge of all the mysterious mechanics of actually having sexual intercourse. Lucas and I have engaged in heavy petting, but we always stop just in time before surrendering and "going all the way." The last time we parked and were touching and kissing and exploring each other bodies, getting more and more excited, Lucas asked me to put my mouth on his erect penis, which was trying to push its way out of his jeans. Truth be told, I had never seen a penis. I've never seen my father or brother naked, and the only idea I had of what one looked like was from pictures in medical books, or from a coffee table book in our living room showing great works of art, sculptures being included, and the most famous being the exquisite sculpture of David by Michelangelo. So, when Lucas gently pushed my head down on his emancipated penis, I wasn't exactly sure what I was supposed to do, and just stayed there, not moving. I felt inadequate and clumsy. Lucas was gentle and coaxed me along. I didn't flinch, and pretty soon, I took over and was eagerly enjoying the new experience. The phallus at rest is one thing, but one that is fully engorged and at strict attention is an impressive sight. Other than the initial sense of gagging, I thought this was something I could become proficient at, and I was ready to find out what else lay ahead in my erotic journey.

Della saw Lucas pull into the driveway and she felt the situation was out of her control now, if it had ever been in her hands at all. Della wanted so to dislike Lucas, but she couldn't. He certainly was not what she and Henry had in mind as a suitable match for their daughter, but he was polite, pleasant and handsome, but lacked any credentials that were essential, in their minds, to be acceptable.

"Hello, Mrs. Cane." Lucas said smiling as Della opened the front door.

"Come on in Lucas, Ella shouldn't be but a few minutes." They went into the living room and sat down to wait for Ella to emerge from her room.

"I'm sure you're excited about leaving tomorrow for college," Della said, trying to make conversation and keep her mind's eye from glimpsing the things Ella and Lucas probably would be doing later. She shivered slightly and stood up, turning to Lucas. "Can I get you a Coke or something, Lucas? You know how

Our Erring Sisters by Carol Henwood

Ella is. Everything has to look just so before she will leave the house."

"No thank you ma'am. Ella always looks perfect to me anyhow. I am looking forward to school, and playing ball especially, but I have to keep my grades up to keep my scholarship, so I'll really have to be disciplined, but I think I can do it."

"I'm confident you can, Lucas. You appear to be a focused young man, and I know it must be difficult with all the responsibilities you have between home, school and work," said Della with the intention of emphasizing where his focus needed to be, and it wasn't on her daughter.

"Oh, here she is now," Della exclaimed as she saw Ella walk into the room, her eyes glowing, as she smiled sweetly, almost innocently, at Lucas.

Della examined the clothes that her daughter had chosen to wear tonight. She had changed clothes since Della had left her room. At once she began going through a scenario where Ella was taking her clothes off, and the dress she had changed into would be easy to get out of.

"Why did you change clothes, Ella? I love that skirt and blouse you had on earlier. Why did you change?" Della insisted on asking, thinking the blouse, which had many small buttons, would be too much trouble to take off.

"I just felt like wearing this sun dress tonight. It's warm out and besides, it shows off my suntan," I answered as I smoothed the material on my white dress, which showed more skin than Mama liked.

Forcing a smile, Della looked up at Lucas as she patted Ella on her bare shoulder. "Okay, you two, run on now and try and make an early evening of it. You both have a busy day tomorrow. Best of luck to you, Lucas, I know you will excel at Batesville, and hopefully, we'll see you around Thanksgiving," she said as she closed the door behind them and leaned back against it, and closed her eyes, feeling as if she had just turned her daughter over to the big, bad wolf.

Our Erring Sisters by Carol Henwood

"You sure look handsome tonight, Lucas," I said, grabbing his hand as we walked to the car.

"Thanks, Ella, I like that dress. You look real nice tonight, too" Lucas replied as he gave me the complete once over.

"It is our last night together until I don't know when, so I wanted to look my best. It makes me sick to know that we won't see each other for a while," I said.

"We can't start to worry about that now. I'll figure something out. I got into a big argument with Dad about taking the car tonight. I told him it wasn't right that you had to ask your parents all the time if we could use one of their cars for a date. I ended up having to beg him for it, and he still almost didn't let me have it. He had a date with some old floozy tonight who agreed to come pick him up. I told him this was the last time we would see each other for a while, so with some help from Miles, he gave in. It's tough not having my own transportation, but that's just the way it is," Lucas said as he opened my door.

"Your brother always supports you, doesn't he, Lucas?" I asked as we were backing out of my driveway.

"We look out for each other, but Miles knows he's the favorite son and if he can help me out, he does."

"Okay, Ella Lou, what is it we're doing on our last night?" Lucas asked as he turned to me.

"I thought we'd go get a hamburger at Hardee's or the Dairy Queen, and then go to the drive-in when it's dark enough, and see *The Russians Are Coming, The Russians are Coming*. I've heard it's really funny," I said, knowing I wouldn't watch five minutes of the movie.

Smiling at me Lucas turned the radio on and said, "Good choice, Ella," and we drove down Broad Street headed to Hardee's.

By the time we got to the drive-in it was already filling up. Everybody wanted to park as far in the back as they could and there were just a few secluded places left. We found a good one on the end. We parked the car, and Lucas reached out and got the speaker and hung it on the window.

"Do you want popcorn or a coke, Ella?" Lucas asked.

Our Erring Sisters by Carol Henwood

"No thanks, I'm plenty full from the hamburger and milkshake."

"I don't know how you're full, you hardly ate any of it, forcing me to finish it for you," Lucas replied laughing and playfully hitting her shoulder.

"Well, I have to watch my waist line. A girl can't be too thin or too rich, you know," I said immediately regretting the flippant comment, especially the part about too rich.

"I sure wouldn't know about being rich, but I know I like to eat."

"That's just something a silly woman said in a magazine, Lucas. I don't care about being rich at all, you know that," I said as I snuggled closer to him.

The movie screen came alive as darkness enveloped us. We watched the movie for a while, and it was a funny story. I would have to watch enough of the movie to be able to tell my mother something about it when I got home. Soon, Lucas started massaging my neck, which I loved. He had such strong hands I told him he could have been a professional masseuse. He stopped and took my chin in his hands, and leaned down to kiss me. We gently kissed, then passion overtook us as we were kissing, touching, and panting, the way we normally did. I stopped abruptly and looked at Lucas.

"Lucas, I want you to make love to me tonight. It's been hard for us to wait this long. We've been so good not to give in to each other, but I'm tired of waiting and I know it must be torture for you to get so close to actually, you know, and then have to stop. You have a lot of experience in this department, and I don't, but I'm ready and tonight's the night, so let's do it," I declared, sounding like a football coach giving a pep talk to his losing team at halftime.

Lucas pushed himself up to a sitting position, wiped his brow, and pulled his unbuttoned shirt together.

"Ella, you know I would never insist on going any further than you want, so don't worry about me, I'm just fine with it," Lucas insisted, half-heartedly.

"Lucas, you've always treated me with respect, but I'm telling you, I want us to make love tonight. Now is the right time, I know it, so don't tell me no," I insisted like a child who wanted something and her parents explained all the logical reasons why she couldn't have it.

"Ella, are you positive about this, because if ….."

"Shhh," I whispered as I held my finger to his lips. I lifted myself up and put my hands under my sundress and slipped off the new bikini panties I had bought today, just for this auspicious occasion.

Lucas watched, almost reverently, as I showed the panties to him then let them drop unceremoniously on the floorboard. I continued the striptease, shedding my strapless bra and casting it away to join the panties on the floor. By this time, Lucas couldn't say a word he was so mesmerized.

I never took my eyes off of Lucas as I reached back and finished unzipping my sundress and slid it off under me and kicked it away.

"Well, here I am Lucas," I said as I spread my arms wide for him to take my nakedness in.

"You're not going to refuse me now, are you? I said I was ready and I meant it, and from what I can see, you are too," I said playfully, as I placed my hand on Lucas's bulging jeans.

"Ella, you know I've wanted to make love to you since the first time I laid eyes on you, and it would be the height of rudeness for me not to grant you your wish, 'specially since your sitting next to me buck naked and I'm about to die," Lucas said as he pulled her over to him. Ella's wish came true that summer night. Lucas and Ella would not be able to share their newly found intimacy again until Thanksgiving. Their wondrous journey of discovery and passion brought with it trials and troubles Ella had never bargained for.

Our Erring Sisters by Carol Henwood

Chapter Three

"Slade, phone's for you," Bobby Meadows yelled to Lucas from the hall phone in the athletic dormitory at Batesville State University. "It's Wednesday night, so it must be your honey," he joked as they passed in the hall, Lucas popping Bobby with a towel.

"Hey, El, you're about thirty minutes early tonight aren't you, baby?" Lucas affectionately asked as he toweled himself off. "I just got out of the shower, so let me get dry and then we can have our little chat."

I listened to the sound of him toweling off and pictured him standing there in the hall, naked, wet and glistening, all six foot five inches of his well-toned berry brown body, his Indian ancestry evident in his coloring.

"Ella, are you there?" Submersed in my visualization, I didn't hear Lucas and was jolted back into the moment. "I was gonna go over to the library after talking to you and work on some damn paper I've been putting off for my U.S. history class."

The enormity of the lie I was about to tell caused a gut-wrenching pain in my stomach, and made breathing difficult. I was about to spin a yarn worthy of Mark Twain and I didn't want to do it. I wanted to tell Lucas the truth; I was pregnant with his child and wanted to marry him if he would have me. But, instead I was going to give him a list of reasons why we should break up and date other people, the main one being we never get to see each other, and any other lame reason I could think of. After I presented my unconvincing case, there was a stunned silence.

"Ella, where in the hell did all of this come from? What did I do, or not do?" Lucas insisted in a stern tone I rarely heard from him.

Our Erring Sisters by Carol Henwood

"Wait, it's all a lie, I just made it up," I almost shouted out, but I didn't. "Lucas, let's just give it a chance. It will be a true test of our love, won't it?"

"Something's not making sense here," Lucas said sounding confused and anxious. "Everything was fine the last time I was home, and the last time we talked, which was just last Saturday night. I know you haven't found someone new in the last four days, Ella, so what's the real reason?"

"Honest, Lucas, I just think we should take a break for a while. You know, my grades at Desota Community have been really awful for the last couple of months, and I need to concentrate on pulling them up, or I'll never be able to get into a real college. I haven't been studying like I should, I'm always thinking about you, when we can be together, and ...,"

"Wait a minute. Is this coming from your parents? I get that they don't think I'm good enough for you, but that's something we can change. I just have to prove to them that I am the right man for you, if they'll just give me a chance."

My heart was breaking, but I continued down liar's lane. "When you think about it, Lucas, we are both pretty young and maybe we should see what else is out there. If we still feel the same about each other after a year or so, we can get back together." Words I never thought I would say came forth almost effortlessly. I was trying to convince myself as well as Lucas. Bracing myself for his response, I closed my eyes so tightly I saw fireworks.

"Ella," he spoke in a calm and gentle voice, "some folks might think we're young, but I'm twenty years old and I've lived a lot in those years. I've pretty much raised myself, as well as Miles and Rennie, and you know that. I wasn't brought up like you; I wish I had been. We've been together for almost a year and a half and never once talked about dating other people. I know what I want, and it's you, I thought that's what you wanted, too. I'm sorry I can't get home every weekend, but I can't, it's not possible. You always seemed to understand that. I've hitch-hiked home many times just so we could spend a few hours together, so if you're testing me to

Our Erring Sisters by Carol Henwood

see if I say I want to date around, the answer is no, I don't. I hope that's what you're doing, because if it's not, you're not the Ella Cane I know and love. That girl wouldn't have said what you just did, unless she was forced to. Tell me, Ella, what's really going on here?"

I was sitting on the bed in my room squeezing a pillow to my chest, wanting to scream at the top of my lungs, but I kept spinning the tale. "Well, it's sort of my parents' idea, but I think it's something we need to do. You know I love you, Lucas, and I think this may be the smart thing for right now. You've got your grades to keep up, too, so you can hold on to your scholarship. I'm probably a huge distraction for you, always asking you to come home and to call me on the phone three times a week, which is expensive, and I know you don't have much money. I'm probably keeping you from studying as much as you should, too," I was rambling now and I just wanted to say anything to make my story sound legitimate, without much success.

"Stop it, Ella, just be quiet. I don't believe you, but if your hell bent on this I will concede defeat, for now. I can't believe this is happening, but I know when I'm out-numbered. I'll go along with this, but I don't want to hear about anyone you're going out with – ever. I love you now, and I'll love you in ten years, time won't change anything. Take care of yourself, Ella. Call me if you need me, I've got to go now."

Click, the line went dead. I stared at the receiver not wanting to believe Lucas had hung up and was gone from my life because I told him he had to go, and I never even said good-bye. He was gracious in his grief, never saying a hurtful word to me after I had inflicted such pain on him. I'd heard the anguish in his voice and, once again, I had been the deliverer of heartache in another person's life, and each time it was someone so dear to me. I was waiting to experience an overwhelming sense of relief, or at least to feel a bit self-righteous, knowing I had done the right thing for all concerned, and that good deeds should be their own reward, but I didn't feel relieved, I felt anger. I was angry at myself for being a gutless wonder, and at my parents for not considering how Lucas and I might feel, or what we may want. But they didn't care. It was

Our Erring Sisters by Carol Henwood

all about keeping it a secret so our family wouldn't be disgraced and humiliated because of my trailer trash behavior. In the final analysis, I agreed to go along with whatever they decided, I'd had a chance to fight for what I wanted, but I didn't, I caved. The wheels are in motion so hold on, Ella, you silly, spineless girl. This train is pulling out of the station, and you're the only one on board.

The next day turned into the next week, and then the next month. I was already under house arrest, with no one to talk to or share my terrible secret with, or even seek comfort from. I felt like a pariah in my own home, someone to be avoided, but I tried my best to please and demonstrate my gratitude to my parents for supporting me in this very difficult time. I was lost without Lucas and had picked up the telephone to call him and spill the beans on more than one occasion. I had been warned, "don't ever tell Lucas about this business, he does not need to be involved." I continued spring classes at the community college and managed to hide my condition successfully. I was small anyway, so no one noticed anything, plus I didn't socialize with any of the students there. Unlike me, most of my friends had gone away to college. My grades in high school were not good enough to get in to the state university, so I attended college at Desota Community College in hopes of pulling up my average and transferring. I enjoyed English literature and history and did well in those subjects, but despised math, I was terrified of it and had the poor grades to prove it. I was unable to concentrate or focus on anything other than my current state of affairs and what was going to happen. As a result of my poor study habits and skipping class to boot, my status at the community college was now in jeopardy.

Before I knew it, Easter break was here and my good friends were all home from college. They called and wanted to come over and visit, and I was thrilled at the possibility of seeing them. When I told Mama, I thought she was going to jump out of her skin.

"Ella, call them and tell them they can't come. Tell them you forgot you had a dentist appointment, or tell them anything, just don't let them come over here."

Our Erring Sisters by Carol Henwood

I was fully loaded with extra hormones now and I was on an emotional roller coaster. "No, I want to see my friends; I want to see somebody, anybody. I'm sick of hiding every time the door bell rings. They won't notice a thing, I'll make sure. I want to talk to a person my own age, and you're not going to stop me," I yelled as I flicked tears of anger and frustration from my cheeks.

I ran out of the kitchen and into my room where I rummaged through my closet and found a blouse and a pair of pants that still fit and didn't reveal my expanding middle. It was a navy blue and white striped blouse that was cut full and hid any suspicious bulge, and a pair of jeans that wouldn't button at the waist, but my friends would be unaware of it. I concluded that I was sufficiently camouflaged for a visit, and might make a joke about putting on extra weight since I lived at home and not in a dorm, and I ate well and didn't have the exciting, busy life they enjoyed living on a college campus. That was a plausible argument for any extra pounds.

Ginny Myers, Sue Ellen Smith and Luanna Lindsey were my best friends from high school. We had been cheerleaders together and shared most all of our deepest secrets with each other. Ginny had gone away to an all girls' school in Virginia, Sue Ellen to the University of North Carolina, and Luanna had stayed in Georgia, attending the state university. She decided to go to college with Billy Reeves, her long time sweetheart. Why Luanna wasn't the one who was pregnant was a mystery to me. She used to brag about, and describe in great detail, all of the sex she and Billy were having. Most of us had never "gone all the way," so this was uncharted territory and both exciting and frightening to us. Well, she didn't get pregnant, I did, and this was one secret I was not going to be able to share.

Mama was pacing around the house looking out of every window like we were bootleggers and expecting a raid by the Feds any minute, instead of a visit from my friends. She agreed that my clothes didn't reveal anything, so maybe my condition would go unnoticed.

Our Erring Sisters by Carol Henwood

"Ella, tell the girls you and Lucas broke up and you are doing just fine, that he wasn't right for you anyway, and you're looking forward to being a camp counselor in North Carolina this summer. Keep the conversation away from Lucas as much as possible." Having heard all I could stand, I flippantly told Mama I would act natural and carefree in an attempt to hone my skills as an accomplished liar. She didn't like that comment.

"Well, you know that Ginny Myers has the biggest mouth in Desota, just like her mother, and she would probably love to get a rumor started about you being pregnant, just for spite since you beat her out for homecoming queen your senior year."

"Oh, pleeze Mama, Ginny and I are best friends and she would never start a rumor about me, plus, she could care less about being homecoming queen. Big deal! She would stand up to anyone who said one mean word about me, and so would Sue Ellen and Luanna." It was true we were best friends, which made this so much harder. If I ever needed someone to talk to, it was now. Ginny and Sue Ellen would be sad for me, cry and carry on about the unfairness of it all. Luanna would casually say, "you and Lucas should just run away and get married, that's what I would do. Parents don't always know what's best." And she would have done just that. Luanna had more courage and determination than any girl I knew. Nothing seemed to scare her. I could use some of her determination and courage about now.

I heard a car pulling down our driveway and looked out of the living room window to see Sue Ellen's car, a bright, shiny red mustang convertible. I observed them extinguishing their cigarettes before piling out of the car, joking and laughing as they walked up the sidewalk to the front door.

"Oh, my stars, they're here," Mama nervously shrilled as she cast a sidelong glance at me to assure herself that I didn't look obviously pregnant. "Remember what I said, Ella. No talk about Lucas Slade, just keep the conversation moving along, talk about anything but him."

I resented the way Mama referred to Lucas as some insignificant peon who was unworthy of my mentioning his name in

Our Erring Sisters by Carol Henwood

polite company. "Well, that's about the most ridiculous thing I've ever heard. Lucas will be the very first thing they want to ask me about, so I will have to talk about him. It would be more suspicious if I didn't." The doorbell rang and Mama shrieked, "Oh, no!" I started toward the front door, and made a detour to take a last look at myself in the hall mirror, was satisfied, and I shooed Mama into the kitchen to get some refreshments for us, just to get her out of the way. I opened the door to greet my best friends, knowing I was going to perpetuate my perfidious story and I felt disloyal for including them in my web of lies. They descended on me with open arms, and I embraced them all, holding their hands and hugging them, all to the sounds of shrieks and laughter.

"Ella Lou, it's so good to see you, girl," Ginny screamed. "It feels like it's been years, not months." We continued to stand at the front door laughing and talking over each other, and getting louder and louder.

"Come on in ya'll before the neighbors call the police on us for a public disturbance." I closed the front door and we continued chattering and went into the living room where everyone found a seat and plopped down.

"You got your hair cut and the color changed, didn't you Luanna?" I asked, as her naturally long, light blonde hair was now short and a bright copper color. "It looks fabulous! Does Billy like it?"

"Thanks, El. I just needed a change; I was tired of the same ole do." Leaning in and curving her finger for us to lean in close, she whispered, "Billy loves it, matter of fact, he's the one that wanted me to change it. It makes him feel like he's with another girl, without actually being with someone else, if you know what I mean," Luanna smiled provocatively as she winked at us.

"Good God, Luanna, is sex all you ever think about?" Sue Ellen chimed in. Her all American girl next door looks, freckles and all, made her appear more innocent than she actually was.

"Ella, she has been going on and on about things we have no business hearing. Really, Luanna, not everybody is interested in your sex life!" Sue Ellen said smiling sheepishly.

Our Erring Sisters by Carol Henwood

"Well, at least I have one, Sue Ellen, and it's not like you couldn't have any boy in the state of North Carolina you wanted. You're too prim and proper when it comes to interacting with the opposite sex. You need to lighten up a little, and lose some of those Victorian values your mama instilled in you, and you know it; we've had this conversation before. Listen to your old friend and love master, Luanna."

"Honestly, Luanna, you are shameful!" Ginny added as she gently poked Luanna's shoulder.

"Oh, don't give me your holier than thou shit, Ginny Myers. Everybody knows you and Clay Bethea were getting it on last summer, so don't act like butter wouldn't melt in your mouth." Luanna had an uncanny ability to know things about other people's lives, and that made me slightly nervous.

"I don't have any idea what you're talking about. You know perfectly well that I went out with several different boys last summer, and Clay was just one of many. He was always a perfect gentleman." With a puzzled look on her face, Ginny asked, "How did you know that anyway? You are amazing, Luanna; I'm glad you're my friend and not my enemy."

Pulling out a pack of cigarettes from her purse with a self-satisfied expression on her face, Luanna stood up and sashayed toward the dining room door, just close enough so she could see into the kitchen. "Ella, let's get down to business. What's the story with you and that hunk of a man, Lucas?" This was asked quietly as Mama was in the kitchen with the swinging door slightly ajar, just enough so she could pick up any tidbits that might interest her.

"Will Miss Della mind if I light up? We are grown up women now, you know, sexually liberated and everything. Hell, she knows we all smoke anyway, we sure left enough butts in her car ashtray last summer."

I remembered our last summer together, cruising around at night in Mama's 1955 Cadillac we aptly named the Gray Grunt, due to its color and propensity for breaking down. We'd ride around town looking for boys, talking about boys, and sharing our inner most thoughts and feelings with each other, all the while smoking as

Our Erring Sisters by Carol Henwood

much as we could in the span of three hours. Those were the last crazy, lazy days of summer before everyone left for college. That was the direction I tried to guide the conversation.

Ginny sighed and sat back with her eyes closed. "Gosh, we had such fun. I can't believe that part of our lives is over with. We had no idea how lucky we were, with no real responsibilities, just enjoying life. I wish we could go back, don't ya'll?" My success was brief.

"Okay, Ella, is it true, did you and Lucas break up?" Luanna insisted as she tilted her head back and blew smoke in the air. I took a deep breath and started to give them the approved version of the fairy tale when Mama pushed open the kitchen door, and walked through the dining room and into the living room, carrying a tray full of little sandwiches, cookies and a pitcher of lemonade. Ginny, Luanna and Sue Ellen all jumped to their feet and gave a group hug to Mama.

"Miss Della, elegant as ever, and Johnny on the spot with the refreshments," Ginny said as she made room on the coffee table for Mama to set the tray down.

"Girls, it is so good to see you all. Can you believe how fast this year has gone? I miss seeing each one of you over here all the time, but I do keep up with you through your mothers and it sounds as if you are all doing well in school." Mama walked over to me and put her arm around my shoulder, drawing me close as she said with a deep sigh, shaking her head. "We all know Ella could have been accepted to a good school if only she had studied a little harder, and not been so interested in other things. She wishes she had now, right dear?" Mama never missed a chance to rub it in.

"Well, I don't know, Mrs. Cane. Staying at home and going to school has its benefits, too. Ella has good home cooking and a good bed, not like dorm life," Sue Ellen volunteered as she dove into the sandwiches.

"That's right, you never know who you'll get for a roommate, either. My first roommate was a big, fat slob from up North, so at least you're not living with an obese Yankee. Anyway, I bet Ella will be at State next spring," Ginny cheerfully said. Luanna continued to smoke her cigarette and didn't offer a comment at first. Just as Mama was going back into the kitchen, Luanna brought the subject of Lucas up again.

"Okay, Ella, are you and Lucas still together or not?" Mama stopped dead in her tracks, turned around, and headed back into the living room. "Girls, can I get something else for you before you leave?"

"They just got here, Mama," I said giving her a bewildered look.

"I know, Ella, I just thought that ...," Luanna jumped up, sensing an awkward moment, and steered Mama toward the kitchen. "No thank you, Miss Della, this is just perfect. We just want to have some girl talk and catch up with Ella's news and any hometown gossip she knows about. You go on now, no need to babysit us. Sit down and relax in the den while we visit, we'll come and say good-bye when we leave." Unsure if it was safe to leave me unmonitored, Mama unwillingly left the room looked over her shoulder at me and gave me a warning look, a silent reminder to stick to the script.

"Mothers are all the same, aren't they? Afraid they're gonna miss something. I hope I didn't hurt her feelings, but we need some privacy. Let's have it, Ella," Luanna said as all three girls looked intently at me.

"Well, nothing much to tell. I just thought it was about time for Lucas and me to take a break and date other people to see what else is out there. He agreed, so we decided to do it. You never know what you may be missing until you see what else is available," I said doing my best to sound convincing.

"That's not what I heard. I heard that Lucas didn't like it at all and he thinks you were forced to break up with him because your parents wanted you to. Is that true?" Sue Ellen asked, as she had her second brownie.

"You know my parents. They never wanted me to go steady anyway, so this seemed like the right time to break up. We don't even see each other much anymore, and as far as I know, Lucas could be going out with other girls right now. How would I know? Three hundred miles is a long way from home, and he may

Our Erring Sisters by Carol Henwood

get lonesome. I couldn't blame him, and besides, we are from different backgrounds. It probably never would have worked out." What a crock I was unloading.

"Oh, baloney, Ella, that boy didn't want to date anybody else. I'm surprised at you for giving in so easily. You should have put a big fight, that's what I would have done," Luanna said as she examined her manicured nails. I wanted to end this conversation quickly, without the interference of Mama, so I continued my bogus story adding a few details here and there to make it sound believable. Ginny's huge puppy dog brown eyes glistened with tears as she walked over and put her arms around me.

"Oh, Ella, you are so brave. I know you did it to please your parents, but your heart must be breaking. Maybe you two will get together again someday."

Holding back the tears that were stinging my eyes, I shrugged it off nonchalantly as if I didn't care. "There are lots of fish in the sea, and I plan on diving in." With that said, Mama was back in the room with Camp Rollingbrook brochures to show the girls where I was going to be a summer counselor. Luanna casually walked over to Mama and took a cursory peek at the brochures and walked away.

"Camp Rollingbrook is where I went for five summers, Ella. Remember how I hated it? The counselors were real bitches, too! Oh, sorry Mrs. Cane, but they were really mean to us," Sue Ellen said.

"Ella, you'll be a great counselor, it might even be fun. You know, there are always male counselors for the boy campers, too," Ginny said, trying her best to sound excited about my summer plans.

"A camp counselor, Ella? That doesn't sound like anything you would ever consider. We both hated that god-awful Girl Scout camp we went to the summer before the sixth grade. You don't even like the great outdoors, much less obnoxious, pre-pubescent girls! Why in the world did you sign up for that?" Luanna asked suspiciously while glaring at me with her piercing hazel eyes.

Thinking of a good answer as fast as I could, which was pretty quick these days, I came back with "I thought this summer I would

Our Erring Sisters by Carol Henwood

do something constructive and fulfilling, plus earn some money to boot. After all, it does seem a tad bit shallow for us to lie around the country club pool all summer working on our tans, or tagging along on the golf course with Bobby Gray and Taylor Brooks, or whoever is playing golf on any given day," I sanctimoniously offered.

The truth was, I hadn't followed any boy around the golf course in two years. Cheerleading camp and practice occupied most of one summer, and last summer I was with Lucas, who didn't belong to the club.

My mother, sensing an opening, hastened to add, "Why I think it is a marvelous idea, Luanna. Girls and boys from nice families work as counselors in the summers and what a fine way to meet other young people from similar backgrounds," she said with a smug look on her face. Picking up on her thinly veiled inference to Lucas, Ginny, Luanna and Sue Ellen nodded and slightly smiled at her. Realizing we were not going to be allowed any time by ourselves for serious talk, my good friends gave in.

"We really should get going, Ella," Ginny said as she stood up from the rose brocade sofa and collected her purse and the others followed suit.

Admiring her reflection in the mirror above the sofa, Sue Ellen half-heartedly added, "Yes, I need to do some shopping for an Easter bonnet for church on Sunday. Don't you just love Easter hats?"

Rolling her eyes, Luanna hugged me and said, "I'll call you later on this week, Ella. I'd like to see you again before Billy and I go back to school." As we walked to the front door, Luanna whispered in my ear, "Are you sure you're okay?"

Startled by her uncanny ability to read me, I nervously laughed. "Of course I am, silly. I may be getting a little crazy living here with Miss Manners in there, but everything is just fine. You know how Mama can harp on certain subjects ad nauseam, but I'll be out of here soon enough," I said under my breath as I squeezed Luanna's hand. After hugs, kisses, and promises to stay in touch, I waved good-bye to them as they drove away in Sue Ellen's cherry red convertible, seemingly without a care in the world. I joylessly

Our Erring Sisters by Carol Henwood

walked up the boxwood lined sidewalk to the front door, realizing for the first time that I was about to undergo a monumental change in my life, a change that would set me apart from my friends, that would make me become a grown-up woman before I wanted to be, and the realization that I would be leaving the carefree world of youth behind me forever. I opened the door and stepped inside, suddenly feeling old and very much alone.

Our Erring Sisters by Carol Henwood

Chapter Four

June, 1967

The spring flew by and before I knew it, summer had arrived. I had completed my freshman year at Desota Community College in less than an auspicious manner and I was elated to be finished with classes, and just in the nick of time. I couldn't button my pants anymore and they barely made the trip over my hips. My breasts were plumping up and I had gone up two bra sizes in the last two months. Any other time I would have been thrilled to have this voluptuous new body, but for right now I would have to keep everything under cover, and avoid nosey neighbors and friends which was getting harder by the day.

One early summer afternoon I was helping unload groceries from Mama's car, thinking the coast was clear, when our next door neighbor, Alice Babcock, came rushing out of her back door. There was nothingAlice liked better than a good, juicy morsel of gossip. She was a professional busy body, and her house was rumor control headquarters. My comings and goings were planned around her comings and goings. I hadn't seen her in at least a month and a half and I only had a few weeks left before my confinement. Mama lived in daily fear that Alice would find out and spread the word.

"Why, hello there Ella Cane, I haven't seen you in a month of Sundays. Where in the world have you been? I thought you might have moved on over to Alabama to be with that handsome young man of yours."

She said this while looking me up and down with her beady eyes and long nose, like the rat that she was, sniffing out something to gnaw on. I held a grocery bag in front of my stomach and talked to her over the top of it.

"Oh, hi, Mrs. Babcock, I've been here, just running around trying to get ready to go away this summer to North Carolina to be a camp counselor at Camp Rollingbrook. I'm surprised I haven't run

Our Erring Sisters by Carol Henwood

into you before now. How is Lila doing?" I asked, trying to change the subject.

"Well, dear, Lila is just doing splendidly. She's applying to Vassar, Smith, as well as Agnes Scott. My stars, all that girl does is study. She is the incoming president of the senior class of 1968, as well as the president of the Honor Society this fall. Right now she is taking a six week course for star students at Emory University in Atlanta. I don't know where she gets the energy, but then she is a dynamo," she crowed. "How are your studies coming along at the little community college?" she asked condescendingly.

"I'm through for the summer, thank goodness, glad to be out. That's fantastic about Lila, Mrs. Babcock, tell her I said hello. I'd better get these groceries inside before the ice cream melts," I said as I tried to get away without moving the bag, which was beginning to slip.

"You certainly have a nice, healthy glow about you Ella, you must let me know what you're doing to look so robust." I nearly dropped the bag with that comment.

"It's probably just because I'm overheated from lifting these heavy groceries," I said as I laughed nervously and practically ran away. "Bye, see you later, Mrs. Babcock, tell Lila I said hi." I felt her eyes burning into my back as I walked through our gate and into the house.

Emily Anne had come home for a short visit before she and a sorority sister moved to Atlanta to live and work for the summer. While she was home we talked about everything under the sun, except my pregnancy and the impending birth. Emily Anne was a smart, self-assured girl who was both popular and pretty. She looked more like Daddy's side of the family with glossy, brunette hair and an aquiline nose, but had inherited Mama's greenish-brown eyes that would dazzle you as they changed colors right before your very eyes.

I am sure my parents instructed Emily Anne to act as if she knew nothing about my condition, and she was following the rules. Deny, deny, deny. I was the ten ton elephant in the room no one acknowledged and tiptoed around. Mama was busy helping Emily

Our Erring Sisters by Carol Henwood

Anne get ready to move and I was delighted she had something else to occupy her mind. Tarleton, who was driving now, was unaware of the family drama taking place. He was with his buddies most of the time now, and football camp would begin soon and that would dominate his summer. I was grateful for small favors.

Tarleton did give me a scare one early June day. I was in the kitchen leaning over to open a lower cabinet, putting the dish washing detergent in its place, when I heard footsteps behind me and felt a pop on my rear end. Straightening up and turning around quickly there was Tarleton with a devilish grin on his face.

"Putting a little extra padding on the old caboose aren't ya, Ella? For a minute there I thought you were Mattie," Tarleton cracked as he made reference to Mattie, our corpulent maid for the last twenty years. Alarmed and embarrassed by his observation, I subconsciously put both my hands on my expanding fanny.

"Well, maybe I have put on a little weight, but its hard not to living here in this twenty-four hour diner. Besides, I have always been skin and bones, you said so yourself, so a few pounds can't hurt. Anyway, I'm sure I'll lose any extra weight I may have gained working at Camp Rollingbrook this summer," I declared as I opened the freezer and took out Eskimo Pies. Tarleton took the Eskimo Pies from me and opened the box. Taking one of the delectable frozen bars out, he unwrapped it and started toward the kitchen door.

"I'm just messing with you, Ella. You needed some meat on those bones."

God bless that sweet boy for lying. Finishing up the ice cream, Tarleton asked,

"Oh, yeah, when do you leave for the woods?"

Feigning excitement I eagerly answered, "The counselors are supposed to arrive next Saturday for orientation and cabin assignment, and the campers come Sunday afternoon. It should be a lot of fun, I can't wait!" You would have thought I had won a free trip to Disney Land by my feigned over-the-top enthusiasm.

Balling up his ice cream wrapper and tossing it expertly across the kitchen into the garbage can, Tarleton winked at me and in a tone

Our Erring Sisters by Carol Henwood

dripping with sarcasm commented, "Sounds like a blast Ella, a real blast. See you later. Gotta go," and he sauntered out of the kitchen door.

Daddy had received a phone call from the director of Emmeriah Parrish informing him that a place was now available for me and we would be leaving Saturday, a mere four days away. Everything had become very real to me now; it was actually going to happen. I thought this must be the way prisoners feel once they have lost their last appeal and their execution date is looming. I would be leaving my home and family, and going to live in some institution, asylum, or sort of prison for girls of questionable character. I didn't know what to expect, and was told very little. My confinement would be at least two months, maybe longer, the doctor wasn't sure of my due date, but we thought early September was pretty close. I tried to project a brave front by appearing stoic and strong, but I was scared to death. I did not want to go, but going I was.

Mama had purchased some maternity clothes for me in Atlanta on an earlier trip she made with Daddy. He would drop her off downtown at a department store and go on to his office. Occasionally, we were allowed to take a day off from school and go to Atlanta to visit my grandmother and go shopping. These trips were fun, exciting and a treat we savored. But, I wasn't invited on this particular shopping excursion; I understood. We certainly couldn't take any chances buying maternity clothing in Desota, too much of a risk of running into someone we knew or answering questions asked by an overzealous sales clerk. If I had been a young married girl, expecting her first baby, Mama and I would have gone shopping together and had such fun picking out cute maternity outfits for me, as well as spending time in the baby department and marveling at the tiny sleepers in pink and blue, as well as the booties, blankets and all the small and necessary items babies require.

I had taken that pleasure away from my mother and I was relieved not to be present to witness that cheerless task. Unfortunately, this was not an occasion for joy between a mother and daughter anticipating the arrival of a new life, that of a child and grandchild. This was a shared agony, one we never spoke of, but endured privately. I longed to put my head in Mama's lap and cry and be soothed and comforted as a child would, to tell her of my fears, how frightened I was of what was happening to me, but I didn't, and I wasn't encouraged to. I believe my mother was struggling immensely from this blow I had dealt my family, barely hanging on, and the emotional distance she put between us was a safety valve for her, as well as for me. Maybe it was her way of getting me prepared for being alone for the birth of my baby.

July 4, 1967

The fourth of July fell on a Saturday in 1967, the same day I would leave the familiar and comfortable surroundings of home and move into a world of secrets and seclusion. I had never been away from home for more than one week, and then it was with family or friends. I was petrified about the unknown and being thrown together with strange girls from God knows where, and yes, the possibility of dying while giving birth with no family around me.

Putting on a brave face was becoming more difficult as the day to leave drew near. Over the past two days Mama and I had packed my belongings, adhering to the list we received listing suggested items to bring. One thing I knew for certain, there would be no need for party dresses. Being a voracious reader, I packed as many paperbacks as I could squeeze into my small suitcase.

Included in the letter explaining what we should bring, was a daily schedule of chores we would be expected to perform and a list of classes we could participate in – pottery, art, music, typing – anything to keep us busy. There was even a school for the girls who were still in high school, and, yes, even some in junior high.

A bus would transport us to Crawford Long Hospital for our weekly and monthly doctors' appointments to ensure our babies would have good prenatal care; better late than never in my case. The fear of the unknown was paralyzing to me. I had no idea what to

Our Erring Sisters by Carol Henwood

expect or what I would encounter once I arrived. Should I be afraid for my safety? Would the girls who were there be members of a gang that delighted in making the life of the new residents a living hell? Would it be necessary for me to pay for protection from the elite group that ran the home? I had no clue about the dynamics of the place. My active imagination was working overtime and I was fearful of having an anxiety attack, carrying on like a crazy person, screaming, foaming at the mouth and finally being dragged, kicking and screaming to the car for the inevitable trip. But I didn't. I maintained what little composure I could gather and bucked up. My plight was not unlike that of a first time traveler to a far off land where a different language was spoken and peculiar customs practiced. Before the sun set today, I would be a member of an obscure sorority, one where grades, achievements, and family background were of no consequence. Unmarried and pregnant were the only credentials needed, and I met the requirements. This sorority of dejected and shamed girls was one I didn't want to join. The initiation would be excruciating, the results long lasting.

****

I was awakened from a restless sleep by the rattling of pots and pans in the kitchen. A welcome sound which usually filled me with anticipation as to what scrumptious delights would be forthcoming, but not today. After fully waking up, I realized this was my last day living at home as a carefree teenage girl. My life as I knew it would soon be turned upside down and there was no way I could get it back. The familiar morning sounds of breakfast being prepared and my father getting dressed for the day were reassuring, but sad and unwelcome knowing this was the end of my happy-go-lucky days.

I decided to stay in bed for a little longer, not wishing to face the day just yet, but after ten minutes of trying to wish myself somewhere else, I gave up and got up. I put on my short summer robe and slippers and headed to the kitchen.

"Good morning, Ella," Mama sang out as she kneaded biscuit dough, "I was just about to come and wake you up. I thought you

Our Erring Sisters by Carol Henwood

might like a good breakfast this morning since it's going to be a long day and you need something to sustain you," she said in one breath.

"Oh, great, I'm really hungry," I said, watching my mother expertly manipulate the biscuit cutter and place the fat biscuits on a pan and pop them into the oven. Bacon was sizzling and scrambled eggs were up next. I was always hungry these days, and I didn't hold back either, I ate! I was gaining weight steadily now, and I was beginning to look pregnant, so it was a good thing I was leaving today.

Emily Anne was staying in Atlanta for the fourth of July for a big barbeque with friends from college, and Tarleton was at his best friend Lanky's lake house for the weekend. It was just me, Mama, and Daddy, which was fine, no extra drama needed.

"We should leave here no later than 10:30 this morning, it will probably take two hours to get there, since I'm not certain where the home is located, and I don't want to be late. We have to fill out a good deal of paperwork and get you checked in, so we need to get moving soon."

Taking the bacon out of the frying pan and laying it on a paper towel lined plate, Mama had barely glanced at me, just talking a mile a minute. Breaking off a piece of bacon from the plate, I went over and began to set out three placemats for breakfast.

"Just set two places, Ella. Your father has already eaten his bowl of cereal and fruit. You know he's back on that diet again trying to lose another fifteen pounds. He is not going to ride down to Atlanta with us after all," Mama stated finally looking at me.

"I can handle the details and we think it is better that he stays here and plays golf as usual," she concluded and turned around to scramble the eggs. Boy, was I relieved!

"There's no need for him to go anyway, and I don't want him to miss his Saturday golf game on my account," I said as I took up the third placemat from the table. I could think of nothing worse than having both of my parents drop me off at my unhappy destination and have to witness the looks on their faces as they drove off. It was going to be hard enough to have Mama there, but both of them, unbearable.

Our Erring Sisters by Carol Henwood

Daddy was an imposing man with a seemingly hard exterior and could be intimidating to the people who didn't know him, especially young lawyers coming before him for the first time. But, they were pleasantly surprised at his kind and helpful manner. In reality, he was a soft hearted marshmallow of a man. I didn't need to see my father turn to mush in front of my eyes today.

"You're right, Mama, we can handle this," I quickly offered, as if I knew what the hell I was talking about.

"Daddy loves his weekend golf games and his buddies might wonder why he had to go back to Atlanta on a Saturday," I said.

"You're right, Ella. Those men would give him the third degree if he missed his regular game."

My father's partners were serious golfers and were affectionately referred to as the "terror squad" around the Pro Shop. They played twenty-seven holes of golf every Saturday and Sunday unless there was a family or national emergency. Daddy made sure he attended the early worship service at First Presbyterian before he hit the links; he and God had an understanding. I took the platter of bacon and biscuits over to the kitchen table as Mama scooped the eggs onto a platter. I poured myself a glass of orange juice and sat down.

"You want a cup of coffee, dear?"

I had just recently started drinking coffee and enjoyed it, although I probably didn't need any extra jitters this particular morning.

"Yes, I can get it. You go ahead and sit down," and I walked over to the coffee pot and poured a cup. As Mama brought the eggs to the table and sat down, Daddy walked into the kitchen.

"Good morning ladies. Smells good, Della, wish I could have some," he said as he pulled out a kitchen chair and sat down with us. Surveying the bounty in front of him, he picked out a golden brown biscuit and slathered it with butter and jelly; so much for his diet.

"Just this one biscuit won't hurt, I guess," he said as he took a bite.

Our Erring Sisters by Carol Henwood

Fearing the possibility of an emotional farewell speech from Daddy, I immediately started babbling about anything that came into my mind, trying my best to avoid an uncomfortable, melodramatic moment. It didn't work. After five minutes of inane commentary concerning the weather, national politics and the brassy new hair color of Alice Babcock next door, I ran out of gas. Daddy allowed me to complete my obvious attempt at dodging the inevitable.

Solemnly he interlaced his fingers and placed them on the table in front of him, turned toward me and sighed deeply.

"Ella, I don't need to tell you how difficult this is for us. I know you think you are the only one suffering here, but that is far from the truth. This family is suffering right along with you. Having said that, I strongly believe this is the only course of action we could have chosen for everyone's sake. One day you will look back on this difficult time in your life and realize it was the right thing to do. After this is over, you should put it behind you, forget it ever happened and resume your life, as we all hope to do. Everything is on hold for the next three months or so. Remember that we love you and always will, no matter what, but this is a sad, sad day for the Cane family."

I sat as still as a cat preparing to pounce on an unsuspecting mouse, every muscle in my body tensed, dutifully listening, but not acknowledging the words. I didn't look at either of my parents. My mother, pushing the eggs around her plate, and stifling the tears that were near the surface, my father, still staring at me waiting on a response.

Predictable and obedient as ever, I responded, "I know. It'll be okay." Not wanting to prolong the torture, I picked up my plate and walked over to the sink and began rinsing it off and put it in the dish rack.

"Well, I guess I'd better get a move on if we are leaving anytime soon," I said, as I started heading out of the kitchen. Daddy stood up, came over and awkwardly hugged me, and just as awkwardly, I returned the hug. He started toward the kitchen door that led to the back porch where his golf shoes, clubs, and all the other golf paraphernalia were kept.

36

Our Erring Sisters by Carol Henwood

"My tee time is in five minutes. Della, drive carefully, you know how those Atlanta drivers are. It should be relatively easy to find, the directions Ben got are very detailed. Pull over somewhere and call the home if you get lost."

Looking at me and searching my face one final time, he opened the door and stated in a matter of fact tone, "Be brave, you can do this Ella."

Mama jumped up and began clearing the dishes with unnecessary urgency. I started to help her and she snapped at me.

"Go on and get ready, Ella, I can do this."

I understood she needed to be alone right then. I softly touched her arm as I left the kitchen, but the sound of her muffled sobs permeated my heart as I closed my bedroom door.

I was packed and waiting in the den for my mother to come downstairs so we could get the show on the road. Punctuality was not Mama's strong suit, and I didn't expect today would be the day she turned over a new leaf. I was wrong. She came into the den looking lovely in a dark blue linen suit with white buttons, blue leather open-toed high heels, and matching purse. Her salt and pepper hair had just been styled yesterday and still looked new and fresh. She was a young looking fifty-three, with a petite frame, hazel eyes, and shapely legs she claimed were her best asset. It was Mama's contention that the way one dressed made a big difference in how people treated you. If you were unkempt and disheveled, you would not be taken seriously. On the other hand, if you were dressed nicely and neatly, not necessarily expensively, you would be treated with respect and given every consideration. Mama was dressed for business.

"Well, let's get started and maybe we can get there by noon. I don't want to be driving back to Desota after dark."

For the first twenty-five miles or so, we engaged in safe conversation, commenting on the building boom along Highway 41, the new McDonalds that had just opened, the only one for miles around, and I even managed to create the illusion in my mind that this was another fun shopping excursion to Atlanta like so many others we had taken together. After exhausting my limited resource of non-threatening subjects, Mama saw an opening and took advantage of it.

"Ella, I realize this going to be a stressful and frightening time for you, being away from home and among strange people, and especially under these circumstances. It is going to be hard on us as well. We have been assured that this facility is above board and highly respected among social and medical professionals. You will be treated well and all your needs met by the staff to the best of their ability. Remember, privacy is essential, tell no one anything about yourself or your family. The matron of the home, Miss Sallie Mellete, will give you a temporary identity and you will assume it, and answer only to that name. They will inform us of all the details at our meeting. Above all, we need to have an assurance from you that you will not try and get in contact with Lucas. It would serve no purpose and only bring more heartache and turmoil in your life. I firmly believe our decision is the right one, and the only way out of an unfortunate situation."

Taking her eyes off the road briefly to glance at me and gauge my reaction, I didn't respond and continued looking out of the window as we were coming into the city limits of Atlanta.

"Ella, do we have your word that you will not try and get in touch with Lucas?"

Slowing turning my gaze from the passing landscape to my mother, I answered in a slightly irritated and bored tone. "Yes and no."

Jerking her head toward me so quickly she caused the car to swerve briefly out of her lane, I instantly knew my cavalier answer was a mistake. Safely getting the car back in her lane of traffic, Mama kept her eyes on the road ahead and spoke slowly, in a low deliberate tone, the way she did when she had reached her boiling point.

"In case you were not aware, Ella, your reckless behavior has turned this family inside out. Stop acting as if we are to blame for the mess you find yourself in. Your response had better mean 'yes' you have my word and 'no' I will not get in touch with Lucas.'"

Not wanting to anger Mama further, and without hesitation, I answered respectfully, honestly, and meekly.

Our Erring Sisters by Carol Henwood

"I will not get in touch with Lucas, I promise. I don't even know where he lives anymore."

"Good," she answered as we exited onto Peachtree Road.

Before Atlanta became a cosmopolitan city, it is my belief that people from outside the South, who had never visited, thought of Peachtree Road only as the address of Scarlett O'Hara's Aunt Pittypat. It is the most famous street in the South, made so by Margaret Mitchell's *Gone With The Wind*, and is a vital, much traveled artery running north and south through Atlanta. Traveling south on Peachtree will take you into downtown Atlanta. If you go north, you will pass beautiful old neighborhoods, new upscale neighborhoods and shops, and continuous construction of new malls, businesses and restaurants. We were traveling north, passing familiar places Mama and I had been together in happier times. A sudden unexpected lump in my throat took me by surprise. Fumbling around in my purse while clearing my throat, Mama looked over at me.

"Are you okay, Ella?"

I didn't want to cause any extra anxiety or worry about my state of mind, so I continued to aimlessly scrounge around in my purse as if I had a hidden treasure in there.

"Yes, I'm fine. I thought I'd better run a brush through my hair. We must be getting close by now."

Brushing my hair seems to be something I always resort to in times of stress.

Why, I don't know. Possibly appearing neat and put together on the outside disguised the utter chaos inside.

"We should be coming up to the turn any minute now. It's on North Peachtree Road, and I think its right up here," she said as she craned her neck to see beyond the next traffic light.

"Yes, this is it."

We turned left and the first driveway on the right was the entrance to the Emmeriah Parrish Home for Unwed Mothers. It was not marked with any sign, no indication of what lay beyond the towering hedges that hid the facility from the outside world. We slowly drove down a long, winding driveway toward a large two story red brick home that had a long dormitory-like addition on one

Our Erring Sisters by Carol Henwood

side. It looked similar to many of the large homes in this area of Atlanta, and for the first time the mental picture I had etched in my brain of a gray, concrete, prison-like structure with bars on the windows and a barbed wire fence surrounding the perimeter was replaced with a welcoming feeling. Maybe I wasn't going to be subjected to torture for my transgression after all. Whatever lay behind those high hedges and red bricks would soon be revealed to me as I took my place as one of the lost and fallen girls.

The Home

Mama drove down the driveway and parked in a small parking area at the side of the house and next to a small red brick building that I soon discovered was the school house.

We got out of the car, walked up a sidewalk leading to the front door, and rang the doorbell. Within a few minutes the door opened to reveal a stern looking, gray-haired lady of undeterminable age, wearing a drab, shapeless dress, black sensible shoes and holding a feather duster. I was immediately reminded of the matron at a women's prison as portrayed in vintage Hollywood movies, and my heart sank. An audible gasp came out of my mouth. I looked at Mama who was wide eyed as well, and for a brief moment I contemplated fleeing the scene. Then the woman smiled and whatever fears I harbored were wiped away by the infectious smile that lit up her entire face. My first impression of a whip yielding ogre was replaced with that of an impish, grandmotherly looking lady with twinkling blue eyes, who greeted us as if we were long, lost relatives. Taking us both by the hands, we were escorted into the foyer where this little lady began to put us at ease, which was where we needed to be.

Putting the duster on a nearby table, she began. "First of all, let me introduce myself. I am Sallie Mae Mellette, Miss Sallie to most everybody, and I'm the one responsible for keeping things running smoothly around here," she said cheerfully as she took my suitcase and placed it beside a settee in the foyer.

Our Erring Sisters by Carol Henwood

"Welcome to Emmeriah Parrish, ladies, I know you are the Canes," she said as she looked at Mama.

"We have been looking forward to your arrival, and now that you're here, let's sit down and visit a little bit. Let's go on into my office and have something cool to drink. Happy July 4th, by the way, I must look a fright," she exclaimed as she gathered stands of her untidy hair that had fallen from her tightly wound bun, and pinned them back in place. Then smoothing her dress over her wiry body, she continued.

"We are having a cookout this afternoon and have been cleaning and getting ready for it all morning. Some of the home's board members are coming, and we want everything to look tip top and organized. It's not usually this chaotic around here."

As we followed her through a room that I surmised was a small library, I had my first glimpse at some of the residents. Two girls who looked to be my age or younger, and very pregnant, were taking paper plates, napkins, and plastic cups outside to a covered patio area where tables and chairs were set up and July 4th decorations adorned the tables. Red, white, and blue streamers were strung along the poles of the awning of the patio area, and if I didn't know differently, I could have sworn I was at one of my friend's houses for a summer cookout. As we passed by the kitchen and dining room, I saw several more residents in all stages of pregnancy, busy as bees, laughing as they placed American flags on the picnic tables and put plates, napkins and plastic utensils on the tables for the party. The cheerfulness of the girls made the entire scene appear surreal. What did they have to be so happy about? I was sad and downhearted and felt very out of place at that moment, thinking to myself, 'I can't stay here, something's wrong with these people.'

Miss Sallie brought me back into focus.

"You'll meet all the girls this afternoon, dear, and I'm sure you will like them. Everyone here gets along just fine, and if they don't, we fix the problem," she said with a wink and a smile.

Miss Sallie led us up a stairway to the second level of the home where we followed her into a small office. Sitting down at a

Our Erring Sisters by Carol Henwood

well organized desk, Miss Sallie opened a drawer and produced a file with my name on it.

"Here we are. Let's get started on this paper work, then we'll take a quick tour, and we can get you on your way home Mrs. Cane and Ella can get settled in and meet the other residents at this afternoon's festivities."

Miss Sallie informed us the staff consisted of an executive director, three social workers, a nutritionist, three registered nurses, clerical support, and maintenance support staff. Mama was given a packet to take with her explaining the history, purpose, board members, expenses and anything else related to procedures and the day to day running of the home. We both signed many documents and at last, after forty-five minutes of reading and writing, we were finished.

"Now, I will give you a quick tour of the dormitories, the kitchen, common area where the girls gather, and the main part of the house which we just came through."

We followed the quick stepping matron through the small library which was cozy and inviting, and I knew I would be spending some time here. The dining area was next and reminded me of a smaller version of my school cafeteria, and off the dining room was the kitchen where all residents had a turn at cooking and washing dishes. I wasn't thrilled at the prospect of kitchen detail. We continued to the common area where I saw more of the residents sprawled out on the two large couches, others relaxing on plush, oversized chairs. Some were watching television, others playing cards at tables scattered around the room, while a few napped or read, and one girl was giving another one a manicure. Typical teenage girl activities; maybe this wouldn't be so bad after all.

As we left the common room, we walked down a hall, past a wall with a large bulletin board which had many announcements for activity opportunities, weekly menus, as well as the list of girls who would be going to the doctor that week. Continuing down a ramp, we entered the dormitory wing.

Our Erring Sisters by Carol Henwood

"We have twenty rooms, two girls to a room, and we are just about at full capacity right now. Last night two of our girls went into the hospital and delivered early this morning."

We continued walking and Miss Sallie stopped at a room with the number eight on the door. "This is your room, Ella. Your roommate's name is Andee, and you will love her, everyone does. She's a feisty little thing, came all the way from Hawaii. Let's see if she's in."

She knocked loud enough to wake the dead and called out Andee's name.

"Andee, are you in there dear?"

Miss Sallie slowly pushed the door open, locks were not allowed.

"Oh, well, she's not in, but come on in and take a look."

I cautiously entered the room with Mama close behind and we were pleasantly surprised to find a bright, colorful room decorated with posters of Hawaii, the Pacific ocean, and two blond, tan surfer boys.

There were two small desks with chairs, one with a typewriter on it, the other piled high with text books. The room had twin beds across from each other and two closets, one filled with clothes, the other one empty. One large window looked out onto the wooded lot the house sat on, the woods filled with rhododendrons, wild azaleas and many other trees and scents I knew, but couldn't identify. A nice, secluded room in the woods; I liked it.

"As you can see, Andee loves reminders of Hawaii. She misses the vibrant colors of the island. Hope you don't mind. I suspect she is out helping set up for the party. You can meet her there in a few minutes. The bathrooms and showers are across the hall. This is a good room, close to the bathroom, which I know you have found you spend a lot of time in."

Hurrying us along, we retraced our steps and found ourselves back in her office.

"The only thing I forgot to show you is the nurse's station, which is off the common room. I will have Andee show you around for a more extensive tour later on today.

Our Erring Sisters by Carol Henwood

"Now, the final bit of business we have to address. While you are here, Ella, you will have a different name than your given name. It is for your protection and privacy. You can either pick a name if you like, or we can assign you one. I know it must feel very strange for you to assume another identity and answer to a different name, but you will find it easier than you think and will become accustomed to it. After all, it's only for a short time. Any suggestions?"

How many times in a lifetime do you have the opportunity to pick a new name for yourself? Not many and I was stumped. I looked at my mother and she looked as puzzled as me.

No doubt Miss Sallie was used to this reaction, so she offered a suggestion.

"What about Elizabeth, since your first name starts with the letter E, and let's see, how about the last name of Nash?" she asked as she looked at a piece of paper I assumed was a list of possible names, yet to have been chosen.

"Elizabeth Nash. Does that suit you, dear?" she asked sweetly as she patiently awaited my answer.

I pondered the sound of my new identity for a moment, and then answered enthusiastically, "Yes. It will do just fine, I'll be Elizabeth Nash."

All of a sudden I liked the idea of not being me for the next few months. If only I could change everything else with as much ease, my life would be a dream. I was now Elizabeth Nash, but my life was still in shambles.

"Ladies, I promised you something cold to drink, and I forgot. Let me get Jessie to bring us something right away."

Getting up from behind her desk, she walked past us to the door, opened it and yelled, "Jessie, could you come in here for a minute? Jessie likes to help out in the office, she is sort of my girl Friday."

A freckled faced, red headed and very pregnant girl of maybe fifteen appeared at the door.

"Yes, Miss Sallie," she said as she squeezed by my chair and smiled down at me.

Our Erring Sisters by Carol Henwood

"Jessie, this is our new resident. Elizabeth Nash, and her mother."

Looking at Jessie, Miss Sallie beamed with maternal pride as she continued, "Jessie has been here for almost the entire nine months of her pregnancy and should be delivering any day now, correct dear?"

"I'm due next week, but I keep hoping it will be today or tomorrow. I don't have any more room inside me and this baby is gonna kick right through my belly if it doesn't come on out," she cooed as she patted her bulging belly.

She wore a pair of white shorts and a sleeveless red maternity top that barely covered the enormous protrusion. She couldn't have been five feet tall and had skinny arms and legs, giving her the appearance of a stick figure with a melon ball stuck in the middle. My mouth hung wide open in awe, taking in the sight of this tiny girl at the brink of bursting, and Mama elbowed me and I closed my mouth.

"Well, Jessie we know it cannot be too much longer, love. Would you mind bringing in a pitcher of lemonade and some glasses on a tray, and some of those nice shortbread cookies?"

"That sounds delightful" said Della, "and after our refreshments, I will help Ella unpack and then I should start back home"

"Oh, there's no need for that, dear," Miss Sallie said as she got up from behind her desk and walked over to where Mama was sitting, and patted her gently on her shoulder.

"Let us take care of everything from here; you've done the hard part by bringing her to us. It will be easier on both of you if you say your good-byes here in my office. I will give you some time for that, then our staff, and the girls themselves will make Ella settle in and feel at home in every way. She is safe in our hands."

I suppose my mother thought she would unpack my bag, place everything neatly in the drawers, hang my clothes up, and arrange all of my toiletries. Why wouldn't she? She'd always done that for both Emily Anne and me.

Our Erring Sisters by Carol Henwood

"Well, if you think that is best," Mama replied, noticeably ruffled, as she realized her presence here was no longer required and Miss Sallie was trying to move things along.

Jessie backed into the room holding a silver tray with a pitcher of lemonade, tall glasses with ice, scrumptious looking cookies on a lace doily, and two linen napkins. Etiquette and manners were very important in Mama's world, and the suggestion that social graces were alive and well here in this most unlikely place had to give her sagging spirits a boost. The very thought of me being exposed to girls from God knows where, was enough to make her swoon, so this small detail hopefully reassured her in some way that I would not leave here as a foul mouthed, vulgar and coarse girl due to the influence of girls with no breeding or background.

"Thank you, Jessie, dear," Miss Sallie said after Jessie placed the tray on the table. "You can go on back downstairs now."

"I'm going to leave you ladies now. I've got a few more things to take care of before this afternoon's festivities. Mrs. Cane, please be assured Ella will be fine here, and you know, of course, you can call here anytime to speak with me, or any of the staff if you have questions. Also, there is a telephone in the dormitory wing and the residents can make and receive calls there. The brochure I gave you should answer most of the questions you may have."

"Ella, why don't you walk your mother out to her car when you two are ready, and then come on back in and I'll introduce you to everyone."

Turning to face my mother, Miss Sallie smiled and took Mama's hands in hers.

"Take care, drive carefully, and most of all, please try and not worry. We take excellent care of our girls."

Miss Sallie quietly closed the door behind her as she left us alone to say our good-byes.

Waiting for Mama to say something first, I busied myself by pouring a glass of lemonade and reaching for a cookie.

"Would you care for some lemonade, Mama? These cookies smell delicious. I think they must have just come out of the oven." I tried to act as nonchalant as possible, struggling to keep my emotions

Our Erring Sisters by Carol Henwood

in check. Standing up and wandering around the office, Mama ran her hand along the back of a chair, picked up a photograph from Miss Sallie's desk and studied it intensely, and walked over to the office window and stared out focusing on the cars in the distance traveling along Peachtree Road. She stood there, not moving a muscle, with her arms folded in front of her. I guessed she was gathering her thoughts before she spoke. I let her.

"No thank you, Ella, or I suppose I should say Elizabeth," she added with a mirthless laugh, accentuating each syllable.

"I'm not very hungry at the moment, but you should eat something, you might get light headed if you don't," she advised as she turned around and walked back to the chair and sat down next to me. The Canes are not very good at heart to heart talks, especially if the subject matter is uncomfortable. Avoidance, if at all possible, is our way of dealing with things. The less said the better, which works for a while where minor issues are concerned. This was no minor issue. This was excruciating for my mother and my heart bled for her. I felt I had to say something, anything, because if I saw tears, I was a goner, the flood gates would open wide.

"Mama, you have got to try one of these cookies, they are out of this world, really, try one," I blurted out, making a lame attempt at keeping things light. Looking at me with such sadness, she took my hand.

"Ella, sweetheart, I don't know what to say or where to start, but I feel confident you will be taken care of here, and that is our main concern, your welfare. If I cannot be here for you, I believe Miss Sallie will be an excellent stand-in for me. She seems to be a caring, compassionate woman who loves these girls, and understands the stress and difficulty of each individual situation. It appears to me that she tries very diligently to make this a home away from home. This isn't an ideal situation, of course, but it was what we had to do under the circumstances," she finished by clearing her voice and looking away from me.

Not wanting to bring up the alternate solution at this late date, I agreed.

Our Erring Sisters by Carol Henwood

"I will be fine, Mama. This place is not at all what I thought it would be, you know, sort of prison-like, it's actually pretty nice. When I meet the rest of the inmates, sorry, residents," I said sarcastically, "what do you want to bet we'll have a lot in common?"

My mother didn't care one iota for the inmates remark, nor my contention that I would have something in common with the others.

"I don't believe you will have anything in common with these girls Ella, possibly one or two, but no matter, you are not here to make friends. We will stay in touch with you by phone and letters, which reminds me, you should write to Mimi and your friends, describing your camp experience, and include some anecdotes about being a counselor."

As I started to protest, Mama raised her hand much like a crossing guard would, indicating to stop right there.

"Make it up, Ella. You love a good story, just make one up. We will do what we have to do to keep this quiet. The letters will be forwarded to a camp in North Carolina where they will be postmarked there and sent to the addressee. It has all been arranged, so don't concern yourself about the details."

I was amazed at the extraordinary steps that were being taken so my cover wouldn't be blown, and I again started to protest the charade.

"Ella, I know you want to do everything you can to cooperate, so no more arguments, please."

I reluctantly conceded. What was the point? "I will write some letters to Mimi, but I don't know about writing to anybody else." I didn't want to risk the possibility of Luanna Lindsey doing some private investigating on her own. No letter to Luanna for sure.

Looking at her watch, Mama stood up and sighed.

"I should get going."

I jumped up and faced her. We hesitated for a moment and then fell into each other's arms. We were both sobbing now, albeit controlled, but tears were falling, no words needed. We allowed ourselves the moment, then pulled ourselves together in typical Cane fashion, swallowed our emotions, and walked out of Miss Sallie's

48

office, down the stairs, and out the front door to the car. Not wanting to linger too long for fear of another unwanted display of raw emotion, we hugged each other tightly, forced smiles, and promised to talk soon. I turned and almost ran back into my new home so I wouldn't have to see my mother drive away. I was now Elizabeth Nash, on my own and ready to become one of the girls.

Chapter Five

I followed the sound of voices from the foyer and into the main area of the house, proceeding cautiously, looking and listening for the gathering, but not wanting to barge in, just slip in unnoticed. Spotting a group of people outside on the covered patio, I stopped abruptly before I ventured out.

I am more of an introvert than an extrovert, which is something my parents have never been able to understand, and I'm pretty sure it is a source of irritation to them. Mama has an outgoing personality, is very gracious and cordial, and puts people at ease immediately.

"It's not as if you have a reason to be so timid, Ella. You're a pretty, popular girl from a well respected family. Try and be a little more bubbly and vivacious for heaven's sake."

Daddy is much the same, but to a greater degree. He is a larger than life figure, whom people gravitate to, and he is that one person who takes up all the air in the room. Then there is me. Meeting people for the first time, especially by myself, is not something I do well. My bashfulness and lack of self confidence often are mistaken for aloofness. I am not aloof, I am unsure of myself, and therefore I tend to be quiet and remote. But, I have been given an opportunity to re-invent myself as Elizabeth Nash. She will be a very different girl than Ella Cane. Elizabeth will initiate conversations with other girls, get to know them and try and make a friend or two. She might even prove my mother's prediction of having nothing in common with these girls to be completely baseless. Sharing the same burden, as well as the miracle of a new life growing inside each one of us, is reason enough to acknowledge our similarities and overlook any differences.

I found a powder room near the library, and went inside to use the facility, as well as to freshen up from the trip. My bladder

Our Erring Sisters by Carol Henwood

was full almost all the time and it was a major nuisance, so I never passed up a bathroom. After taking care of that pressing matter, I checked myself in the mirror. I still had my purse with me, so I took out my cosmetic bag, loaded with all the necessary items for quick fixes, and applied some pink lipstick and a little powder, brushed my hair and said out loud, "Who really cares?" and turned quickly to leave the restroom. Catching a glimpse of myself in a full length mirror that was on the back of the door, I paused before exiting. I was dressed in white shorts and a red and white checked maternity top, and looked every bit of the seven months pregnant that I was. This was the first time I had not tried to hide my condition and it felt good, very liberating to just let it be; maybe I would even enjoy the remaining time my baby and I had together. I had no one to talk to about all the changes I was going through, physically and emotionally, or to share my innermost thoughts with. Mama didn't want to discuss it, she just wanted it over, and I didn't press her. I was in dire need of a friend, so lately I had started talking to the baby inside of me, telling it the mess I had gotten us into, and how sorry I was, but that it was going to be okay in the end. I was trying hard not to become attached, knowing the outcome. Maybe I was going over the edge, losing it, or maybe this was the way all mothers-to-be react. Patting my stomach, I opened the door and stepped out as Elizabeth Nash.

The Lost and Fallen Girls

The 4th of July party was well underway as I made my way toward the patio. I walked into the common area where I had my first encounter with several of the residents. Miss Sallie was having an animated conversation outside with a tall, well groomed socialite looking woman, whom I assumed was a member of the board of the Emmeriah Parrish Home. There were two other women and men, equally as elegant, talking and laughing with each other and some of the girls.

51

Our Erring Sisters by Carol Henwood

Miss Sallie saw me enter the room, excused herself from the group and came inside.

"Hello, Elizabeth, I see you've joined our party," she sang out as she walked over and hugged me.

"Did you and your mother have enough time together, dear? I hope you did, I know it is hard to say good-bye at a time like this, but the transition will be easier for you now," she said looking at me with soft, understanding eyes.

"Now, I want you to meet some of our girls," she said as she motioned to a group of four to come over.

"Girls, I want you to make welcome Elizabeth, our new resident. She arrived earlier today, just in time for our July the 4th party."

A pretty brown-eyed brunette stepped forward and put her plate down with a half eaten hot dog on it.

"Hi, I'm Bonnie, nice to meet you Elizabeth."

"Nice to meet you, too, Bonnie," I replied with sincere enthusiasm. Mama would have been proud.

"I'm due in late August, when is your baby due?" she asked sweetly.

"I think around September 3rd, it could be a little sooner, or later for all I know," I answered with an embarrassed giggle.

"That's the same for most of us here, nobody is sure about their actual date, it's just an educated guess on the doctor's part anyway," Bonnie added.

"That's what we get for being such sluts, you know," said a girl who looked maybe twenty-one years old, with short, dirty blonde hair and an attitude.

She was smoking a cigarette and blowing smoke rings in the air.

"I'm Lacy. I should be getting out of this place in October. Seems like I've been here my entire life, but it's only been since May 15th. I was getting too big to hide anymore, so my mother begged one of her new boyfriends to pull some strings and get me in here pronto. She couldn't take a chance that one of her hoity-toity friends might see me at the summer soiree she throws every June

Our Erring Sisters by Carol Henwood

and disgrace her. Strings were pulled and I was shipped here and all is well in the world of wine and roses. Anyway, B-day is October 15th for me," she said as she continued to blow smoke rings.

"Lacy, you know the rules about smoking inside, and smoking in general. Please extinguish that cigarette now, dear," Miss Sallie stated firmly while patting Lacy on her back. Lacy rolled her eyes and smirked as she turned away.

"See you around, Elizabeth", she sang out as she smiled and winked at me and sauntered away. All of a sudden the tough girl images I had expected to find here came back with a vengeance.

Sensing my uneasiness, Miss Sallie took me by the arm.

"Don't mind Lacy, she is one of the sweetest and most caring girls we've ever had here at the home. She wants to project a hard exterior, when in fact, she is very tender hearted. She is planning on keeping her baby, in spite of her mother and father's objections, and that is causing much anxiety in her life. She's like a big sister to everyone, isn't she Kylene?"

A strikingly beautiful platinum blonde girl with green eyes and a golden tan walked over and joined us.

"Lacy? Her bark is much worse than her bite. Hi, I'm Kylene, welcome to the funny farm, Elizabeth. My sentence is just beginning, as you can probably tell," Kylene demonstrated turning sideways to emphasize her small bump of a tummy.

"I haven't been here very long either, so I'm still one of the newcomers."

"Good," I said with relief. I was relieved to have met two girls, Bonnie and Kylene, who seemed to be very much like me. I couldn't wait to have long, late night talks sharing so much of what I had kept inside for months.

All of a sudden an imp of a girl appeared, eating a chocolate ice cream cone. She was wearing a flowing, flowered sun dress which hid her condition and complemented her dark skin and hair, which was pulled back in a pony tail.

"Andee," Miss Sallie said with delight as she pulled the unsuspecting girl over to where we were.

Our Erring Sisters by Carol Henwood

"Here you are. I want you to meet your new roommate, Elizabeth. She has just arrived and I was hoping you would take her under your wing, show her around, introduce her, and help get her things to your room. Just make her feel at home, all of this after she has something to eat, of course. You must be famished by now, Elizabeth. Those little cookies won't hold you for too long."

Andee and I looked at each other for a moment, and simultaneously laughed out loud. That was a good sign; I could tell I was going to like her.

"Great, let's do it. Elizabeth, do you want to get something to eat? The hot dogs are really good. I made the slaw and it is fantastic, if I say so myself," Andee crowed as she polished her fingernails on her shoulder.

"Then I will just have to try some," I told her as we almost skipped to the patio. Once outside, we descended upon the food table. I made myself a hot dog with catsup, mustard and relish, spooned a large serving of slaw on my plate, as well as chips, and I opted for an ice cold Coke.

"Let's go over here and sit under this big ole tree."

Andee led the way out into the grass off of the patio, which was well kept and had some flowering shrubbery around the perimeter. There were two comfortable looking lawn chairs under a large oak tree and we plopped down in them.

"I wanted to get away from board members and any pain in the ass staff so I can give you the skinny on our prison," she said irreverently as she swallowed the last of the ice cream cone. I bit into my hot dog with gusto, I hadn't realized how hungry I was. Chewing and swallowing in a hurry, I quietly inquired, "Is it awful here?"

Clapping her hands together and laughing simultaneously, Andee leaned in.

"I know what you're thinking because we probably had the same gruesome picture in our heads about what this place would be like. You know, turn of the century women's prison place with a cruel matron and dangerous girls. That's what I thought when I found out I was coming here, and when I say here, I mean from

Our Erring Sisters by Carol Henwood

Hawaii to the Mainland, then traveling all the way across the country to the deep South. Hell, I thought I might never be seen again."

Riveted to Andee, I dreamily spoke saying, "That is a long way for you to come. "Hawaii," I said with a wistful sigh, "it must be beautiful there. I'd love to see it one day. Have you always lived there?" I asked as I continued eating and hung on her every word.

"Yes, for most of my life. My dad is in the army and has been stationed at Pearl Harbor for the last twelve years. It's great, I miss the ocean, but most of all I miss my boyfriend," she added sadly.

"But, we'll talk about all of that good stuff later. Now, to get back to your question. No, it's not awful here. Miss Sallie is a sweetheart and cares about all of us, maybe too much. She doesn't have any children of her own, so we are kind of her family. I just wish my parents had been as caring and understanding as she is. Most of the staff is okay too, some of the social workers are cold, judgmental, double-barreled bitches, but that's just my humble opinion. My baby is due in October, near the middle of the month. I'm almost six months and not very big," she said as she stood up and pulled her sun dress taunt against her belly.

"Candy over there is six months too, and looks like she is going to pop any minute." Andee pointed to a very sexy looking girl with long, lustrous auburn hair, dancing and swaying to a song on the radio as others watched and cheered her on. She had on short shorts and a maternity top that did not cover her huge stomach, but that didn't deter her, she didn't miss a beat.

"Yeah, that's Candy, our resident slut and all round party girl. This pregnancy has put a dent in her active social and sex life. She's not even sure who the father of her baby is, and doesn't care either. She's going back to exotic dancing, which is just another name for stripping, as soon as this is over. She is a piece of work. Miss Sallie just throws up her hands when talking about Candy."

'Lord help that child, she is headed down a path that can only lead to her destruction, and I cannot make her see it.' "We tell

Our Erring Sisters by Carol Henwood

Miss Sallie not to bother about Candy, she has no intention of changing her life. She likes it."

I was fascinated by Candy and wondered what it must be like to be a stripper, and how brave or crazy you had to be to get up in front of all those men and take your clothes off. I didn't think I would pursue a friendship with Candy, not that she would be interested in having a small town, provincial girl like me as a friend. The music stopped, Candy curtsied to everyone, laughed, and pulled a pack of cigarettes out of her bra and went to look for a secluded place to smoke.

Tapping me on my shoulder to get my attention, Andee said, "Shows over for now, Elizabeth, but there will be more believe me, Candy loves the attention. Anyway, what about you, when's your baby due?"

I brought my attention back to Andee and answered. "I think my due date is around September 3rd, give or take a few days. I have a pretty good idea when I got pregnant, but didn't keep up with anything, and I didn't go to a doctor until my mother made me go. She knew something was going on, but never asked about it, hoping she was wrong. When I finally went to the doctor, I was already four months pregnant. I had been in full blown denial, thought it would all go away. That's a good one, huh? I finished my hot dog and slaw and started looking for the ice cream.

"Your slaw was real tasty, and I don't even like slaw," I told Andee as I looked around the grounds which were quite lush and beautiful. There were day lilies and an array of colorful summer flowers growing by a back fence, as well as gardenias and hydrangeas blooming all around us. Geraniums and impatiens in ornate pots were strategically placed around the patio. The entrance to the back yard from the parking area was through an arbor with a Confederate Daisy growing up and over it with abundant, fragrant, tiny, yellow flowers. I could have been in an English garden at a lawn party, but I wasn't, and I wouldn't have been invited to a party in my current condition, either. The point is, someone cared enough, and worked

Our Erring Sisters by Carol Henwood

very hard to make this into a picturesque and restful area for us. The pre-meditated conceptions I had about Emmeriah Parrish were being replaced by feelings of safety and love by those in charge. I think I'll survive.

It was about 4:00 in the afternoon when the visitors to the home started to leave and the assigned clean up crew begun bagging the trash and cleaning up the patio and surrounding area. Some of the girls were napping in the comfortable lounge chairs scattered around the yard. Others were back inside stretched out on the sofas in the common room, playing cards or watching television. Miss Sallie took the opportunity to speak since everyone was quiet.

"Girls, this was a lovely day for us and our guests. Thank you for making it so very nice, as it was you who did most of the work, and you can be proud. Give yourselves a pat on the back." In unison, every girl lifted her hand and gave themselves a pat on the back, then broke into hysterical laughter. I found out that was Miss Sallie's way of building self esteem in each girl. It may have been childish for this group, but they indulged Miss Sallie's theory and secretly felt good about it.

"Now, the girls who have been assigned initial clean up, go ahead and get started, the majority of the heavy work will be done by Willie and Anthony. I believe we will delay our dinner tonight by one hour since we did have a late lunch today. Dinner will be at 6:30 tonight and snack time is still 9:00 p.m. Enjoy your leisure time, and for those of you have not met our newest resident, Elizabeth," Miss Sallie looked toward me and Andee under the big oak, "make a point of welcoming her. I will see everyone at dinner."

"Okay, Elizabeth, let's go get your suitcase and whatever else your brought from home and move it in with me," Andee said as we both got up and took our paper plates and cups over to one of the trash cans and dumped them in.

"I got out of the clean up detail thanks to you, and you had the good luck to get me as a roomie," Andee said as she slapped me on the back.

For the rest of the afternoon I unpacked and placed the few personal effects I had brought on my desk – a picture of my dog,

Our Erring Sisters by Carol Henwood

Lady, a loving, needy mutt, and a few favorite knick knacks, and on my bed I put an old, worn out stuffed tiger Daddy had bought for me at the county fair years ago. The room looked pretty good; it could have been a college dorm room if you didn't pay attention to the occupants.

"I love your posters of Hawaii, and especially that one of the surfer boys," I commented admiring her decorating style.

"Yeah, well, they don't all look like that, but most everyone is really tan, and surfs, but not all are blonds. I've been surfing for about eight years and I met Kalani, my boyfriend, or Lani for short, at the beach in a surfing contest two years ago. My parents never approved of him because he is Hawaiian, and that doesn't work for them. He is not an army brat like me, he was born and raised in the islands and even has royal blood running through his veins, and a better pedigree than me, but I was forbidden to mix with the natives, if you can believe that crap! 'Stick to your own kind, Greer.' That's my real name, Andrea Greer Gibson. So, I opted for the alias of Andee. Cute, huh? I know we're not supposed to reveal our real names, but I don't care, we'll probably never see each other again after this is all over," Andee spoke softly as she laid back on her bed tossing a tie-dyed pillow up in the air.

Thinking about it for a split second, I felt rebellious as I revealed my name also.

"I'm Ella Louise Cane. Miss Sallie chose the name Elizabeth since it starts with the same letter as Ella. I don't mind, though," I said as I leaned on my elbow lying on my side on the bed. "Do you get homesick being so far away from your family?" I asked thinking she wasn't the type to get homesick.

"Homesick?" she laughed. "I get homesick for Lani, the ocean, the beach, and my friends, but not particularly for my parents." I talk to them once a week, and they still make me feel like a loser over the phone, so I don't miss the constant guilt trip, but I guess I do miss some things about them. They just want to make sure I'm not talking to Lani."

Wanting to hear more of Andee's story, I continued to ask questions.

Our Erring Sisters by Carol Henwood

"Did Lani know about the baby?"

"Of course he knew. I told him in the beginning when I suspected I might be pregnant. When I confirmed that I was pregnant, we were going to tell our parents and get married. Even though we were both still in high school, we'd worry about that later. Obviously, that's not the way it turned out. My mother overheard a telephone conversation I had with Lani, she was always listening, and that was the end of that. My parents and Lani's got together and decided what should be done and, Voila!" Andee said as she sat up on her bed, smiled, and turned her hands out, palms up.

"We're you and Lani included in the decision making at all?" I anxiously inquired.

Andee got up from her bed and walked over to the shelf above her desk and took a picture down and brought it over for me to see.

"That's Lani," Andee said with obvious love and pride.

I took the picture from her and saw a very dark skinned, handsome, native Hawaiian teenage boy, smiling as he pointed to his surf board with the Pacific Ocean in the background.

"Oh, Andee, he's adorable. I bet you two really looked good together."

Taking the picture frame from me and placing it back on the shelf, Andee sighed and said, "Yes, I think we did. We were not included in any decision making about the fate of our baby. We were told separately by our parents that we were far too young and immature to come to a logical decision ourselves, and certainly too young to get married. Plus, the Hawaiians have very old and stringent rules about marriage, and they are not in favor of their children, especially their sons, marrying Caucasians. So our plans were doomed from the beginning. Lani wanted to marry me, but he couldn't disobey his parents, grandparents, and all the ancestors that his family consults with. Weird, I know. He was angry, sad, and helpless. But we're going to see what happens after I get back home," she said with a sinister gleam in her eyes.

Our Erring Sisters by Carol Henwood

"I've been here since April and have written Lani almost every day. He wrote back for a while, but his mother intercepted some of the letters and made it clear to him that he would not be allowed to correspond with me anymore. I called him once on a Sunday morning, hoping he might be by himself, and he was. He told me he was forbidden to stay in touch with me and that he was miserable. We decided I would call him on Sundays. His parents own a restaurant and they go in real early every day, I just have to be careful and hope they've left when I call. But I still call him, we talk fast, and I keep putting quarters in until they're all gone. It's worked so far, but I have to save every single nickel for phone calls. I'm a long way from home and I can't control what happens when I'm not there, but I know Lani loves me and wants us to be together. That's all I've got to hold on to."

Andee stood up and using her hairbrush as a microphone said in a most serious, news commentator's voice, "Just one of many soap operas unfolding here at the Emmeriah Parrish Home for unwed, knocked up young women. Stay tuned for further developments."

Andee threw her brush across the room hitting the wall. She lay down on her bed, propped up on one elbow facing me across the room where I lay on my bed, and asked,

"So, Elizabeth, does any of that sound familiar?"

We spent the next couple of hours sharing stories about our life experiences and how similar our situations were in many ways. We were both frightened about the future, wondered where we would be one year from now, and what life would be like after we left. Andee was two years younger than me and still had one more year of high school to complete. She was taking classes here at the home so she can make up the three months she missed when she dropped out of school for an "undisclosed illness."

"That's a good one, isn't it? 'Undisclosed illness;' I told my mother why not just tell the school I have leprosy, and at least people would stay away. She wished she'd done that once the word got out and friends from church, the base, and the neighborhood starting calling and coming by. They wanted to know if there was

Our Erring Sisters by Carol Henwood

anything they could do, and of course they tried to find out what terrible disease I had, and was it contagious?

She had to scramble to come up with an answer, but she managed to invent a non-life threatening condition that required complete rest and a mandatory trip to Atlanta, for further tests. Way to go, Mom, pretty creative of her. My Aunt Marcie does live here, so it all came together. That's the real reason I was sent to Atlanta, because of Aunt Marcie. She told Mom about this place and promised to keep an eye on me. She's great, not judgmental or anything, we talk every few days and she comes by a couple of times a month. She's Mom's younger sister by ten years and is married to a great guy named Rob. They have an adorable little boy who's two. Marcie's not nearly as uptight as my mother, and we get along famously."

Leaning up on her elbows to see the clock on her desk, Andee said, "I can't believe we've been lying here talking for almost two hours, and I've done most of the talking. I guess you're sorry you got a blabber mouth for a roommate!"

I sat up on my bed, stretched.

"This has been so great, it sure doesn't seem like two hours have passed by. You haven't done all the talking either, but just wait, I've got a whole bunch to unload on you, too. I haven't had a soul to talk to about this mess, except my parents who don't want to discuss it. The less said, the better. Just out of curiosity, if you've been here since April, have you always had a room to yourself?

"Nope. When I arrived they moved me in with Ginger, who delivered the very next day. Then within the next couple of weeks they moved another girl in with me who was about two months pregnant and cried every day and night for two weeks. I told Miss Sallie I couldn't take the nonstop tears; I sympathized with her, but it was constant and it was starting to make me a little crazy. She finally left, her family came and got her and took her back home, somewhere in Tennessee, I think. She was real young and it was pretty sad. I had one more roommate that moved in and she delivered the next week. Who knows? Maybe that's a good sign for you, Elizabeth, could be something about me that starts labor. Let's get up and go on down to the common room, named for us common girls," she said with a sly smile. "We all sort of congregate there before dinner every night, talk, watch a little news, see what's happening in the outside world and usually catch a sitcom or two before bed. I'll introduce you to the rest of the girls. You'll like most of them, we all get along pretty well."

I got up and stretched my arms above my head and moved from side to side.

"I'm ready to move too, but first I've got to pee, I'm about to pop."

"Yeah, me too, we're so lucky to be right across the hall from the bathroom, although it would have been sweet to have our own private bath, but this isn't exactly a resort; I have to keep reminding myself of that minor fact."

We laughed as we left our room and hurried across the hall. It was good to have another girl to talk to, and even better to laugh again.

Our Erring Sisters by Carol Henwood

Chapter Six

Della Cane drove most of the seventy miles from Atlanta to Desota in a fog. She could have driven it blindfolded, knowing the road so well, which was a good thing since her mind was not focused on the road, but on Ella. She wondered if Ella had broken down after she saw the car was out of sight, and would she really be okay there, despite her brave front. Della had been encouraged after her meeting with Sallie Mellete, but the entire day had been strange and stressful. Henry would be impatiently waiting her arrival back home, probably cutting his golf game short. Golf was a game of total concentration, and Della knew Henry would be distracted and worried. He would beg off early with an excuse for his poor playing, and go home to wait for her arrival.

Della allowed herself more tears after she was on the highway, wanting to get it out of her system for now. She needed to appear in control, not only for Henry's sake, but there was Tarelton to consider. He had been told of Ella's condition two weeks ago, but informed his parents he had already figured it out.

"I'm not an idiot, you know. I knew something was going on with Ella, and it wasn't a good thing. She seemed edgy, plus she had put on weight and I kidded her about it. I wish I hadn't done that now, but I thought maybe she might open up and tell me about it. It wasn't until later that I put it all together," Tarleton said sadly, shaking his head. As if he had forgotten something important, he quickly looked at his parents and asked, "But what about Lucas? I thought they would end up getting married anyway, what does he think about her going away to have his baby?"

Della immediately responded, "Don't be absurd, Tarleton. They would never have gotten married. It was a high school romance, if you want to call it that, but they were on different paths. It is better like this. Lucas Slade does not need to know,"

Our Erring Sisters by Carol Henwood

Della answered with finality. Looking puzzled, Tarleton asked, "You mean Lucas doesn't even know about the baby?"

Henry was quick to answer. "No, Tarleton, he does not, and as your mother just said, that is the way it is going to stay. Do you understand?"

Realizing the futility of any further questions, Tarleton replied, "Yes, I understand. No one will get anything out of me, and if they say anything about Ella, I'll kick their ass."

Henry Cane patted Tarelton on the shoulder saying, "That won't be necessary, son. We have managed to contain this so no one outside our family knows, except of course Dr. Graham, and I trust his professionalism to keep this to himself. You just stick to the story that Ella is a counselor at a summer camp in North Carolina and we'll make it through," Henry assured Tarelton.

It was close to 5:00 in the afternoon when Della pulled into the driveway. She saw Henry's car in the garage as she had suspected he would be home. Usually, on a Saturday he wouldn't be home before 6:30, playing twenty-seven holes of golf and partaking of a libation or two in the tap room afterwards; not so today. Della checked her face in the rear view mirror for redness and puffy eyes. She powdered her nose, smoothed her hair and was satisfied with her appearance. Gathering all the brochures and paperwork she had received from Miss Mellete, Della got out of her car and walked up the sidewalk to the back door and went inside. There she found Henry sitting at the piano, playing and singing one of his favorite songs, *"Some Enchanted Evening."* She quietly entered the den, sat down on the sofa, and listened as he movingly sang the last notes of the song. Henry was a man of many talents, music being his first love, and Della felt very fortunate to be married to such a gifted man.

Henry turned to her and in a soft and sorrowful voice asked, "Did you leave our girl in good hands?"

They spent the next three hours discussing the events of the day, Della reporting every last detail of the home itself, down to the number of stalls in the bathroom. She informed him of her meeting with Miss Mellete, the medical care Ella would receive, and what a routine day would be like for her. The conversation took place in the kitchen as Della prepared dinner for them, a supper of ham, tomatoes, deviled eggs and leftover potato casserole. They sat at the kitchen table eating and talking about the unanticipated upheaval in their lives and what the repercussions would be for the future.

The long day was coming to a welcome end and Henry and Della were exhausted, both physically and emotionally. Henry locked the doors, turned the lights out in the living room and den, and started up the stairs to the bedroom, with the unread daily newspaper under his arm.

"You coming up, Della?"

"You go on, Henry. I'm going to finish the dishes and I'll be up directly."

Della wiped the kitchen counters off after drying the dishes and putting the leftovers away. For a split second Della experienced an eerie sensation, almost an actual presence, as the hair stood up on the back of her neck. She shuddered and crossed her arms across her chest. Then it hit her. It was the quiet; the screaming silence of her surroundings that intensified the absence of Ella, but heightened the awareness of her ever present spirit. Della knew she was mentally drained and the mind played tricks in such a weakened condition. She could not have put a coherent sentence together, even if she'd wanted to continue the discussion with Henry, which she didn't. The answer to the ubiquitous question that continued to torment her was unknown for the time being. Sending Ella away, all alone, to have her baby and put it up for adoption, her very own grandchild whom she would never know, had it been the right thing to do? She and Henry had prayed for guidance, and shed tears over the answer. Della turned the lights out in the kitchen, stood up straight and said to no one, "We did the right thing. We will be stronger and closer as a family because of our decision. Good night, dear Ella, sleep tight. You are loved and never alone."

Our Erring Sisters by Carol Henwood

Chapter Seven

Andee and Ella walked into the common room where everyone was gathered. Ella was startled as Andee starting clapping her hands and yelling at the top of her lungs, "I want everyone to meet our newest mommy-to-be, and my roommate, Elizabeth, lucky girl that she is."

Amidst the sounds of groans and laughter, Lacy shouted out in her smoker's husky voice, "I don't know if I'd consider her lucky, other than the fact that none of your roommates last very long."

"I'm going to go around the room and everyone say your name, starting with you, KC," Andee said pointing to a tall girl with a blonde, pixie haircut, and huge brown eyes, who was reading *Seventeen Magazine*.

"Hi, Elizabeth, I'm KC. I'm from Virginia and I've got four months to go. It's not so bad here," she said quickly and sat down.

"I'd say that's a matter of opinion," chimed in Candy who was lying on her back, one leg propped up on the other, arms behind her head.

"Hi, I'm Candy, and that's my real name. I don't need any of that secretive shit. I've got three more months to go, maybe less, then I'm back out enjoying the good life."

"The good life is what landed you in here in the first place isn't it?" someone in the back sarcastically commented.

"We can always depend on Pollyanna over there to chime in," Candy said as she faced a girl who wore no make-up, had brown braids hanging down her back, and wore a long, loose dress that reached down to her ankles. She stood rigidly with an open Bible in her hands.

Sitting up quickly, Candy looked over her shoulder toward the voice and said, "Elizabeth, meet our resident moralist and Bible beater, Dedre. Now, refresh my memory, Dedra. How is it that you

Our Erring Sisters by Carol Henwood

came to be here? Immaculate conception, right? No, wait, I believe you and the preacher man got a little too cozy, and he came to know you in the Biblical sense. Now, isn't that more like it, Deeedra?" Candy asked with a sneer, drawing out Dedra's name.

Dedre turned red and splotchy and looked as if she might explode.

"How dare you, you whore of Babylon. You don't know what you're talking about. There is no truth to that lie, and I won't listen to it. Preacher Josiah is a moral man and I'm a moral girl. You are the spawn of the devil, Candy." She shrieked at the top of her lungs as everyone stared at her and stifled laughter. Dedra snapped her Bible shut and left the room, going through the library and up the stairs.

"Candy, now you've gone and done it. She's gone up to Miss Mellete's office to tell her she's being picked on again," Andee said, obviously annoyed with Candy.

"Oh, who cares? She's a royal pain in the ass."

Looking at me, Candy continued, "No one will be her roommate either because all she does is preach to you and read scripture all night. Poor Jessie agreed to room with her for her last couple of weeks, and she just tunes her out. I think Dedra is gonna go over the edge pretty soon, further out in la-la land then she is now. Serves her right for being so self-righteous, she's no different than any of us."

"She's harmless, Elizabeth; obnoxious, but harmless. Okay, where were we?" Andee asked, trying to get back on track.

"Hi, Elizabeth, we met earlier. I'm Kylene from Dallas, Texas. Some days are better than others here, but we do manage to have a pretty good time, in spite of everything."

"It's nice to see you again, Kylene."

I spoke to Lacy and Bonnie whom I had met earlier, as well as Jessie from Miss Mellete's office. By then it was time to go into dinner.

"You can meet the rest at dinner. There are not too many more that you'd want to meet anyway," she said with a grimace.

Our Erring Sisters by Carol Henwood

Dinner was prepared and served by the residents. Miss Mellete helped in the preparation of the meals, but mainly supervising. The menu was meatloaf, green beans, macaroni and cheese, and dinner rolls. Dessert was ice cream left over from the cook-out today, as well as iced tea, water and milk, chocolate and whole milk.

I sat at a table with Andee, Kylene, Bonnie, and Jessie. I finished my dinner and was pleasantly surprised.

"Well, that wasn't too bad, I'm impressed."

Andee pushed her half eaten plate away and commented, "It wasn't too good, either. But, I've never had a bad meal here, which is surprising since we do the cooking. The staff puts together a menu for each month, buys the groceries, and Miss Mellete gets all the ingredients out and ready. She stays in the kitchen to instruct the girls who are the cooks for the week on how to prepare everything. It's kind of like a mini chef school for pregnant girls, which I might add could come in pretty handy once we're out in the workplace. That is, of course, after we've delivered our babies, signed them away, and need a fresh, new start somewhere," she said in a mocking tone.

Pushing back her chair, Jessie picked her tray up and said, "I'd better get going, I promised Miss Mellete I would finish the paperwork she gave me to do. By the way, Elizabeth, new chores are assigned on Sunday and posted on the bulletin board in the hall. So look in the morning and see what your chore will be for the week. I guess Andee already told you that, but just in case, that's the way it works."

Jessie turned and walked into the kitchen with a couple of others who had the same assignment.

"I would have told you," Andee said, "but Jessie is very organized and always on top of everything, she's kind of the secretary of the group, and Miss Mellete's helper. She lets us all know what we are supposed to be doing, or not doing. It's fine, it keeps her busy and she's about to get out of here any minute."

I noticed a table on the other side of the room where a very pale girl sat alone. She had carrot red hair, thick glasses and looked

Our Erring Sisters by Carol Henwood

different, but I couldn't put my finger on what it was. She was dressed in an out of style, worn dress, even for maternity clothes.

She looked unkempt and almost dirty. I didn't want to stare, and Kylene saw me looking and explained.

"That's Elma you're looking at. Poor thing, it's such a sad story. She's not quite right in the head, has the mental age of about a ten year old, and she's twenty. She was living with her grandmother in a trailer park in south Atlanta somewhere. Her parents got tired of dealing with her, so they dumped her off there and split. The story I heard through the grapevine, which is pretty reliable," she said with authority, "is that she didn't go to school or do anything, just hung around the trailer park all day with the low life high school drop-outs. Her grandmother tried to keep her away from them, but there wasn't a whole lot she could do by herself. One night, five or six of the good ole boys decided to get her drunk, and have a little fun. She didn't know what was going on, just was happy for the attention. Long story short, they got her drunk, they all had a turn with her, and she ended up pregnant. Elma doesn't even know how she got pregnant, or much less what it means, and she told her grandmother her 'boy friends were loving her.' The grandmother didn't want any trouble, and didn't want Elma anymore either. Since there was no way they would ever find out who the father was, Elma was made a ward of the state and sent here to have her baby. God knows what will happen to her when she leaves here. Nice story, isn't it?"

What a place of contrasts, I thought: Candy, the party girl, Dedra, the religious zealot, Kylene, the stunning beauty from Texas, and Elma, the homely, pathetic creature who reminded me of the female characters from Steinbeck's *The Grapes of Wrath*.

Feeling sorry for her and feeling guilty for coming from a nice home and loving parents, I asked, "Does anybody talk to her, sit with her, or do anything with her?"

Bonnie took over where Kylene left off.

"The thing is, Elizabeth, Elma's a special case and Miss Mellete looks after her for the most part. She can't carry on a conversation with any of us because we have nothing in common. She can't help it, she's still a ten year old mentally. For instance, she wants to watch cartoons on Saturday mornings and kids' programs during the day, and it's almost like babysitting. We're not mean to her, but it's difficult. We all try to be kind and tolerate her juvenile behavior, sort of like an annoying little sister."

"Okay, I get it. Who's her roommate?"

"Roommate?"

"Elizabeth, no one could be her roommate," Andee whispered.

"First of all, she has to have someone help bathe her, and believe me, she needs lots of baths. She's not very fragrant; she gets dirty and smelly and has to be reminded to wash her hands after using the bathroom, just like a kid. Miss Mellete put her in a room near the nurses' station and she's looked after like the child she is."

I saw a girl whom I hadn't met yet go over to Elma, speak to her, and sit down at the table beside her.

"Who's that?"

Kylene peered around and looked at the table where Elma was sitting.

"That's Penny. She's the kindest person in this entire place. She's from a real small town in Alabama and goes out of her way to be nice to Elma. She looks at comic books with her and even watches those stupid cartoons with her when the rest of us just leave the room. Penny's another sad story. She wanted to keep her baby, but her parents said absolutely not, they would disown her if she did, so she cries more and more as her due date gets closer."

"She is so quiet, and never speaks above a whisper, not like some loud mouths in here," Andee added glaring at Candy and her groupies.

"As much as I hate to end this fabulous dining experience, I think we should go for our after dinner walk," Andee said to me as we picked up our plates and took them to the dirty dish station in the kitchen.

"Kitchen duty is probably going to be your first chore, Elizabeth, we'll see in the morning. Either washing dishes, or cooking, neither of them is too bad. The easiest detail is setting the

Our Erring Sisters by Carol Henwood

tables for meals, cleaning up after them, and dusting the house; the worst is cleaning the bathrooms. You'll get a chance to do them all before it's over with," she said with a cheery smile.

I listened to everything very carefully, and I hoped I would remember the other girls' names, and the inside information on the workings of the home. I was excited about taking a walk, and eagerly asked Andee, "Where do we walk around here? Looks like there's nothing but woods to me."

"We walk up and down the driveway at least four times. It's a long driveway, as I'm sure you noticed, and back and forth four times equals one mile. It's a good work-out; it's got a slight elevation at the end, just enough to make us huff and puff a little. We are encouraged to walk by the doctors, since they know we have no other form of exercise, or entertainment for that matter."

Andee and I stopped in the hallway on the way to our room, and looked out of the glass window that faced the woods and beyond that the outside world.

"You know, Elizabeth, I never would have thought that taking a walk would be something I looked forward to, but it's the highlight of my day. Now, there's something that's downright pitiful!" she said grimacing. "We all love our morning and evening walks, it helps clear out the cobwebs and all the snakes in our heads, for now anyway."

Hardly able to contain my enthusiasm, I told Andee about my restrictions at home, how I was unable to go out of the house very much, and always had to be careful not to be seen. So taking a walk outside anywhere was a treat and I couldn't wait to get started.

"First we need to get some tennis shoes on, I hope you brought some. After our walk we come in, take a shower, get in our PJ's , and watch a little Saturday night TV, if you want to, then go to our rooms by 10:00. We can read, study or write letters for a while, but lights out at 10:30. Just like camp, huh? Who could ask for a better Saturday night than this? No way for us to get into any trouble here; just good, clean fun – what a bore!"

Our Erring Sisters by Carol Henwood

We broke into laughter as we went to our room to change shoes for our walk. I was feeling more and more relaxed, almost enjoying myself and I was happy to have a friend.

Our Erring Sisters by Carol Henwood

Chapter Eight

I was in the suspended state of being half awake and half asleep when I heard strange voices and noises I wasn't accustomed to. Concluding that I was still asleep and in the grips of a weird dream, I turned over. The noise persisted, my eyes flew open and I gasped for air and remembered. I had made it through my first night at the Emmeriah Parrish Home for Unwed Mothers. There was much activity outside in the hallway, and across the room from me Andee was stirring in her bed. I saw the clock across the room and it said 6:45 a.m. There must be a fire drill or something else going on to cause this much noise and activity this early in the morning.

"Good morning, Elizabeth," Andee said sleepily, as she swung her legs to the floor.

"I've got to pee like a race horse. You don't need an alarm clock around here, everybody gets up to go to the bathroom at the same time," she said as she sprung from her bed right into her slippers. "I'll be right back," she said as she ran to the door. Before she was out of the door, she turned and asked in amazement, "You mean you don't have to pee?"

I was still trying to adjust to my surroundings when I realized my bladder was about to pop. "Yep, I've got to go," I answered with sudden urgency and I slid into my new slippers and was close behind on Andee's heels.

I had a quick look yesterday at the communal bathroom on my mini tour, and was pleasantly surprised at how clean it was. It sparkled and shined from the porcelain toilets and sinks to the chrome faucets. The tile floor was clean enough to eat off of, and I assumed a professional service did the work, but I had found out that cleaning the bathroom was one of our chores. The bathroom was indeed a beehive of activity. A roomful of pregnant girls

Our Erring Sisters by Carol Henwood

wearing bathrobes and slippers or bare feet and pajamas, shifting from one foot to the other, impatiently waiting their turn; six stalls and they all were occupied. Other girls were at the six sinks brushing their teeth, washing their faces, all the usual morning routines the entire world engages in. There were no bathtubs in this bathroom, and only three showers, so you practically had to make a reservation to get one, and there were already three girls waiting their turn. Andee told me the only bathtub in the home was in the large bathroom near the nurses' station, used mostly for the girls who had delivered and were back at the home for several days and needed to soak their bottoms. I could have gone a long time without hearing that delightful bit of information. Two stalls opened up simultaneously, and Andee and I each hurried into one. After the relief of an empty bladder, I stepped out and timidly spoke to Lacy, who was the next girl in line for my stall.

"Good morning, Lacy," I said cheerfully, as I came out and moved aside, using my best bathroom etiquette.

"Morning to you," Lacy replied in her smoker's raspy voice. "How was your first night here, get any sleep?" Lacy asked as she went into the stall.

"Okay, I guess, I don't think I moved all night," I answered feeling conspicuous speaking out loud as she used the toilet. "Andee and I were talking after we turned the lights out, and that's the last thing I remember. Then a little while ago I heard all this noise in the hall, and thought I was dreaming. I woke up wondering where I was; then it hit me."

"That happens for a while, at least it did to me," Lacy said as she flushed and emerged from the stall. We went over to two available sinks, washed our hands, checked ourselves out in the mirrors and groaned in unison, then laughed.

"It's Sunday morning, isn't it?" I asked Lacy as we left the bathroom. "What's everyone doing up so early? I thought Saturdays and Sundays we could sleep in until at least 9:00 or so?" I asked baffled.

"8:00 maybe, but it hardly ever happens. Miss Mellete says we can sleep or just stay in our rooms until 8:30 on the weekends,

Our Erring Sisters by Carol Henwood

but there is always something or somebody making noise, and besides, we're all up peeing half the night and first thing in the morning; might as well just stay up. Where's your roomie? She's usually the first one up around here."

"I don't know," I answered looking around, realizing Andee wasn't in the bathroom. "We came in together, I guess she's faster at taking care of business than me."

"There you are," I said as Lacy and I walked into my room and saw Andee sitting in the middle of her bed with a pile of silver coins and she continued to count as we sat on my bed.

"If Andee hasn't already told you, every Sunday morning she calls Lani in Hawaii."

"You got it Lacy girl," Andee said as she starting putting stacks of quarters, dimes and nickels into a drawstring bag of some kind. "Yep, I have to time the call just right, you know, so Lani's mom and dad are nowhere in sight. If they are, he tries to answer the phone before they do, and say something like 'wrong number, jerk,' so I'll know it's not a good time to talk. What we girls go through for love, right ladies? Toodles," Andee flippantly said as she left the room.

"Don't get me started, Andee," Lacy quickly responded as Andee waved at us and left the room.

"Everyone here lets Andee have the phone Sunday mornings so she can make her phone call. They can never talk for very long because she'll run out of change. It makes her happy and she deserves a little happiness. She's so far from home and she's been here the longest of any of us. I just hope things work out for her and Lani when she leaves here. I'm betting against it, but don't you tell her I said so," Lacy instructed, as she looked at me sternly.

"Don't worry, I can keep a secret, believe me," I said as I patted my belly. "Andee told me she and Lani are going to get back together and maybe somehow get their baby back. I don't see how that can happen, especially after she signs any papers consenting to an adoption, but maybe she has another plan in mind; Andee seems pretty resourceful."

Our Erring Sisters by Carol Henwood

"That's an understatement! Andee can come up with more ideas to keep us busy and actually have fun. This place would be a real drag without her around," Lacy said, as she looked around the room at all of the Hawaiian posters and leis Andee had decorated her side of the room with. "Okay, enough talk, time to get dressed for breakfast. We can't show up for meals in pajamas, just in case you didn't know. Do you go to church, Elizabeth?" Lacy suspiciously inquired.

"Well, yes, at home I do, I mean, not obsessively, but yes, my family does attend the Presbyterian Church, but not every single Sunday," I assured her hastily, not wanting her to think of me as another Dedra.

"I was just wondering because there's a bus that takes those who want to attend church on Sundays to the local denominations around here. Hey, it's just fine with me if you go to church, I was raised Baptist myself, but right now God and I aren't speaking."

Lacy stood up to leave and said as she left the room, "If you want to take a shower before breakfast, you'd better get on the stick. See you in the dining room."

I lucked out and got a shower stall as soon as I entered the bathroom. I was again very impressed with the sparkling tile in the stall and floor and thoroughly enjoyed my shower experience. I was appreciating small things now more than ever before. I didn't have time to wash my hair, roll it up, and sit under my portable hair dryer before breakfast, so I would have to postpone that important part of my beauty routine until later. When I walked back in to my room, Andee was lying down on her bed, and I could tell she had been crying.

"You okay, Andee?" I asked stupidly. "Did you talk to Lani?"

Wiping away the wetness on her cheeks, Andee managed to reply.

"If you consider two seconds a conversation, yes, I guess you could say I talked to Lani. Something is going on and he's not telling me about it. The last two times I've called him, he can't talk, at least that's the signal he gives me. He could at least go to a pay

Our Erring Sisters by Carol Henwood

phone like me and call from there just to let me know something – anything. But maybe he just doesn't give a damn about me anymore. Out of sight, out of mind; I guess I've been kidding myself thinking Lani would still want me after this is over," she sobbed and turned over on her side.

I did my best to console Andee, even though I had known her less than twenty-four hours, but I could identify with her pain and what she must be going through. There was a knock on the door and Lacy popped in the room.

"You two had better get a move on or you're going to be late for breakfast, and you know how Miss M. feels about punctuality, Andee. We don't want to get Elizabeth off to a bad start, now do we?" As soon as the words were out of her mouth, she was on Andee's bed beside me, asking what had happened.

"Elizabeth, I'll stay here with Andee for a few minutes, you go on down to breakfast and get your tray and sit down with Bonnie and Kylene if they are there. If Miss Mellete asks where Andee is, tell her she is coming, just running a little late this morning, she won't question you much since this is really your first full day. We'll be down in a few minutes, and don't mention anything in earshot of Miss Mellete about the phone call. We don't want her calling Andee's parents and getting things stirred up."

I hurried and got my clothes on, primped a little, and assured them I wouldn't say a word to anyone. With that I was out the door and on my way to breakfast as one of the girls, and had learned that most everyone looked out for each other here, and I felt very much a part of the group already.

I could smell the aroma of the bacon once I was in the main hallway going to the dining room. I still had the nervousness of being the new girl, but felt bolstered by Lacy putting her trust in me to help cover for Andee's tearful breakdown. I walked in with some of the other girls so I wasn't the last to arrive. Everyone spoke and asked how my first night had been and made small talk in general, putting me at ease.

Bonnie came over to me as I was going through the breakfast buffet line which, I might add, looked scrumptious.

Our Erring Sisters by Carol Henwood

"Mornin," Elizabeth, how'd you sleep?"

"Hi, Bonnie," I cheerfully replied, grateful to have someone seek me out. "I slept great, I don't think I moved all night. I guess yesterday pretty much wiped me out," I said, as I surveyed the many breakfast choices. "This is quite a spread, and it all looks delicious." There were pancakes, waffles, scrambled eggs, bacon, biscuits, grits, and an array of cereals and fruits, as well as yogurt. Orange, grapefruit, and tomato juice, as well as coffee and tea were offered.

"Yeah, Sunday morning breakfast is one meal nobody misses, and we can have as much as we want," Bonnie informed me as we piled our plates with a little of everything.

"You'd think since we do the cooking the meals wouldn't be very tasty, but they're usually good. You know we all have to have a turn or two in the kitchen, depending how long your stay here is, cooking and washing dishes. I love doing the cooking, and I guess if anything good comes out of this, we've learned our way around a kitchen, and that can't hurt," Bonnie said as I followed her over to a table where Kylene and KC were sitting with another girl I didn't recognize.

Kylene, as beautiful at 8:00 in the morning as she was at 8:00 last night, chuckled and said, "I see you survived your first night here, Elizabeth. Congratulations. I bet you didn't know where you were when you woke up this morning, am I right?"

"You're right. I experienced that scary moment when you don't recognize anything, and you think you've gone crazy, or something very strange is happening to you, then, bam, it hit me, and I was relieved at least to know I wasn't nuts."

"I'm Sarabeth. Nice to meet you, I was sick yesterday and didn't leave my room all day, I'm much better now, just a rotten summer cold."

Sarabeth was a gorgeous girl with olive skin, thick black hair, and eyebrows that framed her gray-green eyes.

"Hi, Sarabeth. It's nice to meet you, too. Nothing in the world worse than a summer cold," I added sympathetically.

78

Our Erring Sisters by Carol Henwood

"Sarabeth teaches our pottery class here, Elizabeth, and she's very good. We make all kinds of things, like vases and bowls, and then we stain them or whatever she tells us to do," Bonnie said as she smiled at Sarabeth and sat down next to her.

I pulled out the chair next to Kylene, sat down and dug into my inviting breakfast. We continued to chat as we ate.

"I was thinking about taking the pottery class, even though I'm not crafty or artsy at all, but sewing and poetry don't interest me, so I think pottery it is, especially since the teacher comes highly recommended."

"I don't know how good a teacher I am. I took a pottery course one semester in college at Auburn, and enjoyed it, made a few pieces that I liked, so I offered to teach it here after the instructor the home had recruited to teach had to back out."

Kylene was finishing up her plate of waffles and bacon. "She's just being modest. You are a fabulous teacher and everyone loves that class. It's offered on Wednesday mornings at 10:00, downstairs. I'll show you where later on, Elizabeth."

"Is anyone going to church this morning?" I asked, as I looked around the room to see if anyone was dressed in church clothes.

"I am," Bonnie announced. "I promised my mother I would try and go a few times while I'm here. Last time I attended the Episcopal Church not far from here. I just pray no one recognizes me while I'm there, but that's unlikely since we're miles from my neighborhood, and I'm a Baptist, anyway."

"So, why do you go the Episcopal Church if you're a Baptist?" I asked Bonnie.

"The Episcopalians aren't as narrow minded and strict as the Baptists are. I don't think the Episcopalians will be too judgmental if they discover I'm from the "home." You remember Dedra, right, Elizabeth?" Bonnie asked as she nodded her head in the direction of the unmistakable Dedra, in her floor length cotton dress, no make-up and braids to her waist.

"She always goes to church, every Sunday, but there is no Primitive Baptist Church around here, that's her denomination, and she bitches and complains about the services she attends on the way back to the home, as if she is the authority on all things holy. She's a major loon, and I'm embarrassed to be seen with her. I wonder what the members of these churches think when they see us come in on Sundays? I'm sure they're all non-judgmental and accepting," Bonnie said with a smirk on her face.

"Oh, right," Kylene chimed in. "They're all sweetness and light to your face, and tear you apart as soon as your back is turned. That's the way it is in my hometown, anyway."

"Are you planning on going to church, Elizabeth?" Bonnie asked.

"No, not today, I think I'll stay here and try and get a little more familiar with everything; maybe another Sunday. My mother's plan is to come and visit on Sundays and bring a picnic lunch. I don't know where she thinks we will have a picnic, but she doesn't think it's a good idea to leave here and venture out to a restaurant. My parents are so afraid we might run into someone they know."

"Awe, that's so nice of your Mom, Elizabeth. Is she coming back today?"

"Oh, no, next Sunday, so today is probably going to be a long day for me, but I'm going to try and stay busy."

Bonnie looked around the room and asked, "Where's Andee this morning? She's usually the first one here on Sunday mornings. That girl can put away some food for someone so tiny."

Just as I was about to expound on the whereabouts of my roommate, Lacy and Andee came into the dining room. Andee seemed to be in good spirits as she and Lacy were laughing as they got in line for breakfast.

"How's everybody this glorious morning?" Andee sang out as she pulled out a chair and squeezed in at our table.

"You sure are peppy this morning, Andee," Kylene exclaimed. "Do you have some exciting news, or is that just your natural Mary Sunshine personality coming through?" Kylene jokingly asked.

Lacy came up behind Andee with her tray and caught Kylene's eye, and shook her head to imply "don't ask."

Our Erring Sisters by Carol Henwood

"Good morning to all," Lacy said as she slid in beside Andee. "Nothing like Sunday morning breakfast here at the old home, one of the many perks we enjoy," Lacy sarcastically stated. "What's everyone up to today?"

"I'm off to church this morning, back for lunch and studying for a math test I have tomorrow morning," Bonnie said.

Kylene got up from the table, headed to the kitchen to drop off her tray, and came back over to the table. "I'm going to take a nice walk before it gets too hot, go over some college applications my mother keeps sending me, snooze a bit, and just be a lazy, fat pregnant girl for the rest of the day. How about you all?" she asked looking at Lacy and Andee.

"I like the lazy, fat, pregnant girl scenario; that sounds good to me. Andee and I have a test tomorrow too, so I guess we'll have to devote some time to studying."

Lacy looked at Andee who seemed to be in another world.

"Andee, let's you and me go for a walk with Kylene. It's supposed to get really hot this afternoon, and you know I don't like to sweat."

Perking up, Andee answered Lacy, "Sure, Lace, that sounds like a plan, but first we need to go check the bulletin board in the hall to see who's going to the doctor tomorrow morning. Elizabeth, you'll probably be on the list since you're new and the doctor has so see you and make his own evaluation, and all that good stuff. The way it works is, everyone goes once a month until eight months, then you go twice a month, and the ninth month, you go every week. Of course, if you're having problems, or are high risk, like Elma, then you go more often. I hope I'm on the list this week. The last time I was there was the first week in June. We all love going to the clinic, it gets us out, plus, there is one really cute doctor in the group, and if you're lucky, you see him. He is so handsome, and such a dreamboat. We all have crushes on him. The other doctors are okay, except for one Vietnamese woman doctor, who is a cold bitch. I think she considers us scum and treats us accordingly. Dr. Shit Ky or some gook name. Let's go look at the bulletin board."

Our Erring Sisters by Carol Henwood

I followed the others out of the dining room to the hallway where several more girls were standing in front of the bulletin board trying to read the list for the clinic in the morning. Candy was in front reading, taking up most of the room so no one else could see, and a very attractive black girl I hadn't seen before moved in next to her so she could take a look.

"Candy, do you mind if the rest of us have a chance to see the list?"

Candy looked at the girl and immediately moved aside.

"Sorry, Miss Divine, I'm on the list for tomorrow, and I see your name on there, too. I do love going into Atlanta to the clinic, we pass many of my haunts on the way, it brings back memories of good times," Candy said as she moved aside.

The well-groomed black girl, whose name I surmised was Divine, looked at Candy and said mockingly, "Those good times didn't do you much good 'cept land you in here, Candy." She turned around and called out, "Everybody spread out so we all can see who's on the list." More girls came up to the bulletin board to see if their names were on the much coveted list, glad to have Candy out of the way.

I turned to Andee who was scouring the sheet for her name, as well as mine, and I asked quietly, "I didn't know there were any black girls here, not that I mind, but I didn't think any would be in this place."

"Oh, yeah, there are two. Divine, who you just saw, and Sheree, who you should meet today, they're roommates. Divine loves to give Candy a hard time and Candy doesn't do a thing about it, she knows she's met her match."

Andee squealed and turned around to me, grabbed my arms, and excitedly said, "Yay, we're on the list for tomorrow – something to look forward to."

Stopping in her tracks, and shaking her head, Andee turned to me and said, "Is that pathetic, or what? Getting all excited about going to the doctor for a pelvic exam, boy oh boy, I've been here too long."

Our Erring Sisters by Carol Henwood

Kylene looked away with dismay, "Oh, nuts, I didn't make the cut this week. Maybe they've forgotten about me, it's been over a month since I've been there. Well, there's always next week. I'm going for a walk in a few minutes, see you two out there," she called out to Lacy and Andee as she walked out of the room.

I was leaving the gathering at the bulletin board when a felt a tap on my shoulder. It was Divine, the black girl I had asked about a few minutes earlier.

"I haven't met you yet, my name is Divine, and I think I heard your name is Elizabeth, at least in here it's Elizabeth," she added, smiling knowingly at me.

Divine had a warm smile with white, even teeth and smooth, ebony skin and hair. She wore a brightly colored paisley maternity dress and sandals that made her look as if she was on a tropical vacation.

"Yes, I'm Elizabeth, Andee's roommate. Nice to meet you, Divine. Is that your real name or just the one you use in here?" I asked.

"It's my middle name, but I like it better than what I go by on the outside, which is Dorcas. Dorcas Divine Davis. That's some name, huh?" she asked me as we both laughed out loud.

"My granny's name was Dorcas and she said I was a divine blessing when I was born, so that's how that came about. I don't believe she'd think I was too divine right now, if she was still alive."

"Well, I've never heard anything like it, but it's easy to remember. How much longer do you have to go until you deliver?" I asked, trying to figure out how many months pregnant she was, which was hard with the yards of material in her dress.

Putting both hands on her stomach, Divine answered, "My due date is approximately September 6th, but who really knows? It's all a guessing game at this place, unless of course you know exactly when you got pregnant, which is usually not the case here."

I responded with excitement, "That's close to my due date, which is September, 3rd, or there 'bouts, maybe we'll deliver around the same time."

Our Erring Sisters by Carol Henwood

"Could be, there are a few of us September girls. Misery loves company, so let's hope we're in the hospital together."

With a bit of trepidation, I asked Divine, "Is the father of your baby your boyfriend?"

Divine looked at me with eyes of a much older woman. "In the black world, things are a little different, Elizabeth. George, the daddy, and I have been knowing each other since we were babies ourselves. We grew up next door to each other and things just kind of took a natural turn when we got older. My parents like George, but just don't want me to marry him, and I don't much want to either. He's not ever going to amount to much, no ambition, and I've got ambition, I want to do something with my life. We all decided the best thing to do was give the baby up for adoption. My Daddy's a preacher, and let me tell you girl, there's no arguing with that man. So, I'm sad about the way it has turned out, but I reckon I got myself into this, and I got to live with it."

"You know, Divine, that's sort of like my situation, but I suppose I'm not a realist. I thought the father of my baby and I might have a chance at a life together, but that wasn't given much consideration in my family, and my Daddy's a man you don't argue with either, he's a judge. Sounds like you and me have a lot in common."

"See you later, Elizabeth. I'm going to church this morning, trying to stay in good with the man upstairs, as well as my earthly daddy, 'cause girl, you better believe he checks with Miss Mellete to make sure I go to the church house on Sundays."

Divine turned to go outside to the parking lot and see if the church bus had arrived, and waved, saying, "I see you and me are on the clinic list for tomorrow. If I don't see you before, see you then."

I headed in the direction of my room, feeling a little alone and homesick, missing my parents, brother, sister, and my life.

Our Erring Sisters by Carol Henwood

Chapter Nine

Della tossed and turned all night dreaming about Ella in her first pink tutu, and how she insisted on wearing it everywhere they went, as well as sleeping in it. All the childhood memories of Ella flooded her mind from the moment she closed her eyes until she gave in, got up and went downstairs to the kitchen. Why is it, she wondered, that every problem is magnified ten-fold in the middle of the night, but with the light of day the ominous, worrisome issue you were losing sleep over doesn't seem so menacing, even solvable; that is, most problems, with the exception of the current one. Yes, there was a solution for this particular dilemma, and it had been put into place, but the long term repercussions for Ella gnawed at Della's insides.

Della made a pot of coffee and was sitting at the kitchen table in semidarkness, waiting on the percolator to hiss and steam, indicating the coffee was ready when she heard a noise in the den, and saw Henry walk through the door.

"You've been awake too, I see," he said in a weary voice as he sat down at the table next to her, his wavy hair mussed from a restless night. He tied the sash on his plaid robe and patted Della's hands, which were folded on the table, and sat down and leaned back in the chair crossing his arms over his chest.

"Where did we go wrong, Della? Were we not paying enough attention, or maybe too much, being too judgmental in Ella's choice of boys, not liking anyone unless they met our standards, and this was her way of rebelling? I only want the best for my children and sometimes what we want for them is not what they want. I hope Ella's not going to have emotional problems because of this, but we've got all we can say grace over for the present," he said, as he got up and walked over to get two coffee cups out of the kitchen cabinet. Henry poured two cups of coffee and brought the sugar bowl, a bottle of milk, and a spoon over to the table and sat down. "Well, ole girl, if we had any idea about going back to sleep tonight, you can forget that. Might as well have a very early breakfast, what do ya say?"

Della looked at the clock above the refrigerator and answered, "A 4:00 a.m. breakfast might just be what the doctor ordered. Bacon, eggs, and grits sound okay to you?" she asked as she stood up and switched on the overhead light.

"Sounds terrific to me, we'll get a head start on the day and just go to bed earlier tonight, nothing wrong with that."

Della took the bacon out of the refrigerator, put the skillet on the stove and placed several pieces of bacon strips side by side in the pan. Next, she went to the pantry, took out a box of grits, put water in a boiler on the stove and waited for it to boil. Looking back over her shoulder, she continued the conversation with Henry.

"Henry, I don't think we should automatically assume that lack of good parenting was the reason Ella got pregnant. I think we've done an admirable job of raising our children, and should be proud of that. Until now, Emily Anne, Ella, and Tarleton have not caused us one moment's worth of worry, and that in itself is quite an accomplishment. Ella is, and always has been, a very sensible girl, but prone to dreamy, romantic notions, and she convinced herself this was true love, then those raging teenage hormones took over, and her sense of right and wrong went right out the window. Ella is a good girl, not flighty or impetuous, and certainly moral, but Lucas has had her starry-eyed for more than a year now. I saw them on more than one occasion, gazing at each other like love sick puppies and it made me very uneasy. I know they think they're in love, but what do young people really know about true love, for goodness sakes? It's certainly not the fairly tale life that Ella dreams about, no offense, dear," Della added as she winked at Henry and continued cracking eggs into a bowl for scrambled eggs.

Henry had moved and was now standing up, leaning against the kitchen counter next to Della and drinking coffee, watching her as she expertly beat the eggs, adding a little water to make them fluffy, and seasoning them with salt and pepper.

Our Erring Sisters by Carol Henwood

"Well, it sure wouldn't have been a fairly tale life with Lucas Slade if she had married him. I suppose we should have put a stop to the relationship long ago, before it became sexually charged, but how did we even know when that was?"

Groaning and shaking his head, he poured another cup of coffee and added, "I guess we both were putting our heads in the sand, ignoring the obvious and hoping it wasn't true. I can't even entertain the idea of Ella in an intimate relationship, it's too much for my mind to process, plus, I don't want to think about it. I did realize last year, finally, that she was a grown up young woman, capable of having sexual thoughts and feelings, not the same little girl I could bounce on my knee anymore. Ella has many wonderful attributes, and could have had her pick of any boy she wanted in Desota, and she chose Lucas Slade. I don't understand it."

"Get the toaster out for me, will you Henry?" Della asked, as she turned the bacon and got two place mats out of a drawer, along with silverware, and placed them on the table. "Ella has always been unsure of herself, not like Emily Anne who has known since she was six years old what she wanted in life. Not Ella, she is insecure about most everything she has ever done, never felt she quite measured up to the rest of her friends, which is something that baffles me. If she had warts, an unfortunate deformity, or was slow, that might be reason for her to feel inferior, but none of that is the case. She was voted class favorite in the ninth grade, made varsity cheerleader in the tenth grade, was homecoming queen and senior beauty. You would think all those accolades would have given her self confidence, but it hasn't. She doesn't make the good grades that Ginny, Sue Ellen, and Luanna make, but it's not from lack of trying. You know how poorly she performs in math, tutor or not, she just cannot get a grade above a C minus or D. She has some mental block, and the math teacher is less than helpful."

Taking the bacon out of skillet and placing it on a paper towel to drain, Della poured the eggs into the pan. "I know I sound as if I'm making excuses for her, and I guess I am, but it is a mystery to me why she has so little self-esteem."

Our Erring Sisters by Carol Henwood

Henry was sitting down at the kitchen table, staring into space, with his fingers interlaced behind his head. "Maybe it was me, Della. Maybe I've pushed the children too hard to achieve good grades, to always be first in whatever endeavors they undertake, to accomplish things that will matter in the real world. I'm sure they are sick to death of hearing my stories about teaching myself to type, teaching myself shorthand, practicing my voice and piano lessons, studying in law school, never settling for second place. Practice, practice, practice, and achieve more, more, more. I guess they tuned all of that out years ago. I know I've pushed Tarleton to be the best in every sport he ever played, and showed disappointment when he didn't come in first and yes, I was insensitive when Ella was voted homecoming queen her senior year, as you well know," Henry said sheepishly.

Della softly smiled at Henry, recalling the torment he went through after the insensitive remark he made to Ella that a little over a year ago. It had been a long, hard day on the court for him, and after a grueling 2 ½ hour drive back to Desota from Atlanta, Henry arrived home at 6:30 p.m., haggard and worn out. As soon as he walked through the door, Ella excitedly sprang the news of her election as homecoming queen.

"I guess that's fine, Ella, but it would have been more of an honor to be voted 'Most Intelligent' or 'Most Likely to Succeed.'"

Ella was as deflated as a child's balloon someone had heartlessly popped. Her demeanor changed from one of anticipation and hope of approval to embarrassment and shame for thinking her minor victory would be significant in her father's opinion. Ella said nothing and quickly left the room, her face flushed, and her eyes burning with tears.

"If I could take one thing back I had ever said in my life that would be it. Of course, I apologized a few minutes later as you well know, but once you say the words, they're out there floating around forever, and you can't get them back. Ella was gracious in accepting my apology for being so callous and tactless, but the damage was done. So, yes, I feel sure I have contributed to her low self-esteem, and probably Tarelton's, too. Emily Anne is a different child

Our Erring Sisters by Carol Henwood

completely. She knows what she wants, and goes after it. She's also very much like me, and that's why we butt heads occasionally," Henry jokingly added.

Della took the eggs out of the pan and put them on the platter with the bacon. The toast was in the toaster, the grits were ready, and the table was set.

"Go ahead and sit down, Henry, I'll bring everything to the table." Della adjusted the sash on her pink and white seersucker robe as she waited for the toast to pop up. The grits were ready and Della poured them into a bowl, dropped a hefty pat of butter in the middle, and took the bowl to the table, along with the platter of eggs and bacon. Della paused before she sat down, looked directly at Henry.

"Every parent in the world can go back and dissect each sentence they ever uttered to their child and find harm somewhere in it. That's just the way it is when you're raising children. You do the best you can, and pray to God for help with the rest. You are an accomplished man, Henry, more than most, and because of that the bar is set a little higher for our children, but I, for one, am grateful they have such a superior role model to look up to. Now, enough of this pre-dawn analysis, let's have our sunrise breakfast and greet the day like the blessed people we are."

Our Erring Sisters by Carol Henwood

Chapter Ten

I spent most of the day Sunday familiarizing myself with the home, exploring and finding all kinds of nooks and crannies in the former private residence. It must have been quite a showplace at one time. It was still well maintained for its present purpose, but lacked the warmth of a real home with parents, children and family pets. Andee and Lacy were studying for an upcoming math test, so I visited for while with Kylene, ate lunch, met a few more girls and finally, went to the nurses' station and met Nurse Veressa Robbins who was on duty every other weekend.

Nurse Robbins was a very large black woman who almost filled up the entire room. Kylene had warned me so my eyes didn't pop out, but Nurse Robbins was as big as a mountain. I hadn't planned on actually going in the room, but before Kylene and I could quietly back up, a booming voice called out.

"Who's that out there? Don't you be sneaking around. If you need to see me, come on in, now."

"It's just me, Kylene, Nurse Robbins, and this is Elizabeth, she just moved in yesterday," Kylene said as we slowly crept back toward her door.

"Well, I'm sure glad you brought her down here, cuz I was gonna have to go find her myself, so's I can make up a weekend report on new residents. My bursitis is acting up something fierce today, and I don't feel like traipsing around all over the place. Come on in, girls, I'm not gonna bite you, am I Kylene?" Nurse Robbins said, as she laughed and her entire body jiggled.

"Elizabeth, let's see here. Elizabeth Nash, that right, chile?" Nurse Robbins asked as she examined a folder with my name on it.

Our Erring Sisters by Carol Henwood

"Yes, that's me. What is it you need to do?" I asked, fearful I was going to get another examination from this large woman, as well as another one tomorrow.

"I just need to ask you some questions, take your blood pressure, pulse, feel around on your belly some, that sort of thing. Always paperwork involved, you know. Kylene, you can go on back down to the dorm, Elizabeth will be there directly," Nurse Robbins said, as she pried herself out of the chair, groaning and grunting all the while.

"Okay, I'll see you in a few minutes, Elizabeth," Kylene said looking at me and gesturing with her hands, and motioning the words, "I'm sorry."

"Sit down right here, Elizabeth, and let me get your vital signs real quick like," Nurse Robbins told me as she pointed to a chair across from the desk.

"You don't need to be nervous about anything, I know you are, but you don't need to be. This is just so's we'll have an up to date record of your vitals in our files, since this is the first time anyone has seen you here, and it says here," she said looking down at the open folder, "that you'll be going down to the clinic tomorrow, and they need something to compare your current BP and pulse to when they take it at the clinic. Now, roll your sleeve up and let me get a blood pressure."

After fifteen minutes I was freed from the gentle hands of Nurse Robbins, and I was glad I had met her. She reminded me of our maid, Mattie, who had been with us for as long as I could remember. Both women possessed the same, sweet nurturing manner. She assured me that I was going to be fine, and I didn't need to work myself into a frightened frenzy about giving birth, it was as natural as the sun coming up every day, and I could talk to her anytime about my concerns. I felt better, not so homesick anymore, and I went back to my room to relax and wait on Andee.

Our Erring Sisters by Carol Henwood

Chapter Eleven

I was dead asleep when Andee's alarm clock bolted me awake and nearly scared me to death; amazingly, Andee slept right through it. I looked out of the window into the woods and saw the sun shining through the trees, the early morning dew glistening on the leaves, and said out loud, "How beautiful."

"What, are you talking to me?" Andee joked as she rolled over and put the pillow over her head.

I looked back at Andee, laughed, and answered, "No, I'm certainly not talking to you, the woods are beautiful. I know you said your alarm clock was loud, but that thing could wake the dead! Remember, we go to the clinic today, and you said we had to be up and ready after breakfast."

Andee quickly sat up. "Oh, that's right," she gleefully said as she clapped her hands together like an excited child on her birthday.

We both put our slippers on and hurried across the hall to the bathroom. After relieving our full bladders, we brushed our teeth, washed our faces, and went back across the hall to get dressed.

"Okay, this is how it works. We go down to breakfast now, finish by 7:30, and for those of us that are lucky enough to be on the clinic list today, we just hang out in our rooms until the bus arrives for our trip downtown. We usually leave here no later than 8:15, since our appointments start at 9:00. There are between five and ten of us each time, depending on whose due date is close, and the usual monthly appointments.

Now, if you are lucky, you might get to see Dr. Rhett Reynolds, who is a scrumptious hunk of a man, and so, so nice. Then, there is Dr. Wilbur Watkins, an ugly, old guy who gives everybody the creeps by the way he looks at you, like he thinks there might be a little extra something for him later. Yuk! Then there is

Our Erring Sisters by Carol Henwood

the bitchy Vietnamese woman doctor, who goes out of her way to be rough during the pelvic exam, like it's her way of getting back at Americans for going over to her crappy country and trying to help them, which they don't even appreciate. They're a brutal, heartless people; that's what I think. There are a few other doctors in the group, but none like Dr. Reynolds. He has blond hair, and the most beautiful blue-green eyes and long eyelashes you have ever seen on a man. Every girl in here has a crush on him; he treats us like human beings, not untouchables like Dr. Shit Ky, or whatever her name is."

"What do we wear to the appointment, Andee, something a little dressier than our usual outfits?" I asked, feeling as if we were going to a job interview.

"I always dress with a little more care, just in case I see Dr. Reynolds, but no, just the regular maternity shorts or dresses you wear around here is fine,"

We finished dressing, taking special care with our hair and make-up, almost as if we were getting ready for a much anticipated date. We walked down to breakfast, got our trays, and sat down with Bonnie, Sarabeth, and KC, who were also going to the clinic.

Before we could get a word out, KC leaned over and whispered, "Did you hear Jessie went into labor last night and they finally took her to the hospital early this morning. Poor, skinny, thing, she could hardly walk anymore she was so big, but we haven't heard if she's delivered yet. Did ya'll hear anything last night? Her room is on your end of the hall, so we thought you'd know something."

"No, I didn't hear a sound, but I am so happy for her, she's been here forever. Did you hear anything Elizabeth?"

"No, I was out like a light and didn't hear a thing. Who'd you say her roommate is?" I asked.

"Dedra, the Bible beater," Bonnie said. "I'm sure she was a big help to Jessie," she said sarcastically, "probably tried doing an exorcism on the poor kid. Dedra is one strange chick."

"Well, I sure hope everything went okay for her. I guess we'll hear something today," Andee said as she started in on her breakfast. "On a different note, I see we're all decked out in our

Our Erring Sisters by Carol Henwood

best fatty fashions hoping for an encounter with Dr. Delicious today. Am I right, or am I right?" Andee asked, with a big grin on her face.

"Never hurts to look your best. Who knows, there might be an eligible doctor working today who doesn't have a problem with a girl who got into a wee bit of trouble," Bonnie offered, as she looked to the others for support.

"Boy, are you living in fantasy land, Bonnie. That doesn't happen in the real world, be nice if it did, but our chances of meeting any eligible man anytime in the near future looks pretty dim, and certainly not one of our doctors at the clinic," Andee answered.

"Oh, pooh, I'm an optimist – anything can happen in life."

"You got that right, sister, and it happened to all of us. If you get lucky, old Dr. Watkins might make a pass at you, or adopt you, since he's old enough to be your grandfather," Andee slapped the table laughing at her own joke.

Divine walked over to our table along with a very young black girl.

"I bet I know why everybody at this table is so jolly this morning. Could it be we're on the party bus today?" she asked with her eyes twinkling.

"You all make this doctor's appointment out to be an unforgettable experience," I said, mystified at the excitement generated by a mere visit to the doctor.

"Once you've been here a few weeks, you'll feel just like we do, Elizabeth. It is an adventure, and we're out of here for a few hours. Now, what could be better than that?" Bonnie asked.

"Elizabeth, I want you to meet my friend and the only other sister in here," Divine said as she put her arm around the petite black girl who appeared extremely timid, and kept looking down at the floor. "Sheree, meet Elizabeth, she just moved in yesterday."

"Nice to meet you, Sheree," I said smiling, amazed at how childlike she seemed.

In a voice barely audible she answered, "Nice to meet you, too." She looked up briefly, caught my eye, and quickly looked away.

Our Erring Sisters by Carol Henwood

"I'm gonna walk Sheree back down to Miss Mellete's and come on back and grab a quick bite before it's time to go downtown. I'll be back in a few minutes," she said, as she guided Sheree out of the dining room.

"Is Sheree as young as she looks?" I asked incredulously.

"She is only fourteen, Elizabeth, the youngest girl here, and so frightened. Divine has taken her under her capable wing and treats her like her little sister," Sarabeth said.

"So, I guess she and Divine are roommates, right?"

"Yep, and their room is the one at the other end of the house, near the nurses' station, Elma's room is down there, too. Miss Mellete keeps an eye on both of them," Andee added.

Just as I was about to ask more questions, Miss Mellete walked over to our table.

"Good morning, girls, ready for your clinic visits, I see," she said as she scrutinized our clothes and make-up.

"What makes you think that, Miss Mellete, don't we always look this fabulous?" Andee asked, feigning innocence.

Her blue eyes sparkled and crinkled around the edges as she answered, "Of course, I think you are all beautiful girls and look pretty in whatever you wear, and I also know that a handsome young doctor is on staff at the clinic. Could that have something to do with your extra efforts today?"

"Why Miss Melette, whatever do you mean?" I asked in my best Scarlett O'Hara Southern simple voice, feeling enough at ease to join in the fun. "I only wear this ole thing when I don't care how I look."

The whole table got a kick out of my performance and applauded enthusiastically. Miss Mellete seemed to enjoy the playful banter as well.

"Elizabeth, I am pleased to see you survived your first weekend here, and have made friends, too. Now, on to serious business. The clinic bus will leave here promptly at 8:15 and you all should be in the parking lot five minutes before, ready to board. Nurse Knight will be accompanying you this morning, and you know she is a stickler for punctuality, so don't make her wait. Remember, be courteous and mind your manners inside the clinic, you always want to act like the ladies you are."

As Miss Mellete turned to walk away, KC called out, "Miss Mellete, do you have any news on Jessie?"

Turning around with a strained expression on her face, she answered.

"Yes, I was going to make the announcement at dinner time tonight. Jessie delivered twin girls about an hour ago, and all are doing well."

We all gasped and our hands flew to our mouths in shock.

"It was a surprise to the doctors, too, apparently one of the babies was hidden behind the other, and the doctors just thought Jessie would have a large baby. We are grateful to God the babies and Jessie are doing fine, but it is going to make the separation harder for the poor child. We will all have to be especially kind and supportive of her when she comes back to the home. Now, I must go get your charts together for Nurse Knight," she said, as she quickly left us.

We all looked at each other knowing the agony Jessie must be in right now.

"How very sad for her. Twins. She is one of five children from somewhere in South Carolina, the oldest and only girl. How sad," Sarabeth said, tears filling her huge eyes.

"I've lost my appetite," Andee said, pushing away her tray. "The stupid doctors didn't know? At least if she had known, she could have prepared herself for having to give two babies away. Brother, is she ever going to need long term counseling to deal with this. It's probably gonna screw her up for a long time," Andee said, with a hint of anger in her voice as she pushed back from the table.

Stunned, I followed suit and picked up my tray with my uneaten breakfast on it, grabbing a banana in case I got nauseated on the bus. There was a buzzing sound in the dining room. Everyone was whispering about Jessie, and hoping the same thing wouldn't happen to them. It was hard enough trying to come to grips with the reality we would be leaving here without one child, let alone two.

Our Erring Sisters by Carol Henwood

Andee and I went back to our room and lay down on our beds for the next ten minutes, then got up and walked through the house to the parking lot. As we passed through the common room, the girls who were not going to the clinic were watching the Today Show, with Hugh Downs, waiting for school to start or to undertake their chores for the day.

"Ya'll are so lucky. Tell Dr. Delicious I said hello, and I'll see him next week," Lacy called out to us.

There were eight of us going today, and I saw a skeletal looking woman who resembled a female Icabod Crane standing at the entrance to the mini bus with a clipboard and a scowl on her most unattractive face. I could tell she was all business.

"Oh, shit," Divine said as we got closer to the door. "I see we've got Nurse Gladys Knight, minus the Pips, today. If anybody could use a pip or two, it's this old sourpuss."

"Good morning, Nurse Knight," Divine sang out as she passed her on the way into the bus. The woman said nothing, not even acknowledging Divine, just checked her name off.

As I stepped up onto the bus, a booming voice stopped me cold.

"Just a minute young lady. Stop right there."

I immediately froze and stepped back down off the bus. I turned around and looked into the beady brown eyes of Nurse Knight. Her face was so narrow, it looked as if it had been pushed together with a vise. Her long pointed nose hosted a wart on the tip, with a bristle growing out of it; her mouth was home to large, protruding teeth, giving her the appearance of an angry rodent. She had dull, greasy black hair pulled back into a severe bun, stretching the skin around her eyes so taunt, it gave her a maniacal glare. I had never seen anyone quite as scary looking as her.

"Are you Elizabeth Nash?" she demanded.

"Yes, yes that's me. I'm Elizabeth," I answered obediently, with a smile.

She gave me the once over, stopping at my eyes with a look of distaste.

"You can get on the bus, now."

Our Erring Sisters by Carol Henwood

Once inside the bus, I sat next to Andee, and behind Divine and Bonnie. Divine stuck her head around from her seat and said, "Girl, don't you go and be so nice to that old biddy. She don't even pretend to care about us, so don't you go thanking her for nothing," Divine instructed me. "She's the kind of nurse that gives nurses a bad name, you know what I mean?"

"I know, but I didn't want to get off on the wrong foot with the likes of her," I said apologetically.

Bonnie's head popped up over the seat.

"Elizabeth, for future reference, Nurse Olive Oyle is here only twice a week, she's kind of a substitute, so we don't have to deal with her too much. There are three other nurses and they're okay. You met Nurse Robbins yesterday, she's great and our favorite; then, there's Nurse Brooks, who's a young, white woman who just found out she's pregnant, and a mid-forties black lady who is very nice. So, relax, your chances of having any hands on meeting with old ugly out there are remote," Bonnie said and turned back around and sat down.

"Thanks for filling me in," I said gratefully.

"Let's get rolling, Leroy," Divine called out the bus driver. "We've got important business downtown and we can't be late."

"Don't you fret none, Miss Divine, I'm gonna get you all there in plenty of time. Nurse Knight said we be waiting on one more girl, and then we can get moving. So, you just sit back and relax and leave Leroy in charge."

Just as Andee was about to curse whoever it was we were waiting on, we saw Dedra walking slowly up to the bus, sobbing. Miss Mellete was beside her, with her arm around Dedra's shoulder, consoling her. Nurse Knight and Miss Mellete had a few words, and then Dedra got on the bus and sat in the first seat next to Nurse Knight's reserved seat.

"The drama queen arrives," Bonnie said under her breath.

"I didn't know she was coming today," Andee said quietly to me, then aloud to the rest, "Aren't we blessed to have Sister Dedra on board today, just in case we feel the urge to have her quote

Our Erring Sisters by Carol Henwood

scripture on the sin of fornication and how we are all damned to hell, all except Dedra of course, who fornicated with a minister, and he gave her a pass on hell. How caring of him, he knows when he's got a good thing going."

Amidst the laughter, Nurse Knight stood and sternly addressed us. "Quiet down, now!" she yelled. "I will not tolerate that kind of vulgar talk," she spit her words directly at Andee.

"The rest of you could do with a little piety, and less of that arrogant attitude you so proudly display. Dedra had a long night and is exhausted. Miss Mellete added her to the clinic list today because she was so distraught with Jessie going into labor last night. I will not tolerate any more unkind comments," she said in Andee's direction. "That goes for all of you," she added, looking at everyone on the bus. With that she sat down in her seat at the front of the bus, next to Dedra, who continued sobbing.

KC whispered to Andee from across the aisle, "I'd like to know why she is so damn tired? She didn't have twins, she probably hid under the bed and told poor Jessie to pipe down. She's even got that old bat fooled. Dedra is the biggest faker I've ever met, pretending to be so righteous, as if she didn't get in this condition the same way we did."

"I'll tell you the one person who sees right through her and that's Nurse Robbins. Dedra is down there every weekend with a new ailment or complaint," Andee said. "Nurse Robbins told me she thinks Dedra has a psychological disorder of some kind, always needing to be the center of attention, and acting so holier than thou; something's going on with that. I wonder what her family is like?"

Candy, who was sitting in the back of the bus and had been uncharacteristically quiet, provided us with her take.

"Fucked up, that's what her family's like. Her prairie dress get-up and plain Jane appearance is nothing but a cover-up. I guarantee you, she wants to be like the rest of us, but her family belongs to some ultra religious church, or cult, and all the girls have to dress like that, wear their hair in those turn-of the-century long braids, and act so virginal and pure. It's total bullshit," she added with disgust.

Our Erring Sisters by Carol Henwood

We were all facing the back of the bus, listening to Candy's assessment of Dedra's life, and before I knew it, I blurted out, "How do you know about her family?

"I know because she's from the same area of south Atlanta that I'm from and that's also where that church is located. The men who run the place have their pick of any of the girls they want, and it's all in the name of the Lord. I didn't know Dedra, mind you, but I have talked to a couple of girls who sneaked away from a Wednesday night prayer meeting once, and let me tell you, praying is not what was going on in that place, according to them. I don't know if Dedra was the first one to get knocked up, or why they sent her here, maybe because it was the head honcho who got her pregnant. It's all very shady, ladies," she concluded with a laugh.

We all faced forward and were quiet as we tried to absorb what we had just heard. I looked out of the window as we drove down Peachtree Road, all so familiar to me. I noticed the people in the cars driving up and down the road, on their way to work, or school, or grocery shopping, wondering if any of them were friends with my parents, or friends of my sister, and thought for a brief moment, maybe I should move away from the window in case a fellow traveler looked up at the bus while at a stop light, saw me and said, 'Why, that's Judge Henry Cane's daughter, Ella, on that bus. She must have gotten herself into some trouble.' Then, I thought, that's ridiculous, nobody would recognize me, even if we were face to face. There was no sign on the bus, either, proclaiming to the world that a bus load of disgraced, pregnant teenagers were aboard. Dumb. I just sat back, closed my eyes, and waited to arrive at the clinic.

Chapter Twelve

The motion of the bus and the warm sun coming through my window lulled me to sleep for the duration of the trip. I was awakened by the blaring voice of Nurse Knight.

"Everyone wake up. You will conduct yourselves properly inside the clinic, no loud talking or acting up, or you will be sorry. There are always other patients besides you in the waiting room, so try not to bring attention to yourselves, if you can possibly manage," she added spitefully.

"Bitch" Divine said as she leaned over to pick up her purse.

We filed off the bus and I saw that we were at a clinic connected to one of the downtown hospitals. Leroy had pulled into the drop off location and we were de-boarding there. He would go park elsewhere and come back to pick us up at noon.

I followed the crowd, looking all around and taking in everything, and feeling nervous and excited at the same time. It was a busy place. Nurses, doctors, and orderlies scurrying about with clipboards, or guiding people on stretchers and in wheelchairs down the long, busy hallway, filled with poor, sick people, or relatives of poor, sick people. I felt lost and scared, and wanted to have my mother with me, I needed her soothing voice and velvet strength to help me not be afraid. But, she wasn't here and I would have to buck up and take care of myself. I would take my lead from my new friends, because we were in this together, and were each others' advocates.

The waiting room was large, with an aisle in the middle, and filled with rows of folding chairs. There was a magazine rack at the front of the room, next to the window where patients checked themselves in. We were told to find a seat and wait for our names to be called. I had brought the book I was currently reading, *The Dirty Dozen*, because Andee informed me the magazines were all old and outdated, and nothing we would want to read anyway. We were allowed to buy juice or a soft drink and a snack from the vending machine out in the hallway if we got hungry, because we would probably be here through our lunchtime, but would be offered a late lunch upon our return. I was glad I brought the banana; it might be a long morning.

"I didn't think there would be other people here besides us," I leaned over and said to Bonnie, who was sitting on one side of me.

"Oh, yeah, there's a little bit of everything here, but the doctors who work here are the best, at least that's what my mother says."

Time passed slowly as I watched the patients being called back to see a doctor. There was one pregnant woman in the waiting room who had three children with her, and all looked to be under the age of five. She could have been twenty-five or forty-five, it was hard to tell. She just looked worn out and beat down, the three children playing quietly at her feet, one still with a bottle in his mouth. I looked for a wedding ring on her left hand, I didn't see one, but maybe she was married and her husband had never been able to afford one. All the rest of the waiting patients were a mixture of young and old, black and white, all seemed to be down on their luck. Finally, KC's name was called to come back to an examining room, and we all sat up hoping we were next in line. It was getting close to 10:30, so it couldn't be too much longer. I was engrossed in my book when I heard my name, and didn't respond at first.

"Elizabeth Nash," the nurse repeated, standing in the door that led to the hallway where all the examining rooms were.

"Here," I called out.

"Here?" laughed Divine. "It's your turn dummy, maybe you'll get Dr. Hunk if you're lucky."

I was on my feet and on my way when I passed Nurse Knight, who gave me a dirty look as I walked by her.

A very attractive, young nurse, in dark blue scrubs holding my chart in her hand, smiled at me and asked, "Its Elizabeth isn't it? How are you feeling today?"

Our Erring Sisters by Carol Henwood

Stunned to think anyone actually cared how I felt, I happily responded, "Yes, it is Elizabeth and I feel just fine, thank you for asking."

"That's good to hear, Elizabeth. My name is Shelly and I am Dr. Reynold's nurse and I will be assisting him today."

"Assisting him? Am I having something else done other than an examination today?" I urgently inquired.

Gently touching my arm, she guided me past many examining rooms. Shelly hastily responded, "No, not to worry. I will be taking some information from you, as well as blood pressure, the usual things, and I will stay in the room when Dr. Reynolds performs his examination. So relax dear, you're in good hands," she said reassuringly as we approached some scales. Shelly asked to me step on the scales so she could record my weight and height. I stepped up and watched her manipulate the scales until they balanced, landing at 125 pounds, the heaviest I had ever been, and I stood 5' 5". She began taking down information I had given out at least twice before now, but I answered all of her questions politely. Next, she took my temperature, blood pressure, pulse, and pricked my finger, than asked me to go into the bathroom and leave a urine sample in the window. I obediently emptied my full bladder, saving just enough to halfway fill the plastic cup, placed it in the window to be tested, and walked out to a waiting Nurse Shelly. She ushered me into an examination room, told me to strip all the way down, put on the provided hospital gown, with the opening in the front, and sit on the examining table.

"Dr. Reynolds will be with you shortly, dear. Don't worry, you'll love him, everyone does," she assured me.

Easy for her to say, she's not the one sitting here buck naked, getting ready to saddle up in the stirrups. Well, at least I did luck out and am going to see the much sought after Dr. Reynolds. I was twiddling my thumbs and daydreaming, when I was startled by a soft knock on the door. Caught off guard, I called out, "Who is it?"

"It's Dr. Reynolds, may I come in?"

Feeling like an idiot, I quickly responded, "Of course, please come in."

Our Erring Sisters by Carol Henwood

The door opened and in walked Dr. Rhett Reynolds, every bit as handsome as had been described to me. He looked as if he might be early forties, but who knows, I am terrible at determining the age of anyone. He wore a crisp, white doctor's coat with his name embroidered on the pocket, W. Rhett Reynolds, MD. I realized my mouth was hanging open, closed it, and smiled. His eyes. He had the most mesmerizing eyes I'd ever seen. The irises were light blue with dark blue rims and had long, black eyelashes, the kind a girl would kill for. I was completely captivated by them. Not only were they beautiful, they were kind eyes that put me at ease. Dr. Reynolds put down the chart he held in his hands, walked over to me and picked up one of my hands, which had been resting in my lap and patted it gently.

"Elizabeth, I'm Dr. Reynolds, and it is so nice to meet you," he said, and I believed he meant it. "What I would like to do first, is for you and me to chat a little before I begin my examination. Why don't we start by you telling me something about yourself."

"Oh, okay," I answered. "I think I'm about six and a half or seven months pregnant, and haven't had any problems with nausea or …"

"No, no, hold on," Dr. Reynolds said, holding up his hand with a smile. "I meant tell me about yourself, Elizabeth, what you enjoy doing for fun, what music you like to listen to, what your plans for the future are, that sort of thing. Then, I'll tell you a little about myself. I can determine exactly how many months pregnant you are in just a few minutes. I think it is important that you and I get acquainted first, since we will be seeing each other for at least the next three months, and considering the fact that these are unusual, and more than likely stressful circumstances for you, I would like to get a feeling for you, and what's in your heart, and most importantly, for you to consider me your friend. Does that seem reasonable?"

"More than reasonable," I replied wanting to give him a big hug for caring.

Thus began my brief, but meaningful friendship with this genuinely compassionate and kind-hearted doctor.

Our Erring Sisters by Carol Henwood

Approximately thirty minutes later I joined the rest of the girls in the waiting room and we talked about how our appointments had gone, which doctor we had seen, and everything relative to our pregnancies. Bonnie walked over to me from where she had been sitting and plopped down hard in the chair next to me.

"Dedra was the last one called in. Maybe they'll decide she's a nutcase and send her to a place where unmarried, pregnant loons go," she said seriously. Sighing heavily, she continued, "Dr. Watkins said I have gained too much weight and have to cut back on what I eat. The nurses at the home and Miss Mellete will be monitoring my weight and food intake. Can you believe that? No cookies or ice cream for me, I guess," she said sorrowfully.

"Not to worry, Bonbon, we'll sneak you all the goodies you want," Divine said.

Our conversation was interrupted by the grating voice of Nurse Knight.

"Girls, we will be departing in five minutes. Clean up any mess you made, gather your things, and sit quietly until we're ready to go."

"Do you get the feeling we should be in orange jump suits? She treats us like we're female prisoners," Andee said as she gathered up the magazines she had brought with her.

The trip back to the home was subdued, the excitement over, with no more doctor appointments for most of us until next month. Dedra was quiet on the way back. No more fake tears, and she was still sitting next to Nurse Knight with a pained expression on her pale face. Maybe we were wrong about Dedra, maybe she really was traumatized by Jessie going into labor in front of her eyes. I don't know how I would react if I witnessed that, not to mention how I will behave when I go into labor myself; scary thought. The good news is that I made a new friend today in Dr. Reynolds and I am relieved to have somebody on my side. I can't wait to tell Mama about him. I'm looking forward to talking to her this afternoon and telling her about everything that has happened since she left me here on Saturday, which seems like years ago. I miss my family and long to hear the ordinary, hum-drum events of

Our Erring Sisters by Carol Henwood

home, like what vegetables Mama bought at the Curb Market down by the river, if Emily Anne likes her apartment in Atlanta. I have to remind myself we are both in Atlanta right now, albeit, under very different circumstances. I even want to know what Tarleton is doing at football camp, and most importantly, what the local gossip is, as long as it's not about me! It had been an exciting trip to the clinic, just like my friends had promised. I closed my eyes and let the gentle motion of the bus rock me to sleep once again.

Our Erring Sisters by Carol Henwood

Chapter Thirteen

Emily Anne unlocked the door to her apartment and ran to answer the ringing telephone, while holding a bag of groceries in her arms, trying not to drop it.

"Hello," she answered out of breath.

"Did I get you coming in or going out?" Della asked her oldest daughter, smiling to herself as she pictured Emily Anne as the young, almost independent working girl that she was for the summer.

"Hi, Mama," she said, as she set the groceries down on the kitchen counter. "I was just coming in from the grocery store where I stopped and picked up a few things on the way home from work. Cynthia and Dan are meeting for dinner after work, so I'm on my own tonight. How are you doing?"

"Fine, I'm fine. I wanted to see if you would like to go with me to visit Ella on Sunday. I am going to pack a picnic lunch, drive down, and I thought I'd pick you up on the way and we'd swing by the home and pick Ella up and go have a picnic somewhere close by. We can't risk going out to lunch anywhere, there's always the possibility of running into someone your Dad and I know. You could tell Cynthia that I came down to take you to lunch and visit with Mimi. I'm sure Ella would love to see you. What do you think?"

Pondering the idea, Emily Anne didn't say anything for a moment.

"If you have made other plans already, I understand and I wouldn't want you to change them. I just thought since you're not too far away, the three of us could spend Sunday together. I am positive she would love to see you, dear."

"No, I don't have any plans on Sunday, but do you think it will be a little weird for Ella, being so obviously pregnant now? I don't want to make her feel uncomfortable, that's all," Emily Anne said in a concerned voice.

Understanding Emily Anne's reservations, Della continued, "It may be a little awkward at first, but I think the awkwardness will be brief. You're sisters, for heaven's sake, you'll probably take up where you left off before you moved. I just got off the phone with her a few minutes ago, and she had her first doctor's appointment at the clinic today. She had a wonderful, compassionate doctor named Rhett Reynolds, who put her mind at ease about many things, and she seemed very excited about that." Pausing for a moment, Della collected her thoughts and continued, "I am aware that it may be a little weird, as you say, but Ella needs to know her family is supportive of her, and seeing you would lift her spirits. Are you game?"

"Sure. What time do I need to be ready?"

Smiling with relief, Della answered, "I'll be at your apartment at 11:00. Thank you sweetheart, you don't know how much this will mean to her. See you tomorrow."

Chapter Fourteen

The rest of the day was boring in comparison to the anticipation of the morning, and I was grateful I didn't have to begin my assigned chore, which was kitchen duty, until Tuesday. I took an afternoon walk with Lacy, Bonnie and Sarabeth, read for a while, and practiced my typing on an old manual typewriter that had been put in my room to use. That was my mother's request, since I would be interviewing for some sort of secretarial job after the baby was born and needed to beef up my typing skills in order to find a job and work until I could enter college again, hopefully next summer. I was a pretty good typist and could be very good if I practiced, so I did. Mama called and I told her about the charming Dr. Reynolds, my updated September 3rd due date, and I gave her a synopsis of the girls I had become friends with and how I was beginning to fit in.

"I am so pleased you like the doctor you saw today, but you won't be seeing the same doctor every visit, you understand, so don't get upset if you don't see Dr. Reynolds for a couple of months. It's nice that he shows a genuine interest in you girls, I am satisfied he wants to help you deal with this difficult situation. Now, Ella, I don't want you to become too chummy with the girls that are at the home with you. They are not going to be life long friends, just acquaintances you spent a brief period of your life with. Once you leave, you leave them and their friendships there also. Is that understood?"

Rolling my eyes at my mother's constant quest to rid my life of anything unseemly, I responded, "Understood."

Moving seamlessly on to another subject, Mama said, "About Sunday, I am going to pack a picnic lunch with some of your favorite vegetables, fried chicken, and yeast rolls, then Emily Anne

Our Erring Sisters by Carol Henwood

and I are going to come by and pick you up and go somewhere to have a picnic. How does that sound to you?"

Saturday and Sunday were visiting days for the parents, boyfriends, whoever you wanted to come, and we were allowed to leave the grounds, but had to be back by 5:00 in the afternoon.

"Great, that sounds really great. The food here isn't terrible, but I miss your home cooking. Is Daddy coming, too?" I asked skeptically.

"Oh, no dear, you know he plays golf on Sundays, but will call you this week from the office. I am going to keep him well informed as to how you're doing. It's difficult for him, Ella, maybe more so than for me. But Emily Anne wants to see you, so I thought we three girls could have a nice Sunday visit."

Relieved at not having to see Daddy, I quickly replied, "That's fine, I just wanted to know. How's Tarleton doing at football camp?" I asked wanting to change the subject from the uncomfortable subject of how my father was holding up.

"You know Tarleton, Ella, give him a football and he's as happy as can be. He has one more week at camp, then back home, and Desota High will start their practice in August sometime. Your father is thrilled because Tarleton will most assuredly be the first string running back, or some such thing. As you know, he is a very talented athlete, but is going to have to work hard this year to keep his grades up if he wants to keep his place on the team."

"Has he asked about me?"

"Yes, he has. He is concerned about you and genuinely misses you. I've told him you are doing fine, planning for the future, and will be back home before he knows it," Della stated with authority.

"I miss him, and Emily Anne, too, but my stay here isn't going to be too long. Compared to some of the girls here, I'm considered a short timer. Andee, my roommate, has been here for almost her entire pregnancy, and she still has to go until October. I don't think I could do that," I told Mama with a longing in my voice.

"We have been fortunate in many aspects of this saga, Ella – so far, so good. Let's try and keep it that way. Your father and I

110

Our Erring Sisters by Carol Henwood

miss you very much, even though you have been gone such a short time. It's not just the amount of time you will be away, but the change that will have taken place within you when it is over - your transformation from a girl to a woman, and in circumstances where no family member is there with you as you deal with this life changing event alone. I believe you are a much stronger girl than you portray, you have a quiet inner strength that will sustain you during the difficult time ahead." Sighing heavily, Della cleared her throat. "We're all set for Sunday, then. Emily Anne and I will be by to pick you up by noon, and we'll look for a place to picnic. I know there is a spot on the grounds, but I think it would be nice to get away for the day. Agreed?"

"Agreed, I would love to leave here for a few hours, and can't wait to have your home cooking," I said with real enthusiasm. A heavy sinking feeling suddenly overcame me.

"I know I've only been gone from home a couple of days, but it feels much longer. I'm living in an alternate universe, nothing familiar or comfortable here, except the undeniable fact that all of us here are in the same predicament, and the outcome will be the same for most of us. I just hope I can get my life back on track – it scares me to think about trying to fit in again, act normal and do everyday things, after this has dominated my life for the last nine months. Okay, enough of that depressing talk," I said in a much cheerier voice. "I love you, and tell Daddy I love him, too. See you Sunday, Mama," and I hung the phone up and walked back to my room and fell on my bed in a flood of tears.

Chapter Fifteen

Mama and Emily Anne's Sunday visit was a welcome one, and became a weekly event, at least for Mama and me. My mother got up at 5:00 a.m. and cooked fried chicken, green beans, squash casserole, yeast rolls, and brownies. She packed it all in a cooler, put it in the car, and off she went. I know it was a labor of love for her – trying to keep me connected to my family, as if this was a normal Sunday dinner, never mind the fact it was seventy miles from home, in a car, in a deserted parking lot and not at our family dining room table. Seeing me each week with my ever expanding belly, carrying the grandchild she would never know, must have torn her heart out. Once Emily Anne got over the initial shock of seeing my prominent belly, we relaxed and enjoyed the day. We ended up driving around and found a shopping center parking lot, mostly empty since it was Sunday, and stores were not open on Sundays. We pulled in and parked and Mama unpacked a thermos of iced tea, plastic cups, plates, forks, and festive napkins; Mama knew how to do a picnic. We enjoyed the delicious lunch then decided to drive around for a while, Emily pointed out different neighborhoods she had discovered with beautiful houses and lawns. After a while, we decided to head back to the home, since Mama had to drop Emily Anne back at her apartment before she drove the seventy miles back to Desota. We got back to Emmeriah Parrish around 4:30 and Emily Anne and I hugged, she told me to take good care of myself, and we promised to keep in touch by telephone. I told Mama she didn't need to walk me to the door, the staff discouraged any family lingering when the visit was concluded.

"Thank you so much, Mama. Everything was delicious and it was a treat getting away for a few hours," I said as I hugged her tightly.

Our Erring Sisters by Carol Henwood

"No need to thank me, Ella. I'm your mother and I love you, and I want to see that you are properly nourished. I really should go now. Please take care of yourself and we will talk during the week," and she turned and quickly walked to the car. I suspect she was on the verge of tears, as I was, and had to make a quick getaway. One trait my mother and I definitely share is the inability to hold our emotions in check. A Hallmark card will make us cry, so will hearing the National Anthem sung beautifully, even touching and tender moments happening to complete strangers move us to tears. Over the last seven months, the tears, red nose and weepy eyes are our constant companions.

As the weeks slowly passed, the summer grew hotter and I grew bigger and more uncomfortable. The baby was active, kicking and moving around, having hiccups frequently. Whenever one of the babies developed the hiccups, we would all gather around and put our hands on the stomach of the hiccupping baby's mother, and feel the up and down movement with each spasm; it was a form of entertainment for us, as well as a bonding of sorts. Most of us had formed attachments to our babies, as was inevitable, but discouraged. We were advised to try and not get too attached to the babies we were carrying, in an attempt to make the separation easier in the end. How preposterous! You would have to be an unfeeling, cold-hearted robot not to have an emotional attachment to the baby you were carrying and your body was nourishing. Some of the girls had given their babies names, one for each sex, talking to their bellies as they rubbed and patted the large mound. I was guilty of talking to my baby and massaging my stomach as well, it was natural and normal, and gave me a great deal of comfort, not allowing myself to think of the day we would be permanently separated.

Poor Jessie came back from delivering her twin girls, after staying in the hospital for two weeks. The doctors were concerned about her physical, as well as mental condition. She was not the same perky, chatty girl I had met only a few weeks earlier. She quietly moved around the home like a ghost, only speaking when spoken to, and most often stayed in her room, as she was taken off the chore list. She was placed in a different category now, not expectant mother, but delivered of her baby, and just waiting to be picked up by her parents. The cheerful girl was replaced by a despondent waif, who looked as if she could be blown away by a strong wind, and didn't care if she was. I wondered if this is the way I would be. All of us here knew the day was coming soon when we would have to experience the unthinkable, giving away our very own flesh and blood. But until then, we laugh, chatter, and engage in as normal a life as teenage girls anywhere in a college dorm or summer camp would. The difference separating us is our conversation, which is mostly about stretch marks, weight gain, Braxton-Hicks contractions, and how many more weeks we have to go, all the while marking the days off the calendar with anticipation and dread.

One Sunday night in July, most of us were sitting in the common room watching an episode of *Bonaza* when Lacy quickly walked in, looking pale and distressed. She quietly sat down in between Andee and me and whispered, "Candy has gone and done something stupid to make herself go into labor. She is in the bathroom right now, with bad stomach cramps, the runs, and, she hopes premature labor."

My eyes must have gotten as big as saucers as Lacy continued describing the unfolding drama down the hall.

"What an idiot," Andee said with disgust. "That creepy man that came to visit her today, and called himself her uncle, must have slipped her some castor oil. She's been bragging about how she is gonna get out of here sooner than we think." Leaning in close to Lacy, Andee asked, "Is Miss Mellete aware of what's going on?"

"No, but she's bound to find out pretty soon. Candy hid the bottle, but if she does go into labor, the doctors will find out, and Miss Mellete might get into trouble for not taking more precautions when we have visitors. Candy's due around late September or early October, why not just wait it out like the rest of us?"

"Trailer trash, pure and simple," offered Divine as she walked up to us.

"Do you know what's going on, too?" Lacy asked.

Our Erring Sisters by Carol Henwood

"That girl has about as much luck keeping her mouth closed as she does keeping her legs together. Of course, I know she's been bragging about doing this for a week or more."

I was glued to every word that was uttered. I innocently asked, "What happens if you take castor oil?"

Bonnie had now joined our group, and the others in the room were wandering over, wanting to find out what the fuss was all about.

"Castor oil will make you go into early labor, if you're pretty far along anyway. It's not recommended, of course, but I guess if you can stand having diarrhea, terrible stomach cramps and labor pains, that is one way of getting the ball rolling," Bonnie informed me.

KC and Kylene came over from the kitchen where they had an evening snack, saw our tight circle and came over.

"Okay, what's the pow-wow about?" Kylene asked as she sipped a carton of chocolate milk.

Andee leaned on her elbow, propped on the edge of the sofa and said, "Seems like one of our residents just couldn't wait any longer for her baby to be born, things to do, places to go, men to screw, you understand, so she decided do help the process along by swallowing a bottle of castor oil. Sound like anyone you know?"

"That irresponsible whore," KC blurted out. "As if she's the only one who wants to get out of here early. Now, she'll probably get all of us in trouble, as well as Miss Mellete, not to mention the danger she could cause the baby," KC's face turned brilliant red with anger. "She should be sterilized or something, she's just a selfish bitch with no concern for anyone but her sorry self," KC concluded as we all stared at her, never having heard a harsh work come from her mouth before. Seeing the expression on our faces, she continued, "Well, I'm sorry, but it's true, and everyone here knows it." Lacy laughed and said, "Oh, we're not disagreeing with you, I've just never heard you say anything unkind about anyone before, but I couldn't have said it better myself."

"Coming from you, Lacy, that's a compliment," KC said as she smiled and curtsied.

Our Erring Sisters by Carol Henwood

"Who's down there with her now?" Kylene asked Lacy.

"Penny and Sarabeth," Lacy answered. "Penny doesn't care if Candy's a whore and a moron, she's just doing what Penny does best – and that's taking care of people, and Sarabeth's the lookout for her. "Candy took the castor oil about 6:00 this evening, and it's really kicking in now. I guess she'll go down to the nurses' station before too long. She's lucky it's Nurse Robbins on duty tonight instead of the wicked witch of the South, Nurse Knight," Kylene said as she finished her chocolate milk.

We continued to talk, wondering what would happen when we saw Dedra walk into the room, Bible in hand, with a self-satisfied look on her face.

I punched Andee in the arm and she looked at her as she took a seat at the card table, with her back toward us and the television.

"As much as I dislike Candy and her low life ways, I can't stand Dedra and her sanctimonious attitude, and I'm guessing she's gone and told Miss Mellete what's going on in Candy's room. Look at her, she's up to something," said KC.

We all casually glanced in Dedra's direction as she pretended to be immersed in her Bible reading.

"Dedra, why don't you come over here and join us? It's a great episode of *Bonanza* tonight. Little Joe's about to get him some," Lacy, the smart ass said, in a dead-pan voice dripping with sarcasm.

"You people are disgusting. I'm trying to better myself and all you do is wallow in the filth that comes from that television and pornographic magazines," she said, spitting her words at us as she grasped her Bible, which I noticed happened to be upside down.

Lacy started walking toward Dedra and we all perked up, waiting to hear the next exchange, which I knew would be a good one.

Lacy pulled a chair out from the card table and pulled it right next to Dedra's, who starting pushing back from Lacy.

"I think I should clear up one or two things you seem to be confused about, Sister Dedra, or should I say Sister Aimee Semple

Our Erring Sisters by Carol Henwood

McPherson, your heroine, I'm sure. First of all, toting that Bible around all day and quoting scripture doesn't make you better, or holier than the rest of us here, it just makes you phonier, because you got in this condition the same way the rest of us did, with the exception of poor Elma over there. You can give the innocent, virginal girl act a rest, 'cause nobody's buying it anyway. And if I were you, and thank God I'm not, I think I'd be trying to make a friend or two instead of pissing everybody off. Get rid of that prairie girl dress, lose the braids, and try being friendly. We're all here for the same reason, and we try and help each other. We're all in pain, so you're nothing special, so think about it. Oh, and by the way, if you plan on doing any reading, you're either gonna have to turn that Bible right side up, or stand on your head to read it." Lacy pushed back and got up from the table and said out loud, "I think I'll go out for a smoke," and exited the French doors. We all sat in silence, on the brink of applause, waiting for Dedra's reaction when Nurse Robbins and Miss Mellete came storming down the hallway. We all turned to watch and sure enough, they went into Candy's room. I noticed a look of panic on Dedra's splotchy face. Her expression had changed from indignation to fear. We all moved from our positions on the sofa and ran to the door to see what happened. Loud voices and muffled words were all we could make out from our vantage point, but something big was going on. Nurse Robbins came out of the room and approached us, moving her mammoth body quickly and with purpose.

"Divine, go see if Anthony's still here. I'm gonna have to axt him to drive Candy and me down to the hospital, we got no time to call no cab." Before she turned and headed back to Candy's room, Nurse Robbins stopped, turned around, and pointed her finger at us with her dark chocolate eyes glaring, and said, "I don't know who all knew about what Candy was fixin' to do tonight, and I don't want to know. Dedra ratted on her 'cause she don't like her and wanted to get Candy in trouble, but it might have saved her life. You better not go and get any ideas in your heads about trying to make your baby come sooner, too. It's a dangerous thing to do, and it could turn out real bad, for the baby and the Mama. Candy's bleeding heavily now, so you girls make sure you listen to what I'm telling you. Divine, get going," she yelled as she went back down the hall. I looked back and saw Dedra running out of the room and away from us and all the drama.

Divine and Anthony, the home's maintenance man, came blazing down the hall pushing a wheel chair and practically slid into Candy's room. Once again, several voices were raised, all talking at once, Miss Melette and Nurse Robbins shouting orders to Anthony, and sending Divine, Sarabeth, and Penny out of Candy's room, back to join us as we stood at the far end of the hall. As they approached, I could detect a look of pure terror of their faces.

"What's going on down there?" I asked impatiently.

"It's awful, just awful," lamented Divine. "Blood and shit everywhere, and she can't even stand up to walk to the bathroom the pain is so bad. She must have taken way too much of that castor oil and ruptured something inside, I don't know, it's just awful," she groaned again.

Before we could get any more information out of them, Anthony ran full speed down the hall from Candy's room and passed us like a rocket straight into Miss Mellete's office.

Lacy called out to him as he streaked by, "Anthony, are you gonna drive them to the hospital?"

"I can't talk to you right now, Miss Lacy. Nurse Robbins axted me to call an ambulance, too risky to drive Miss Candy, she losing too much blood. You girls better get out of sight, Miss Mellete and Nurse Robbins are boiling mad about this mess and worried about Miss Candy. Go on now, go watch the tee vee or sup'em, but get away from the hallway," he called out as he turned back into Miss Mellete's office.

We all scrambled back into the common room and sat down, ignoring the TV, continuing to listen to the voices and commotion from down the hall. Our usual crew was huddled up whispering about the drama unfolding, when the soft voice of Penny, who had been sitting by herself was heard saying, "Something's happening," and stood up as a flood of pink tinged water poured down from between her legs and made a pool on the floor. Her small features were frozen in a mask of terror as the first labor pain enveloped her and she grabbed her belly and bent over and screamed in agony.

"Go get Nurse Robbins, now," Lacy said, as we all got up and ran over to Penny.

Trying to make light of the situation, in hopes of calming her fears, Divine put her arms around Penny as she helped her sit down on the towel Lacy had placed on the chair, and said, "Well, it's about time, girl. You're over two weeks late. Leave it to Candy to get things stirred up around here."

I ran down the hall to Candy's room and called out before I got to the door so I wouldn't get yelled at for barging in. "Penny's water broke, and she's in labor," I said in an urgent, but matter of fact tone.

Miss Mellete was putting towels in the wheelchair for Candy to sit on as Nurse Robbins was tending to Candy, who was screaming profanities at her as she tried to place a sanitary belt and napkin on her as she thrashed around naked from the waist down. They both stopped what they were doing and looked at me with a stunned expression, as if they didn't believe what they just heard.

"Good God in Heaven," Nurse Robbins uttered as she continued to struggle with Candy.

"Where's the ambulance?" Miss Mellete asked nervously as she finished padding the seat of the wheelchair with towels.

"Veressa, I'll go tend to Penny. I had a feeling it was her day to go. The ambulance will have two patients now, so I'd better get together what paperwork I can to send to the hospital for both these girls. Bring her up as soon as you can, it can't be too much longer before the ambulance arrives."

I stood there frozen in my tracks as I observed Candy lying there half naked, her legs spread apart, as Nurse Robbins fumbled around, trying to clean up the mess, and deal with her screams and cursing.

"You bitch, stop touching me, I don't care if I bleed all over this place or all over you, too. I'm in pain and you won't give me nothing, you heartless piece of shit." Nurse Robbins continued working, not rattled one bit, and told Candy, "You can curse me all you want, Candy, it don't make no difference to me. I'm trying to help you and you're too stupid to even know it. Now be quiet and breathe like I said when you feel a pain coming, the doctors at the hospital will give you something for the pain when you get there, and we'll get there sooner if you stop fight'n me." Candy screamed as another pain overtook her, and in the distance the shrill of a siren from the approaching ambulance blended in with Candy's shrieks.

"Thank you, Lord," Nurse Robbins said as she helped Candy sit up and transferred her to the wheelchair. "Let's go," she said and proceeded to push an uncooperative Candy up the hall with me following behind.

"Elizabeth, go into the nurses' station and bring me my purse, I'm not gonna have enough time to run back in there with both of these girls going to the hospital tonight." I scooted in front of them and passed my friends, who were watching everything going on around them with interest and fear.

Miss Mellete had gotten some towels and had Bonnie clean up the mixture of water and blood on the floor, and asked her to mop the floor, too. Penny and Miss Mellete, walked down to the nurses' station to have more privacy until the ambulance arrived. I ran into the room to retrieve Nurse Robbins' purse from her desk and saw Penny lying on the examining table, softly crying as Miss Mellete consoled her.

"Oops, I'm sorry. I was getting Nurse Robbins' purse for her, she's pushing Candy up the ramp right now," I said as I found the purse stashed in a drawer in the desk, and I did my best not to look at Penny.

"Thank you, Elizabeth. Would you please give this folder to Nurse Robbins?"

"Sure." I stole a glance at Penny, who was looking at me with both arms wrapped tightly around her large belly, not so much in an effort to stave off the next labor pain, but in a futile attempt to keep the baby from being born. I saw the desperation in her face and it pierced my heart.

Our Erring Sisters by Carol Henwood

"I hope everything goes well, Penny, I'll say a prayer for you." I didn't know what I had intended to say, but that's what came out of my mouth, and it felt right. Penny wanted to keep her baby, but her parents would not allow her to, so this was the day she'd been dreading for months, the last day she and her baby would be together. As I turned to go, I was suddenly overcome with fear, anxiety, and a sadness I hadn't experienced before now. Tears filled my eyes and ran down my cheeks and I was gasping for breath, on the verge of hyperventilating. I felt dizzy and closed my eyes and ran head on into Nurse Robbins, her purse flying out of my hands, along with the folder Miss Mellete had given me.

"Elizabeth? What in the world is wrong, chile?" she asked as she picked up her purse and collected the folder's contents from all over the floor.

"I don't know, I guess seeing Candy and Penny like that scared me," I said with embarrassment, looking down at the floor.

"That's understandable, Elizabeth, lots has happened tonight," she said as she put her arms around me. "Now, I've got to follow the ambulance down to the hospital with Anthony, so I need to get out of here. Miss Mellete will have a talk with you girls in the morning, I'm satisfied. Go on back down to the TV room, or to your room; Candy and Penny are just fine. You should try and get a good night's sleep. Good night, chile," she said as she moved as fast as her big body would allow. As I turned and walked back through the house to my anxiously awaiting friends, the ambulance drove off in the night with the lights flashing and siren blaring.

Chapter Sixteen

Sleep visited no one that night, we all tossed and turned wondering what Candy and Penny were going through, all kinds of scenarios playing out in our heads, as we pondered our own labor; would it be that frightening and painful?

It was Monday, and clinic day for those of us who had appointments. This would be my third visit, since it was now early August, and my due date was thought to be early September. I guess I lucked out by coming in so late in my pregnancy, being able to conceal it as well as I had had been a miracle, and I was on the short list for delivery now. I saw Dr. Reynolds two weeks ago, and I doubted I would see him this visit, but I sure hoped so. It was at breakfast that Miss Mellete chose to speak to us about the previous night's events.

"Good morning, girls. I know you are all anxious to know how Candy and Penny are doing, and I am happy to report to you that they are both doing very well. Candy delivered a healthy baby boy at 3:10 a.m. this morning, weighing five pounds, two ounces. He is fine, even though he was in some distress from the forced, early labor. He is early but healthy, and Candy is recovering nicely, in spite of the fact that she lost quite a lot of blood," Miss Mellete reported, looking extremely tired and old today, worn out really, but she continued. "Penny delivered a beautiful baby girl this morning at 4:30 a.m. She is a big girl, weighing ten pounds nine ounces! That is a large baby for our petite Penny. It's a wonder she managed to carry it this long. Now, on a much more serious note, we cannot tolerate anything like what happened last night to ever occur again at Emmeriah Parrish. The risk that Candy took, to both herself and baby was great, and had she not been here where she received immediate attention, things could have gone very differently. Please believe me when I tell you, I understand the emotional and physical stress you young girls are dealing with, but taking unnecessary and dangerous steps to bring on early labor simply will not be tolerated, ever. From now on, every visitor that comes to the home must be willing to show the contents of any package they bring with them, and ladies must be willing to have the contents of their purses examined by the person at the check-in desk. This procedure is being put in place in an attempt to make sure nothing comes into this facility that has no business here. We cannot have contraband being brought in from the outside for the purpose of bringing on the onset of labor. If a visitor refuses to allow the inspection, they will be denied a visitation. I will send a letter to your family members stating the same. Let's try and work together and everyone will have a successful delivery and a healthy baby. Enjoy your breakfast and those of you going to the clinic have fifteen minutes before the bus departs."

As soon as Miss Mellete turned to leave, the room sounded like a swarm of bees had invaded. The buzzing of conversations from all over the dining room was intense, as every table whirred in whispered voices about the excitement of the night before.

"Poor, sweet Penny, she must be so low about now. She wanted to keep her baby more than anything in the world and kept hoping her parents would finally agree to let her bring it home. She was even talking about it last weekend," Sarabeth said shaking her head.

Andee pushed her cereal bowl away and added, "Well, that's not happening, but I know Penny kept hoping her parents would change their minds, even though in her heart of hearts she knew it was a lost cause. I think that's the only thing that kept her going all these months, but now she's going to have to face the reality of leaving here alone. I worry about her, she never shared much with us, did she?" asked Andee as she looked around the table.

"No, she probably talked to me more than anyone, but for the most part, she kept her feelings to herself, except for the ray of hope she clung to for taking her baby home with her," said Sarabeth, and she was closest to Penny because she helped Sarabeth in the pottery class she taught.

"It's too bad her parents won't help her out, maybe rent a small apartment or room somewhere close to them, so she could have her baby, and maybe find a job, and they could help look after it. Take my mother, for instance, Lacy continued, "she knew I was bound and determined to keep my baby, come hell or high water, so she rented a one bedroom apartment for me, probably just to spite my Dad, who is going to help me find a job when I get back home. My snooty mother has now even offered to help with child care if I promise to go back to college. See, miracles do happen," Lacy said as she smiled and pushed back from the table.

"Well, it's a little different in your case, Lace," Sarabeth said. "Your Mom's independently wealthy in her own right, your Dad's a successful attorney, and they each have the means to pay for an apartment, childcare, and anything else you might need. Not so for Penny, her Dad's a farmer, just barely getting by. They managed to scrape enough together to pay for part of her stay here, just so the community wouldn't find out about Penny. They don't want anyone in that dinky little town where she's from knowing about her pregnancy with their strict Baptist beliefs, her daddy a deacon in the church, and her mom having taught Sunday school. News that their only daughter is pregnant at sixteen would be the ultimate humiliation for them. Small towns are notorious for mean spirited gossip and she and her family would probably be shunned." Taking a breath, Sarabeth continued, "This is all according to Penny, but for some reason, she kept thinking her parents would come around once the baby was here. Well, the baby's here, but I'm not holding my breath for any change of heart from them. I've met them, the one and only time they made the trip from south Alabama to see Penny. They are very stern and stoic people who don't smile much, and aren't very warm, but I'm sure they love Penny and are doing what they think is the right thing; we are all familiar with that well used line."

Our Erring Sisters by Carol Henwood

"All of us are going to have to face the same thing soon, so we better start getting used to it and look to the future," KC insisted as we all shook our heads in agreement.

"I guess Candy will be dancing a jig when she comes back, she'll be so happy to get out of here and back to her partying ways. She won't even miss a beat, you wait and see when she gets back Thursday. Penny will be inconsolable in her grief, and Candy will be unbearable in her glee," Kylene said.

As I looked around, almost every girl in the room at that time was within one or two months of delivering. Pretty soon there would be someone going every week to the hospital. A few of the girls had late fall due dates, and as soon as a space opened up, it was filled by a new resident. Our conversation was interrupted by Nurse Jenkins making the announcement that the clinic bus had arrived.

"I'll see you girls later," I said with a smug smile as I headed for the bus. "I'll tell Dr. Reynolds you all said hello."

"It's not fair, Elizabeth", sighed Andee. "Maybe this time you'll have Dr. Shit Ky, that cruel Asian woman, it would serve you right for monopolizing Dr. Reynolds, when the rest of us get the old pervert or that Vietnamese bitch."

"Come on, Bonnie, let's go so we can get a good seat on the bus today," I said as I grabbed Bonnie's hand and waved goodbye over my head. "Toodles."

My luck had run out as Dr. Ky was indeed the doctor I saw. I don't think she intended to be unfriendly and uncaring, but was the product of a culture which was not touchy-feely, but one where only the strong survived, and compassion and tenderness were emotions as foreign to her as a meal of grits and red-eye gravy. Her English was broken and not easy to understand, and she had a dispassionate expression on her face the entire time, as if she didn't consider us humans, but guinea pigs, and her bedside manner was non-existent. She offered no new information to me about the baby, or possible change in my due date, she just gave me a pelvic exam, listened to the baby's heartbeat, measured my belly, and told me I could go. As I was dressing, I attempted to ask her a question concerning my due date, and was promptly told, "You no ask

Our Erring Sisters by Carol Henwood

question, no time, more girls come. You go now." I left, but not before I blurted out, "It's beyond me why the United States is trying to save you people from communism, it's just what you deserve," and I angrily stormed out.

I reported my unfortunate experience with Dr. Shit Ky and my parting shot to the rest of the girls. I was congratulated for my bravado, but we all hoped I wouldn't see her again, and that she would not be the doctor that delivered my baby! Turns out, no one saw Dr. Reynolds, as he was out of town, so we all were disappointed. Elma, the mentally slow girl who had been raped by a gang of thugs, was kept at the clinic and was going to be put in the hospital. The doctors had suspected something was wrong mid-way through her pregnancy, she was having pains and bleeding, and the baby's development was slow, and other signs that pointed to possible retardation. Poor Elma didn't understand much about her situation, but she was happy with us because people were nice to her, and she was treated better here than she had ever been treated anywhere in her young, sad life. We were all concerned for her, more to the point, concerned about what would happen to her after the delivery. The social workers were trying to find a place for her in a home for the mental and developmentally challenged.

The second week in August, I was scheduled to meet with a social worker to talk about my plans for the immediate future and my long term plans. I was downstairs taking my weekly pottery class that Sarabeth taught, trying to decide on what stain to use on the pair of love birds I had chosen, when Miss Mellete came down into the crafts room to tell me my appointment with the social worker was going to be today after lunch. A woman named Molly Muffet, no kidding, would be coming to the home today at 1:00 to meet with me.

"Miss Molly Muffet, now there's a name you won't soon forget," commented Lacy as she carefully stained her ceramic bowl. "I can't wait to get a glimpse of her; she's got to be a new one, fresh out of social worker school."

After class it was time for lunch and I was going to grab a quick bite and go back to my room, clean up and change into

126

Our Erring Sisters by Carol Henwood

another maternity outfit for the meeting. I was sick and tired of my clothes – shorts, tops, and a few summer maternity dresses. Mama loved clothes and shoes, as I did, and on her trip to Atlanta to buy maternity clothes for me, she had done a good job in coordinating clothes that would get me through my stay, and ones that I even liked. But after wearing them day after day, with my ever expanding body, I was ready for some cute, new fashions. We all borrowed each other's clothes on occasion, it gave us a lift to have on something new and different, so I asked Kylene if I could borrow one of her sun dresses for my appointment with Miss Muffet.

"Sure, anything you like, it's just a shame you're not borrowing something for a hot date, instead of a meeting with some old social worker," Kylene said as she made a face displaying disgust.

"What do they want to talk to us about, anyway?" I asked, wanting to prepare myself. Bonnie, who was hurrying through her lunch so she could take a make-up math test filled me in.

"They want to meet you, evaluate you, and make sure you're going to do what you say you are after the baby is born. For instance, if you plan to give your baby up for adoption, they want to make sure you aren't having second thoughts as it gets nearer, or if you are keeping your baby, like Lacy is, how are you planning to care for it. They also ask a lot of questions about how you are doing here, the baby's father, if he's involved at all, and the relationship you have with your parents, stuff like that."

"Right, as if they give a damn about you," Andee said with disdain. "They all attended the same school to learn how to be pompous, judgmental assholes. They don't care about us, or what happens to us, it's all bullshit."

"Andee doesn't like her case worker, if you can't tell," KC offered with a laugh.

"Mrs. Mildred Weatherman is her name, she's my case worker, too," KC said as she leaned in close. "She's not that bad, really. Andee's parents are in touch with Mrs. Weatherman on a continuous basis, trying to find out any information she may have gotten out of Andee about Lani – if he's calling her, if she's calling him, just any tidbit of info. Andee thinks Mrs. Weatherman is a

Our Erring Sisters by Carol Henwood

snitch, so she makes up all kinds of stories to feed to her and she'll in turn tell Andee's parents."

"Little Miss Muffet will be bored by my story, then. No phone calls to or from Lucas, and no plans to get together afterwards. I don't even know where he lives anymore. I'm sure he's moved on from me since he thinks I dumped him. No hidden plans here, just the usual sanctioned secrets and lies," I said.

I got up and made a mad dash to Kylene's room for a dress and back to my room to freshen up for my appointment. I put on Kylene's pink and white silk sun dress and felt pretty for the first time in ages. My hair had lost some of its body due to the pregnancy, and it wasn't quite as full and bouncy as usual, so I pulled it back into a ponytail with a pink ribbon, applied some soft pink lipstick, blush and mascara, and was ready to meet Miss Muffet. The final touch was my favorite pair of white strappy sandals, I was happy I could still get my feet in them. I was lucky I hadn't swollen up yet like some of the girls. I did feel like I was dressing for a date with a cute boy instead of meeting some woman with a ridiculous name who would question me about my personal life and matters I had never talked about with any adult. I was a little apprehensive about meeting with this stranger, but at the same time I wanted to make a good impression, for reasons I wasn't quite sure of. One final look in the mirror and I was off to meet Miss Molly Muffet.

I was talking to Divine and Bonnie in the common room when Miss Mellete stuck her head in. "There you are, Elizabeth, Miss Muffet has just arrived and I'm putting you two on the screened porch since it's a nice day, not too hot. I have put a pitcher of lemonade and glasses on the table for you. She is there now, so go on ahead, dear," Miss Mellete instructed.

"I wonder if Miss Muffet will be sitting on a tuffet, whatever the hell that is," Divine asked as she burst out laughing at her joke.

"I'll give you the complete skinny on Little Miss Muffet, and what she had her butt on, in about an hour. Wish me luck," I said as I slowly walked out with butterflies flitting around in my stomach.

Through the glass-paneled door to the screened porch, I saw a young woman, who didn't look much older than me. She was

Our Erring Sisters by Carol Henwood

sitting in a wicker chair at the glass-topped table, reading what I supposed was my file. I didn't expect to see someone so young. I had imagined an older woman with more experience as my case worker. Miss Muffet looked up and saw me outside the door and waved me in.

Getting up from her chair, Miss Muffet was dressed in a pink pleated skirt, white blouse with a Peter Pan collar, and pearls. She looked as if she had just graduated from college last week. Her hair was shiny and black and pinned up in a French twist, I'm guessing to make her look older; it didn't work.

"Come on in and sit down, Elizabeth. I'm Molly Muffet and I'm here to get to know you, talk a little about how you're doing and feeling these days, and chat about the future. How does that sound?" she asked me while smiling from ear to ear. I guess grinning like a jackass eating briars was her way of putting me at ease. It didn't work, either.

Sitting forward in the chair and clasping my hands together on the table, I answered, smiling modestly "Sounds fine to me."

"Okay, then. It says here in your file that you have agreed to give your baby up for adoption after you deliver in September. I think that's the birth month, correct?" she inquired as she searched the papers in front of her for the information.

"Yes, sometime in early September is what the doctors think."

Looking at me again with the same silly smile, she continued her questioning.

"Are you having any second thoughts or reservations about the decision to give your baby up for adoption, and how does the baby's father feel about the decision?"

Shocked that she had overlooked that important piece of information in my file, I replied in a surprised tone, "The baby's father knows nothing about my pregnancy; it should say that in my file."

Not smiling anymore and shuffling the papers around on the table, Miss Muffet took on a serious demeanor and mumbled something to herself.

Our Erring Sisters by Carol Henwood

"I must have overlooked that, I'm terribly sorry. So, the father is not at all involved in your decision to relinquish the child and has no idea of your pregnancy?" she asked in a tone which signaled disapproval as she continued to rearrange the papers in front of her.

I didn't like the direction this conversation was going, and I answered curtly, with the hint of a smile. "My parents thought it best for everyone concerned if my pregnancy was kept from Lucas, the baby's father, for many reasons and I followed their wishes."

"Yes, of course you should do what is best, but is that what you wanted to do, Elizabeth?" Miss Muffet asked in her practiced social worker voice, using what psychological tactics she had learned in college as she attempted to delve into my deepest hidden feelings.

I was becoming rattled and uncomfortable, not wanting to answer the question.

"I didn't know what I wanted at the time. I was barely eighteen, pregnant and scared to death. I didn't want my parents and friends to know I was pregnant and I was afraid to tell Lucas, not knowing what he would say or how he would react, so I went into full denial until it wasn't possible to deny it any longer."

Miss Muffet placed her elbows on the table and leaned forward, as I sat back in my chair.

"If Lucas had known about the baby, Elizabeth, do you think he would have wanted to get married? It does say here that you two had been dating for over a year. Would marriage have been a possibility?"

I could feel the barricade I had placed around my inner feelings begin to crumble. I hadn't discussed this with anyone other than Andee and Bonnie. "I suppose it could have been a possibility if I had fought hard for it, but I didn't. I knew my parents didn't want me to marry Lucas and I felt I should do what they wanted, since I had gotten myself into the mess and caused a family crisis."

"Elizabeth," she insisted as she leaned in even closer across the table, and asked in an annoying and condescending tone. "Would you have married Lucas if he had known about the baby, and asked you to marry him?" she insisted.   I finally lost the

Our Erring Sisters by Carol Henwood

battle of concealing my well hidden true emotions and I began to sob softly. "Yes, maybe I would have, but what's the point of talking about it now? It's over, decided, and the matter is closed. Why talk about scenarios that didn't happen? I already feel bad enough about everything; I don't want to think about the what if's, and besides, why would you even bring that up now, at this late date?" I guessed what she was trying to get at and I added, "You don't have to be concerned that I'll back out of the adoption at the last minute, I'll keep my word," I stated emphatically, gaining control of my emotions once again.

Realizing she had upset me, Miss Muffet stopped her interrogation and half-heartedly apologized saying she was "only trying to get a glimpse into your heart."

I had become quite adept at guarding my heart and feelings, and Miss Molly Muffet was not going to be the one person I opened up to. I would be more likely to open up to Anthony, the maintenance man at the home, than her any day. He was non-judgmental and kind. Miss Muffet had an imperious attitude and an arrogant demeanor. I didn't care for her.

The remainder of our session was about my adjustment to life at the home; was I being treated well (as if she cared), and finally, was I going to have any contact with Lucas after I had signed the release paper for the adoption?

My answer was succinct. "Yes, I have adjusted well, yes, I am being treated well, and as to contact with Lucas after the adoption is final, well, Miss Muffet, that is really none of your business, now is it?"

We immediately ended our meeting, with Miss Muffet assuring me I could get in touch with her anytime if I felt the need to talk. Was she a total imbecile? Did she actually think she had been helpful to me? I gave her a phony smile, mumbled a thank you and left. I saw a new resident, Millie, sitting in the foyer outside the porch waiting on her turn to be humiliated by Miss Muffet.

"Don't let her get to you," I whispered as I passed by. She looked at me with questioning eyes, but I kept moving.

Our Erring Sisters by Carol Henwood

I felt like a complete and utter fool for dressing up for that silly woman. She must have been feeling very smug and thinking what a pitiful creature I was and how much better she was than me, but she was wrong, she wasn't. Not one little bit, and I didn't need someone like her making me feel bad about myself, I could do that without her help. I suppose I should have been charitable and forgiven her incompetence and stupidity since she must have been very new at her job. No one would intentionally be that insensitive and careless with someone they profess they want to help. I went back to my room to change my clothes and saw Andee sitting in the middle of her bed writing a letter. She stopped writing and looked up at me.

"How did it go with Miss Muffet?" Andee was the recipient of a fifteen minute tirade against Miss Muffet, and all social workers in general. After I was through, we commiserated about our situations for at least an hour, and were so emotionally worn out that we fell asleep until dinner time.

In early August my mother called with the disappointing news that she was not coming down for her regular visit and bringing my lunch on the upcoming Sunday. My grandmother was staying with one of my aunts in a nearby town, and Mama wanted to see her mother. I completely understood, and I felt guilty about keeping her from being able to visit with her own mother when she was in Atlanta seeing me. Since we couldn't have our picnic, she suggested I attend church on Sunday

"Ella, since you've missed so much church over the last few months, this is a perfect opportunity to go, especially under the present circumstances. A church sermon and some quiet reflection by you on your past and future would be very much in order," Mama insisted as I groaned, a little too loudly.

"Well, I don't know, I'll see whose going this week and maybe I'll tag along with them," I unenthusiastically answered.

"I don't believe you are taken downtown to any of the big churches, the ones where we know members, so I think attending church up there in the far northern suburbs is perfectly safe," she added, always thinking of the disastrous possibility of me being

Our Erring Sisters by Carol Henwood

recognized by some lawyer friend of theirs and having to explain away my prominent belly.

Not wanting to have a sermon preached to me over the phone about my sinful ways, I cut the conversation short with the always reliable excuse of a full bladder that needed to be relieved.

I walked quickly up the hallway, looking at the floor, contemplating how I could get out of going to church on Sunday. Granted, I probably could use a little "come to Jesus" preaching, but the thought of going into a church, eight months pregnant with no husband in tow, was an adventure I'd like to avoid at all costs.

As I pondered scenarios where I would be recognized by someone, or asked to leave the premises because I was flaunting my sinfulness, as well as just sticking out like a sore thumb, I almost ran into Divine as she was making her way down the hall.

"Whoa, girl, you better watch where you're going or both of us fat girls are gonna land on our big ole butts," Divine said as she stopped short on her journey.

"I'm sorry, Divine. I just got off the phone with my mother and she's not going to be able to come down here on Sunday. So, she made a request, really more of a demand, that I go to church this Sunday," I unhappily reported.

Divine's face lit up and she smiled from ear to ear. "Elizabeth, come with me and Anthony to the AME Rock My Soul Missionary Church. It's about fifteen miles north of here, almost in Forsyth County, so it's out in the country. I've gone with him and his family a few times, and girl, that place is the place to be on Sundays. We do some singing, swaying, hand clapping, all in the name of the Lord. We also get a good dose of hellfire and damnation, but Preacher Eddie always ends on a positive note, and we do our share of amen'n, too. If you've never been to a black church, girl, you don't know what you're missing. You've got to come with me and Anthony, Elizabeth, and I can promise you girl, you won't see nobody you know there! Plus, we go back to Anthony's house for a big lunch spread, and there's always plenty of food. Well, Elizabeth, are you up for the experience of your young, white life?" Divine asked as she held my hands and waiting for my answer.

"Sure, I'll go Divine. It sounds like it's just the kind of church service I need. I don't have to go incognito, and it doesn't sound like there's any holier than thou stuff going on. It sounds just perfect for me. I'm ready for some old time religion!"

When Sunday arrived, I put on a nice church-type dress and was actually excited about going with Divine and Anthony to church. Anthony came by himself to pick us up from the home, the rest of his large, extended family would meet us there.

The trip to the Rock My Soul church took about half an hour. Anthony's old van didn't have much pick-up or power and was at least twenty years old, but clean as a whistle. The service started at 10:45, and according to Divine, it would conclude whenever Pastor Eddie ran out of steam, which could be anywhere from two to three hours.

"How can he preach for so long?" I asked. "Dr. Scott, the minister at the Desota Presbyterian Church, makes sure he's through with his sermon by noon, and it's a good thing because most all the congregation is falling asleep because he's so boring!

"One thing's for sure, Elizabeth. You're not gonna be bored at Rock My Soul. Ain't that right, Anthony?"

"That's the trooth, Miss Elizabeth, you gonna be wide awake with the Spirit moving all around in the church house today," Anthony proudly proclaimed.

I thought about being the only white face in the church and began to get anxious about being so obviously out of place.

"You don't think the congregation will mind a pregnant white girl showing up today, do you Anthony?" I asked with trepidation.

"What you talkin' about, Miss Elizabeth?" Anthony answered as he turned his body around to look at me in the back seat.

"Everybody is welcome at Rock My Soul Church. We don't discriminate. Every color and condition is welcomed inside the

Our Erring Sisters by Carol Henwood

Lord's house," Anthony answered grinning with pride, his white teeth sparkling.

Once we arrived, the small parking lot was full to overflowing. The church was a modest, white wooden building, which stood serenely in the midst of a grove of pine trees. Two crepe myrtle trees were planted on either side of the steps to the church entrance, their abundant pink flowers a bright and welcoming sight. The gentle setting was reassuring and I felt almost serene myself.

I stayed close to Divine and Anthony as we entered the sanctuary, not wanting to stick out too much; no chance of that. The sounds of laughter and the array of colors dazzled me, neither of which I had ever seen or heard in the Desota Presbyterian Church. The women, men and children wore their Sunday best. The women wore dresses and suits of every color and style, with lots of lace, chiffon or satin, all enhanced with frills and trimmings that made each outfit unique. The ladies wore hats of every size and description, many adorned with flowers, as well as fruit samplers on top. It was almost a sensory overload for me. The little girls wore multiple braids or pigtails with bright ribbons on them, and fancy dresses and white ankle socks with their shiny white or black patent leather Sunday shoes. The little boys were replicas of the men, wearing suits and ties and highly polished dress shoes. I had never seen so much color and excitement in a church before.

Anthony introduced me to his family and many other members of the congregation, and I was made to feel at home and welcome. We all started to take our seats and settle down for the service. The choir came in and sat behind the pulpit in folding chairs. Their robes were a rich magenta color and all looked regal wearing them. As a large lady wearing a bright purple chiffon dress sat down at the piano to play, the choir stood up and broke into song. The congregation stood up and starting singing with the choir, but I didn't see any hymnals in the aisle, so I just stood up and listened until I could figure out what they were singing. Pretty soon the entire congregation was swaying and singing to a resounding

Our Erring Sisters by Carol Henwood

gospel song, and I couldn't help myself, I felt the music through and through to my very soul, and I was swaying and clapping with everyone else. This reserved little Presbyterian-raised girl had just found the Spirit that moved her, and it was a release to sing and clap and be happy for a change. Pastor Eddie started his sermon after a few more songs, scripture readings and announcements. He would start out speaking softly, then gradually his voice would get louder and louder, and would reach a crescendo as he was making an important point in his message. This would happen over and over again during the sermon, and by the time it was over, I was worn out. It was August, and the church didn't have but one window unit air conditioner, and it was getting downright hot inside. Most of the ladies had paper fans with the loving face of Jesus on them, and they were working those fans non-stop. My face was damp, as well as my dress, and I tried to fan myself with a small notebook I had in my purse, but it was a losing battle. Preacher Eddie was mopping his face with a handkerchief every few minutes and had loosened his tie and taken off his jacket. I didn't have a watch on, but I knew we had been there at least an hour and a half. Maybe the determining factor as to when to end the sermon was just how saturated Preacher Eddie became, because by the time his white shirt was sticking to his skin, he wound the sermon up. One more rousing song and the collection basket was passed, then the service was over, much to everyone's delight.

I left the Rock My Soul Church with a wonderful, warm and uplifted feeling, having been accepted and even welcomed by these kind people. The Rock My Soul Church did more than rock my soul, it restored it.

Our Erring Sisters by Carol Henwood

Chapter Seventeen

The second week of August was filled with drama, excitement, and tears. Penny and Candy came back to the home from their hospital stay to recover for three days or so, and then they would leave the home, and the children they had given birth to, and were expected to resume their lives as before. Candy, true to form, came dancing down the hall in short shorts and a tight tee shirt with a deep V- neckline, showing off her new body, sans the big belly. The radio was playing loudly in Bonnie's room and Candy was rocking and rolling to the sound of Jimmy Hendrix's *Purple Haze*.

"How can you do that, Candy, aren't you the slightest bit sore?" asked Bonnie, watching in amazement as Candy shook every inch of her body and ended with several provocative pelvic thrusts.

"I can do it Bonnie, because this is what I do. I've got to stay in shape and this bod needs to look fabulous again, and soon, or I'll be out of a job," Candy informed us all as she lit a cigarette and started to walk away, a little gingerly, "By the way girls, it's not so bad, popping out a baby, that is. They shoot you up with some happy medicine that knocks you out completely – I'd love to have an inside line on that stuff, it was good," she said as she blew smoke into the air. Looking down at the skin tight, low cut tee shirt she wore, she commented, "I wish my boobs would stay this size, but they will be deflating in a few days, since they gave me some pill to dry my milk up. What a shame, I really do like this size," she said as she put her hands on her large breasts. "It's the girls with the big tits that get the big tips, but I have other attributes," Candy said with a smile, as she turned around to flaunt her shapely backside.

I looked up from Candy's breasts and saw Penny walking very slowly down the hall with Miss Mellete, helping her along and carrying her suitcase. I touched Andee on the arm, and she touched Divine, and Divine touched Bonnie, and finally we were all focused on Penny, her demeanor was that of one who has just suffered a great loss, looking despondent and dazed. It brought tears to our eyes to witness her pain, even Candy was moved by Penny's heartache.

"Poor kid, she cried herself to sleep every night in the hospital. She insisted on holding and feeding her baby, which only makes it harder for her, especially since she knows her parents ain't changing their mind."

Penny went into her room and we respected her privacy and didn't intrude. She had enough on her mind without all of us barging in on her now. Each one of us would go and see her before she left.

I sat back on the sofa next to Andee and Bonnie, and sighed out loud, and I knew we were all thinking the same thing. That would be us in the not to distant future; the day was coming and there was nothing we could do to change that.

"I think I heard Miss Mellete tell Nurse Jackson that Penny is going to be here for the entire week since she had such a large baby, the hospital suggested she recover here for an extra couple of days, so we can go pay her a visit and try and cheer her up tomorrow, maybe," Sarabeth said.

"I don't know if anything can cheer her up, she's been down-hearted her entire stay here. She knew this day was coming, but refused to accept it, and now that it's here, she still can't accept it. I'm very worried about her state of mind," Lacy said as she got up from the sofa and peered into the hallway. "They ought to put her on a suicide watch."

Gasps came out of our mouths and Lacy turned around to face us. "I'm serious, she's a prime candidate for suicide. She's in tremendous emotional pain, she's despondent, and you know she doesn't want to go back to that po-dunk town she's from with her strict, somber parents. I think we should ask Nurse Robbins what she thinks."

Our Erring Sisters by Carol Henwood

Sarabeth looked around the room and said, "You may be right, Lacy. She's definitely melancholy and has nothing to look forward to when she leaves here. We may be the only friends she's ever had. Lacy, why don't you go to Nurse Robbins when the shift changes and see what she thinks. I'll go with you if you want me to, and Elizabeth, why don't you come, too. You know the docs at the hospital sent orders back here for Penny. We can tell Nurse Robbins what we think, and I bet she'll agree with our observation."

"Great, let's do it. We've got another couple of hours before Nurse Robbins comes on duty, so let's go right after dinner," I replied.

As we were discussing our fears for Penny and how we should approach Nurse Robbins about it, Dedra walked into the common room. She usually stayed away when we were all gathered there, but she came in, Bible in hand, and sat down as far away from us as possible. She had not been assigned a new roommate since Jessie had delivered, even though there were several new girls in the home. I believe it was because Miss Mellete realized Dedra was not roommate material for anyone, and the best plan would be for her to room alone. On the other hand, Dedra got to have her own private suite, and she smugly credits her good fortune to her high morals and excellent character, rather than the truth, which was no one could stand to be around her for more than five minutes.

Dedra started making her way over to where we were sitting, as we discussed what it was we would say to Nurse Robbins concerning Penny's state of mind. Dedra moved closer and sat down in a chair just outside our circle and cleared her throat a couple of times. I looked over my shoulder and saw her sitting there and forced myself to speak.

"Hi, Dedra, what's going on?" I asked, feigning interest.

I decided to be magnanimous and make an effort to include her in our group and see what happened. I turned around in my chair and said, "Dedra, would you like to come join our discussion about Penny, you know she just got home from the hospital and is feeling pretty low. We're all worried about her state of mind since she wanted to keep her baby and she's not going to be able to. It's very sad for her."

Sitting very erect in her chair, she replied, "I'm on my way to Penny's room right now to read scripture with her, pray, and sing some hymns. I believe that is much more useful than sitting around talking about how sad it is that she can't keep her baby. Pastor Josiah always used the SPS method, or scripture, pray and sing. When a member of our community was in a bad way, it never failed to cheer them up," she stated with authority.

Our mouths hung open as we listened to Dedra's plan.

"You'll go in that room over my dead body," Candy growled as she gritted her teeth and stood up. Now all eyes were on Candy.

"And I suppose you have a better idea? Maybe Penny will be soothed by that devil music you gyrate to, or your disgusting stories of all the men you've been with," Dedra said as she glared at Candy.

The room was filled with tension and everyone got up and moved away from the two girls.

"Let me tell you something, you sanctimonious, hypocritical whore. You think by hiding your body inside that long, ugly granny dress, and reading the Bible all the time makes you any less pregnant than the rest of us? Talk about not wanting to face reality! You live in la-la land. Stop behaving like this is a Saturday night revival meeting in the country and face the fact that you're just as knocked up as the rest of us, and by the way, SPS must stand for Sorry Piece of Shit, if it came from the noble Pastor Josiah's mouth. I haven't seen any sign of him around here on visitation days. Matter of fact, I haven't noticed anyone coming here to visit you. You don't seem to be getting a whole lot of support from the cult, do you?

Dedra's face, a mask of rage, quickly changed to a ghostly pale, with a wounded, hurt look, like a disciplined child, her anger turned into shame and humiliation, accompanied by tears that began slowly and turned into a flood. Dedra began pulling at her hair, unbraiding her long locks, and shaking it loose as it fell down her shoulders, reaching almost to her waist. Screaming and crying at the same time, she started pulling on the bodice of her dress, buttons popping off as she ripped it open.

"Damn him to hell, that miserable, lying son of a bitching preacher man, he ought to be shot, and I may just be the one to do it," Dedra raved as she got up and started running around the room, bumping into furniture and throwing anything she saw. The mild mannered, pious, Bible reading Dedra we had become used to, transformed in front of our very eyes into a profanity spewing, enraged country bumpkin.

"She's come unglued, it was bound to happen, she was a train wreck just waiting to happen," Divine yelled as we all reached for Dedra and tried to subdue her.

"Somebody go get Miss Mellete," screamed Lacy as Dedra picked up her Bible and threw it across the room. KC ducked behind the sofa to avoid being hit by the airborne book. It slammed into the coffee table instead, knocking everything off, and breaking an Oriental vase and a couple of glasses of milk, spilling all over the floor.

Andee, Bonnie, and I were trying to corner her in one area of the room as Sarabeth took off to get help.

"I'll kill that bastard for doing this to me, saying it was 'God's will' that I have sex with him, and if I didn't, I'd be going to hell. Well, I'm in hell, and that worthless, lying son of a bitch put me here. He abandoned me and my family won't have nothin' to do with me, and I ain't got nowhere to go after the baby's born," she wailed, fluctuating between tears and rage as spittle ran down her chin.

We finally got her to be still for a moment and stop tearing at her clothes and hair. She looked like a raving maniac with a crazed expression on her face, the front of her plain, blue dress torn open and ripped apart, exposing her very pregnant belly and surprisingly, very sexy black underwear. Dedra's wavy hair, having been released from the confines of the tight braids, stood out about two feet from her head, making her a dead ringer for the Bride of Frankenstein.

Our Erring Sisters by Carol Henwood

The most unlikely person of all, Candy, was the one who came over and began to calm Dedra down.

"Shh, shh," Candy quietly shushed Dedra, as she gently led her over to the sofa, sat down beside her, put her arms around her and rocked her, softly patting her on the back.

We watched in awe as the tough as nails party girl, who had moments before cussed Dedra up one side and down the other, showed us a side of her we had never seen. If Candy had any animosity toward Dedra now, she was doing a great job of hiding it.

"Forget about him, Dedra, he's not worth the breath it takes to say his name. Don't worry, he'll get what's coming to him soon enough. Now calm down or they're gonna send you some place for crazy people, cause you don't get locked up for being crazy, just for acting crazy," she said soothingly, as Dedra began to sob. At first Dedra was skeptical of Candy's kindness, never having witnessed it before. But after a few minutes it was evident that Candy was sincere in her effort to help Dedra and show some compassion to a very confused girl.

By the time Nurse Jackson and Miss Mellete arrived on the scene, Dedra was composed and talking quietly to Candy. The rest of us were straightening up the furniture, sweeping up broken glass, and mopping up spilled water and milk that had spread all over the floor.

Both women walked over to where Dedra and Candy were sitting on the sofa and Miss Mellete pulled a chair up close to them.

"Dedra, dear," Miss Mellete softly said as she picked up one of Dedra's hands in hers and starting rubbing it. "Sarabeth told me you were very distraught and everyone was worried about you. How do you feel now, dear?" Miss Mellete carefully inquired of Dedra, aware that she was in a precarious state of mind and needed to be handled with kid gloves. If Miss Mellete was surprised to see Candy consoling Dedra, she didn't let on. She more than likely knew that Candy's tough girl act was just that, an act, and in reality Candy was a kind-hearted girl who had been raised up hard, and acted tough to conceal her own pain.

Our Erring Sisters by Carol Henwood

Keeping her head down and trying to pull the front of her dress back together, Dedra answered, "I'm okay, I guess. I'm sorry I broke some stuff in here, I don't know what happened to me, but I'm fine now, really," she answered quickly, afraid that maybe Miss Mellete might send her off somewhere else if she thought she was unstable or a danger to herself.

Nurse Jackson squatted down in front of Dedra, took her other hand, turned it over, and began taking her pulse. "I'm just making sure you didn't get yourself worked up into a state and cause your blood pressure and heart rate to go off the charts – that's not good for you right now, you know," Nurse Jackson sweetly said as she performed her nursing duties. After taking Dedra's blood pressure and pulse, and being satisfied that they were only slightly elevated, Nurse Jackson told Dedra she would give her a mild sedative to take tonight that would help her sleep, if she thought she would need it.

"Dedra, why don't we plan on having a chat tomorrow morning and sort things out. I see your dress is torn, if you want to bring it to my apartment after dinner, I'll mend it for you. Speaking of, it's time for dinner girls, and I bet you are all hungry. The meatloaf smells delicious."

Miss Mellete and Nurse Jackson left the room, heads together, no doubt evaluating the situation. We all were standing around, shuffling our feet near the two girls on the sofa. The newer residents were huddled far away from us, probably thinking this was a loony bin, rather than a home for unwed mothers.

"If you want me to Dedra, I'll ask Miss Mellete if I can stay with you tonight in your room, only if you feel like having company. You know, we're from the same part of town and I've seen you people down around where I live; I don't know how you stayed in that place as long as you did without running away," Candy said.

"I'd kinda like it if you did stay in my room tonight, I do get lonely in there by myself all the time. I know it's my own doing and all, but I'm not really a bad person, I'm just ignorant, I reckon, believing all that hell and damnation I was raised up on," Dedra said appearing embarrassed.

"If there's anything I can do to help, Dedra, please tell me; if you want to talk about anything, anything at all, I'd be happy to listen. It really helps talking to another person, even if they haven't been through what you have," I told Dedra, feeling guilty about all the awful things I had thought about her, made fun of, and for not taking the time to realize she was hurting too. We all took turns apologizing for being so insensitive and not really reaching out to her.

"I've been pretty obnoxious I know, but I'm just as scared as you all are. Maybe now I'll get my fears out instead of pretending to be so prim, proper and holier than thou." Laughing and seemingly a little more at ease, she continued, "You know all those times I was holding the Bible and quoting scriptures like I knew what I was talking about? I haven't even read the first page of the New Testament, let alone the Old Testament. I don't know who said what in there. If I was ever gonna read the Bible, right now seems like a pretty good time to start."

"I think we should go eat dinner, I'm starving," Andee said. "Are you hungry, Dedra?"

Looking at her torn and ripped dress, she answered, "I can't go to dinner in this thing, and I don't have but one other dress, and it's dirty."

"You're welcome to borrow anything I have in my closet," offered Kylene.

Lacy jumped in and said, "You'd better take Kylene up on that offer, she's the best dressed pregnant teenager in these parts. Those Texas girls take fashion seriously, maternity clothes included. She has a fine selection, so go shopping in her closet; you couldn't do better if you went to Neiman-Marcus."

"What's Newman-Marcus?"

Kylene came to her rescue and said, "Oh, it's just a little ole department store out of Dallas. Come on down to my room and have a look at some things. I mean it. I have plenty to go around."

144

Our Erring Sisters by Carol Henwood

"I never want to lay eyes again on those hideous dresses of mine, I hated them from the first time I was made to wear them. I'm throwing them in the garbage after I finish ripping the other one to shreds," Dedra said with resolve.

"What about your hair, Dedra? No offense, but it looks kind of wild right now. Would you consider having it cut and styled, I'm pretty good with hair, and I bet I could give you a great new look," KC carefully asked.

"You could?" I'd love to have a hair cut and a new style. I've never even had a hair cut, I've been wearing braids since I was a little girl. When can you do it?" she asked with enthusiasm.

"First things first," Divine chimed in. "We can eat or we can starve, and this girl ain't about to starve, so let's go eat," and all of us, including Dedra, the newest member of our circle, walked together to the dining room.

Our Erring Sisters by Carol Henwood

Chapter Eighteen

Things settled down again and were back to normal after all the events and excitement of the week before. Dedra got a makeover from KC and looked like an entirely different girl, and a very pretty one. Her brown, wavy hair was cut short and accented her high cheek bones and brown eyes, and with the addition of a little make-up she was transformed into the young, fresh faced teenage girl who had been hiding beneath the dowdy clothes and out of date hair style. Kylene gave Dedra some of her stylish maternity clothes and she was excited as a child on Christmas morning. During that week she told us about her strict upbringing in the church community that her family was a part of, and how scripture was misinterpreted by the leaders of the sect, for the sole purpose of having complete control over the members, particularly the women. Most of the women wanted to escape from the male dominated, abusive lifestyle, but were afraid to try, but within the last two years there were many runaways, including boys, girls and women.

One night after dinner, Dedra told us she overheard Pastor Josiah and some of the elders whispering about a possible investigation of the sect by the state, and then everything would come out.

"I hope the authorities raid that place and find out what's really going on in there, I'll be more than happy to be the state's star witness against that charlatan," Dedra said with a big smile.

The last few days Penny was at the home, every one of us went to her and tried to lift her spirits and draw her out of her depression. We kept her busy and laughing, and she began to cheer up a little. Her parents didn't arrive until the latter part of the week

Our Erring Sisters by Carol Henwood

to take her back home to Alabama. They were a very solemn, dour looking couple, with an uncanny resemblance to the couple in Grant Wood's painting, *American Gothic*. Penny was coming out of her shell, and we all hoped that once back in Alabama she would finish high school, meet a nice boy, get married, and have babies, because that's all she ever wanted to do.

Candy and Dedra were constant companions until Candy left the home. They seemed to share a closeness that comes from having similar childhood experiences, and thus, an understanding of each other. None of us ever thought we'd be sorry to see Candy leave when the time came, but we were.

"Even though you were constantly causing trouble, and getting us into trouble, too, I'm gonna miss you, girl, and I can't believe I just said that," Divine said as she hugged Candy.

Looking slim and fit in her post-baby body, Candy was dressed in a bright floral halter dress that Kylene brought with her from Texas to wear home after her baby was born.

"What do you think of this little number, ladies? Kylene gave it to me as a going away present," she asked as she twirled around in her usual sassy, sexy manner,

"Let's face it, Candy, I never had the body for that dress, you look glamorous in it. I gave it to you in hopes that you will go and get yourself a respectable job, in an office or shop, something a little more high class than stripping. That is just so sleazy," Kylene said, with a disapproving glance.

A momentary flash of anger crossed Candy's face, but it was gone as quickly as it had appeared. "Maybe you're right. I'll see what else is out there; I could probably talk my way into any job I wanted. What do ya'll think?"

"No doubt about that Candy, you do have a way with words," Dedra said with a slight smile, having been the recipient of some of Candy's more choice words.

After Candy's departure, things settled down to a monotonous routine again. Elma was kept in the hospital because she had so many problems in her pregnancy, and she was due in a few weeks anyway. Miss Mellete announced one morning at

Our Erring Sisters by Carol Henwood

breakfast that Elma's baby had been delivered by Caesarean section, but the baby was stillborn. It was very sad, but a blessing, since the baby would have been severely retarded, along with having myriad physical problems. No one would have wanted to adopt a baby with so many complications. As for Elma, the hope was that a good group home would be found for her so she could have a life with others like her, where she would be accepted and loved, not abused and taken advantage of.

After lunch one Wednesday afternoon, I was sitting on my bed reading my mail; a letter from Mimi, and one from Luanna. I'd told Mama I didn't want to write to Luanna, it was too risky, she was so good at finding out everything that was happening in others' lives. Mama saw her one Sunday after church, and Luanna asked her for my address, and Mama gave it to her. I was going to write her back, just to keep her from thinking anything was suspicious, and if I was really where I said I was. As for my sweet grandmother's letter, she asked me all kind of questions concerning the food at the "camp" and if I was making new friends, and she brought me up to date on her simple life of cooking, sewing, attending church, and reading the Bible. She was a devoted servant of God and I hated the fact that I was deceiving her, but I didn't want to break her heart. As for Luanna's letters, there were irreverent as ever, joking about the "boring, wholesome summer job" I had, and her hopes that I had met a cute boy counselor at camp and indulged in some late night make-out and drinking sessions, because according to her, that's what the counselors at these summer camps did after the little campers were tucked in safely for the night. I wrote her back, being very careful not to tell her too much, but that I was having a good time and had met a couple of cute boys, but nothing developed, and I was ready to get back to Desota and enroll in school for the fall semester. I prayed that would satisfy her curiosity, but I doubted it.

Andee was on her bed across from me, totally immersed in writing a letter to Lani. They had devised a plan where she would write her letters and send them to Lani at his best friend's address, so Lani's parents wouldn't intercept them.

Our Erring Sisters by Carol Henwood

"Andee, sorry to interrupt, but have you noticed Bonnie the last couple of days? She can hardly walk she's gotten so big and her feet and legs are really swollen. Her due date is tomorrow, and she's pretty nervous and upset, always on the verge of tears. Her Mom called and told her that a neighbor had informed her that the baby's father, who never even acknowledged Bonnie after she told him she was pregnant, was having a going away party before he left for college at the end of the month. This "neighborly friend" wanted to know if Bonnie was going to be back in town for the big party, after visiting her aunt in Colorado. Every time Bonnie hears something like that, it tears her up. I don't know why her mother thinks it's necessary to tell her everything she hears, especially if it might hurt her. Bonnie told me Sterling, that's the boyfriend's name, had a birthday party right after she told him she was pregnant, and he un-invited her to it, told her to get lost, and neither he nor his parents wanted her around. Of course, all of her friends were there and wondered why she wasn't. She can't seem to get over him, still thinks he might call her or come riding in on a white charger and sweep her away after the baby is born, and the three of them will be together, happily ever after. That's not happening. His family deems themselves high society and Bonnie doesn't meet up to their high standards. They threw her under the bus and moved right along. Truth is, he's not good enough for her, but people like that always seem to breeze through life – but it'll catch up with him one day and he'll get what he deserves. Anyway, my point is, let's be sensitive to Bonnie right now, she's liable to go into labor any minute and needs our support."

Listening intently, Andee replied enthusiastically, "Absolutely, Elizabeth!" I have noticed she's waddling much slower these days and she isn't her usual perky self. Yeah, I know all about Sterling, her snobby ex-boyfriend. With a name like that, what do you expect? He's a real prick, end of story. Bonnie would have been the best thing to ever happen to him, but lucky for her, she dodged that bullet."

"You know it and I know it, I just wish Bonnie knew it. She told me about that birthday party she was un-invited to. She was

Our Erring Sisters by Carol Henwood

very hurt, couldn't believe someone could be that cruel and heartless. Bonnie said, and I quote, "'I didn't care, my parents took me out to a nice dinner and movie, and I had a better time than I would have had at that stupid, old party anyway.'"

"Right," Andee and I said simultaneously.

Andee got up and stretched her hands above her head as she yawned, then using her pen as a microphone turned and eagerly reported, "Just another of the many heartbreaking stories from the files of Emmeriah's Home for Wayward Girls, there are not many happy endings here, just sensible solutions for those pesky teenage girls who find themselves in the family way," Andee lamented as she plopped back down on the bed and groaned.

"You've got a class in a few minutes, don't you?" I asked Andee as she went back to her letter.

"Yes, unfortunately I do. I have an English test that I haven't studied for very much, but Mrs. Walker says I'm doing well and my grades have been pretty good so far."

"When your class is over and I'm through practicing typing for my future secretarial career, let's go out in the back yard and get some sun. I can't go back home pale as a ghost when I have supposedly been in the great outdoors for almost two months. Miss Mellet said its fine for us to sunbathe out there, nobody can see over the hedge and we can take our radios and pretend like we're lying out beside a pool. Granted, we'll have to have a vivid imagination, but what the heck, let's do it. I don't have a bathing suit, that would not be a pretty sight, but we've all got shorts and bras."

"Sounds good to me, I lost my tropical glow months ago, but I do have suntan oil and coconut oil, and maybe the sun will help get rid of our stretch marks," Andee said as she pulled her shorts down and showed off her stretch marks on the side of her small hips, and on her belly. "Those don't even compare to this huge one on my lower abdomen. It keeps getting wider and wider and itches like crazy," I said as we compared bellies.

"Wow, that is a big one, but you're carrying that baby so low, I guess that's why all the stretching is down there. Sorry, Elizabeth, but I don't think that one's going away no matter how much cocoa

Our Erring Sisters by Carol Henwood

butter you put on it. You'd better have a good story to pull out whenever you decide to bare it all in the future!" Andee cackled.

"God, don't even go there, that's the last thing I want to think about now. So, you go on to class, I'll bang away on the old Underwood here for an hour, and then we'll catch some rays. I know Lacy and Kylene will want to come out with us, and be sure and ask Bonnie before class to join us, too. Might make her feel better to lie out in the sun and pretend we're at a pool party and get our gigantic bellies a nice golden tan."

At 2:00 we were out in the back yard of the house, towels spread out on the grass, radios playing loudly, glasses of water, Cokes, and lemonade on the tables, along with chips and dip. We brought out spray bottles filled with water to stay cool, although we did use the hose in the yard to spray each other for fun. What a sight we would have been to any unsuspecting person who happened to get a glimpse of us. Andee, Bonnie, and I had our shorts rolled up as far as we could get them rolled up, and our engorged breasts spilling out of our maternity bras. Kylene, Lacy, KC, Dedra, Sarabeth and Divine came out later on in similar dress and we laughed hysterically at the sight of ten very pregnant teenage girls in makeshift bikinis. Even young Sheree tagged along with Divine and shyly joined in.

"Now, if we only had a pool, a Margarita, and some male companions, this would be fabulous," cooed Kylene.

"If any males did show up, they'd high tail it out of here so fast it'd make your head spin. They'd be repulsed by our big, fat, bodies and terrified they'd get blamed for our condition, the wimps that most males are," Lacy added.

Dedra was enjoying herself so much, it made me think she'd probably never done anything like this, and she shared that she had never had a bathing suit.

"We were not allowed to wear anything this skimpy, it was absolutely forbidden," she said referring to her shorts and bra. "Every inch of skin had to be covered, except for our hands and face. That's why the females have to wear the long dresses with long sleeves and high necks, and socks pulled up so no skin would

151

be exposed, except the hands and face. You have no idea how heavy and hot those dresses are, even in the winter. I can't tell you how wonderful it feels to have on so few clothes, it's liberating," she sang as she whirled around the yard in her short shorts and a black lace bra.

"If the lifestyle is so puritanical there, where did you get that sexy, black lace underwear, Dedra?" sniggered Divine.

Looking ashamed, Dedra timidly answered, "Pastor Josiah gave these to his chosen girls whenever we were to lay with him. He told us never to wear them any other time, only with him, but they were the only pretty things I had, so I wore them a lot and have almost worn them out," she added.

"What a disgusting pervert," Lacy snarled.

"I wish I could get my hands on that sicko and give him a little Divine justice, right where it counts," Divine chimed in.

As we were making up scenarios to humiliate and discredit Pastor Josiah, Laurie, a fifteen-year-old girl who just arrived yesterday, walked out of the French doors and called out, "There's a phone call for an Elizabeth, is she out here?"

"That's me," I said waving my hand in the air and pushing my round body up. "Be right there, well, maybe not right there, but as fast as I can waddle in."

I pulled a shirt over my bra and unrolled my shorts and went inside to answer the call on the hall phone.

"Hello," I answered expecting to hear Daddy's voice.

"Ella?"

Hearing the deep, familiar voice of Lucas on the line shook me to my core. I held the phone away from my ear and looked at it in disbelief, thinking this had to be a joke or most certainly, a mistake.

Lucas?"

"Yes, Ella, it's Lucas. How are you?" he asked sounding like he didn't want to hear the answer.

I was in a state of shock and stammered, "How did you get this number? I mean, the camp doesn't give it out for security purposes."

Our Erring Sisters by Carol Henwood

"It doesn't matter how I got the number, how are you doing?" he persisted.

"Yes, it does matter," I screamed into the phone. "How did you find me?"

"Ella, please calm down, I don't want to upset you, please just hold on a minute. Luanna gave me the number, thinking this may be where you were, instead of being a camp counselor somewhere in North Carolina."

"Luanna, I should have known! I should have never written to her. What business is it of hers to go snooping around?"

"Don't be hard on Luanna, Ella. She was worried about you, especially since the letters you sent her were signed with the name Elizabeth, not Ella. That got her thinking maybe you were not where you said you were and using an assumed name. But, why?"

Damn, I never should have written to her, I thought to myself. I slipped up and signed that dumb letter as Elizabeth, not Ella. Elizabeth – Ella – Elizabeth – Ella, I don't even know who the hell I am anymore.

"Ella, it's okay. Luanna said the last time she saw you, you were acting strange and nervous, and so was your mother." Lucas hesitated momentarily, gathering the strength to continue.

"Luanna thinks you were hiding the fact that you were pregnant, and instead of going off to North Carolina to be a camp counselor, you're at some home for unwed mothers in Atlanta. Is that true, Ella, and if it is, why didn't you tell me?" Lucas asked almost reverently.

Bewildered and confused, and at a loss for words, I didn't say anything for several seconds.

"Ella, I won't be angry with you, I understand the situation, but I do wish you had told me, if it's true. Believe me, I know how your parents feel about me and you did what you had to do, but you know I would have married you, I ..."

"Stop it, don't say another word. This can't be happening. How could Luanna do this, my privacy was supposed to be guaranteed," I said exasperated.

Our Erring Sisters by Carol Henwood

"You know as well as I do, when Luanna Lindsey sets her mind to something, there's no stopping her. She put two and two together and started doing her own investigation. She said she knew all about Emmeriah Parrish Home because her uncle in Atlanta is on the board of directors. She managed to get the telephone number out of his secretary somehow, and gave it to me. She also said she was able to get a list of the camp counselors at Rollingbrook for the summer, and your name wasn't on it. She told me to call this number and ask to speak to Elizabeth and see what happens. So I did, and you answered."

I was reeling from the call, but had so many questions I wanted answers to, I kept blurting them out.

"Where did you see Luanna, and did you ask her to find out where I was?"

"I ran into her a few weeks ago when I was home for the weekend. I was out running and she drove by, blew the horn and pulled over. I got in the car and we started talking, and then everything that had happened over the last several months came out, and she told me she was very concerned about you, as I was, and that the last time she saw you, she thought something strange was going on. Luanna said she was going to find out what was up, and if anyone can do that, it's her. We said good-bye, and she promised to let me know what she found out. Then a week ago she called me at school, I had given her my phone number at the dorm, and she gave me the information, and I finally mustered up the courage to call the number today."

"Well, no sense in trying to pretend any longer. Yes, it's all true. I am pregnant, nine months now, and I'm at Emmeriah Parrish Home for Unwed Mothers in Atlanta, just like Luanna figured out, damn her eyes. Are you happy now? I have agreed to give the baby up for adoption, it's the best thing for everyone concerned, and we will both have to get on with our lives," I said as I regurgitated my programmed speech, as if I believed it.

"I suppose you're right, Ella, but I would have liked an opportunity to have some say so in the decision," Lucas said sounding more hurt than angry.

Our Erring Sisters by Carol Henwood

"I don't want to go back over all the reasons, Lucas, you know them all too well. We thought this was the best course to take, for you, me, and the baby. I was afraid to tell you, to be honest, I'm a gutless wonder. I didn't know what you would say, and I didn't want to trap you in a marriage you weren't emotionally or financially ready for. So, I followed my parents' advice, broke up with you, and took the path of least resistance, and Daddy arranged all the rest, and this is where we are today. I'm so sorry Lucas," I said as my tough act began to falter and I dissolved into tears.

"You deserved to know, but we can be thankful to know that the baby already has a family waiting to adopt him, or her."

Ignoring my tears, Lucas said, "Yeah, that's great, that's great," he said with no emotion. "When is the baby due, Ella? From my calculations it should be any day now."

"Around September 3rd or so, but due dates don't really mean anything, the baby comes when it's ready. After it's born, I'll go back home and recuperate for a few weeks, and either enroll in school or move to Atlanta and get a job until next summer. Emily Anne is transferring to State in Atlanta and she is going to get an apartment, so we could share the apartment until next summer." I was trying to avoid any mention of whether or not we should see each other again, I knew the answer to that.

"Sounds like you have everything worked out, Ella. Just so you know, I'm moving to Alabama permanently this fall. Miles and Rennie have gone to live with Mama again, just an hour from me in Batesville, and I sure as hell don't want to live with Daddy anymore in Desota. So I reckon our paths won't cross again anytime soon." Sighing heavily, Lucas continued with difficulty. "This is not the way I thought things would turn out between us, Ella, but I'm getting used to being knocked down by you, having hope, getting up and trying again, but this time I think I'll just stay down. You know Ella, maybe I'm not financially ready, I've never had the luxury of choosing whether or not I was emotionally ready for things, like whippings, or trying to stop my parents from killing each other, or helping raise my brother and sister. I just took the abuse, sucked it up, and did what I had to do. You're very fortunate, Ella. You came from a loving and secure family and didn't have to deal with unpleasant things in your childhood, and I'm grateful you didn't. Even though we came from backgrounds that are as different as night and day, we had a connection and a chemistry that was something special, and I know you feel the same, but there were too many forces working against us."

Stopping for a moment, Lucas laughed and continued, "Boy, that was a mouthful, wasn't it? Anyway, Ella, I hope and pray everything goes well for you; the birth, your plans, your life. I love you now and always will, and I only hope you find what it is you're looking for one day. Take care of yourself, and don't worry, I won't bother you again. Good-bye, Ella."

"Wait Lucas," I yelled into the phone. "You don't understand. I didn't want to do this, and you don't know what I've had to deal with in my family, Lucas, wait, don't hang up," I shrieked into the receiver. Too late, he was gone and for the second time, I didn't say good-bye.

I hung up the receiver and ran into my room down the hall, fell on the bed crying and pounding my pillow with every bit of strength I had. It had been a shock to hear from Lucas, I had not expected it, and I was going into a tailspin. I had accepted my decision and was beginning to look forward to getting my life in order and letting go of Lucas once and for all. The phone call had brought everything back to the surface, all the feeling I had tried to ignore and forget were front and center again. Damn Luanna Lindsey, at least I knew she'd keep her mouth shut and not tell anyone else. She was a loyal friend, and I guess she thought she was doing me a favor by telling Lucas where I was. Her thinking must have been if Lucas knew where I was, we could talk it out, get back together and get married, keep our baby and everything would just be hunky-dory. Little did she know that speaking to Lucas had only made the situation far worse for us both.

When I didn't return to the sunbathers within twenty minutes, Andee came inside to find me. She found me in a heap on the bed, swollen eyes and tear streaked face, still working my pillow over.

Our Erring Sisters by Carol Henwood

After I was sufficiently calm enough to tell Andee about the call, we talked and I felt better. It was a comfort to talk to someone who knew exactly what I was experiencing, and to be able to share the raw emotions that had resurfaced and were searing my wounded heart. I feared my heart would have many more scars before this ordeal was finally over.

Chapter Nineteen

Della was already perspiring on this hot, sultry Sunday, and it was only 6:30 in the morning. The window units were working overtime in an attempt to keep the large house cool in the dog days of a Georgia summer, but without much success. Della was in the kitchen preparing Ella's favorite dishes for lunch, every eye on the stove was on as well as the oven, and it must have been ninety degrees in the kitchen. After everything was cooked, she would place the food in containers, put them in a cooler, take a picnic basket with her, then drive the seventy miles to Atlanta just to have lunch with Ella in a random parking lot. This was the seventh week that Della had gone through this ritual, but it was a labor of love for her because she knew Ella looked forward to it.

. The cooking completed, Della was ready to go upstairs, get dressed and be out of the door by 9:00.

Henry walked into the kitchen at 7:30 a.m., and jokingly asked, "Any chance of a little breakfast this morning?"

Della knew Henry was being facetious, because when she was in her cooking mode, he knew to stay out of the way.

"Well, if you are referring to a bowl of cereal and can find an empty spot, be my guest," she replied with a smile. Della was grateful for Henry's understanding of her manic behavior every Sunday morning and appreciated his indulgence.

"Smells wonderful, what's for lunch today?" Henry asked as he opened the lids to the pots on the stove looking and sniffing.

Cleaning up the kitchen as she cooked, Della replied, "I cooked a nice, fat hen with dressing, green beans, squash casserole, and of course, yeast rolls, chocolate pie, and sweet tea to wash it all down with. That's your dinner for tonight, too."

Our Erring Sisters by Carol Henwood

"Della, you are one amazing woman," Henry said as she put his arm around his wife. "An entire dinner all cooked before 8:00 a.m. in the morning."

"You know I love to cook for my family Henry, and I get a great deal of pleasure watching them enjoy the fruits of my labor," Della replied as she patted Henry on his chest.

"You realize this might be the last Sunday I cook and travel, if not the last, very close to it, and I am starting to get the jitters. I do so wish I could be there with Ella when her time comes, but I know it's not allowed. I'm going to be a nervous wreck for the next few weeks."

Changing subjects quickly, Della said "Well, I'd better go get myself dressed and ready to go. It's going to be a beastly hot day and sitting in a parked car eating lunch isn't much fun, so I think I might try to find a nice park somewhere in the area." Sighing, and shaking her head back and forth, Della continued telling Henry her fears and apprehensions. "I feel so guilty about not going to see Mama when I'm in Atlanta every Sunday, but I never have enough time, and I would have to concoct some reason for arriving so late and having such a short visit. The end is in sight, and soon we can conclude this charade and get on with our lives. I don't think Ella realizes how much this has affected every single one of us, each in a different way. Tarleton and Emily Anne both miss her and worry about her, and I'm sure they will do anything they can to help her transition back into her life here at home. Tarleton's very protective of her, and will guard her secret with his life. Emily Anne is a good older sister and will give Ella advice on which paths she should take from here. We are blessed to have three wonderful children, Henry," Della said with her voice breaking.

"Yes we are Della, we are truly blessed. Now, don't go and get yourself upset before you have to get on the road. I'll finish cleaning up in here, you go on up and get dressed," Henry told Della as he began to wash pots and pans.

"Thank you dear, I'll take you up on that," she replied as she surveyed the mess in the kitchen, turned and left it in Henry's capable hands.

Chapter Twenty

I was waiting for Mama's arrival in the foyer when I saw the car come down the long driveway. I looked forward to her Sunday visits and the delicious lunch she packed each week. I felt guilty about all the work I knew she went through to get it cooked, packed, and delivered, but we both cherished the time we shared.

I saw Andee out of the corner of my eye, running at full speed toward me, as fast as her ever expanding body would allow.

"Elizabeth, there you are," she said, out of breath. "Bonnie's gone into labor and is down at the nurses' station right now. Sarabeth told me she heard her up and down last night and she finally convinced her to go see the nurse this morning."

"Have you talked to her?" I anxiously asked as I saw Mama coming up the walkway to the door.

"No, but I'm going down there right now to see if Nurse Jackson will let me see her before she goes to the hospital; I think she will, she's pretty understanding, not like that bitch Nurse Knight. Is that your Mom?" Andee asked as she saw Mama walking up the steps.

"Yep, that's her and she's right on time, which is amazing." Turning to Andee I asked, "Would you like to meet her? I know she'd like to meet you. You'll like her, everybody does. Come on and let me introduce you." Mama rang the doorbell and was buzzed in by one of the staffers. She signed herself in and submitted to having her purse searched for contraband, displaying a look of disdain. After those procedures were completed, Mama and I hugged each other tightly for a full minute.

"Hello, dear." Stepping back, she took both my hands in hers and gave me the once over.

Our Erring Sisters by Carol Henwood

"You look just wonderful with a nice, healthy glow and it looks as if you've gotten bigger since last Sunday," she observed with a smile. A puzzled expression came over her face as she looked at the bright, yellow maternity sun dress I had borrowed from Kylene.

"I don't remember buying that dress, Ella, I mean Elizabeth," Mama said, quickly correcting herself. "It's quite lovely, where did it come from?"

"We all go shopping in Kylene's closet, she has more clothes than all of us put together, and she insists that we borrow anything we want to. Pretty, huh?" I asked as I held out the skirt and curtsied.

"It certainly is, and you must take care not to soil it and return it to her in good condition. Whenever you borrow anything, always make sure you return it exactly as it was when you borrowed it, dear."

"Yes, Mama, I will," I said rolling my eyes. I turned around to see Andee fidgeting behind me and I pulled her beside me.

"Mama, this is Andee, my roommate. She's always off doing God know what when you visit on Sundays, so you've never met her.

"Hello, Elizabeth's mother, nice to meet you," Andee said with a nervous laugh. "I know your last name isn't Nash, so I won't address you as Mrs. Nash. We're all incognito here as you well know," Andee said with a wink. "Elizabeth and I have become best buddies, she's a great listener, and believe me, I can talk a blue streak."

"So nice to meet you, Andee. Elizabeth has told me how much she enjoys your company and how you have made her feel right at home," Mama replied politely being careful not to go overboard with too much enthusiasm, wanting to emphasize to me that this friendship was a temporary one. "I know you're quite a long way from home, and that must be difficult for you. Would you care to join Elizabeth and me for lunch today?"

Stunned at my mother's offer, I jumped and turned to Andee.

Our Erring Sisters by Carol Henwood

"Yes, please come with us, Andee, it'll be fun having you along. I want you to taste some of Mama's cooking, it's the absolute best, and there's always enough for a small army. Come on, please," I pleaded.

"Thank you so much," Andee said looking at Mama, "but no, this is your time together, plus, I've got some studying to catch up on, and Mama Mellete always makes sure there is a scrumptious Sunday lunch for those of us who don't get to leave for the day, and I sure don't want to hurt her feelings."

"Whatever you think is best, dear, but we would love to have you come," Mama answered, relieved, I was sure.

"Oh, fiddlesticks, come on Andee, Miss Mellete won't care," I begged.

"Nope, maybe another time, you two go on. It was nice to meet you, Elizabeth's mother, and I have heard about your fantastic cooking. Have a nice day," Andee said as she hastily walked toward the nurses' station, on her mission to get to see Bonnie before she left for the hospital.

I detected just the slightest look of satisfaction on Mama's face, happy that Andee would not be joining us. I was annoyed at her reaction, knowing she hoped Andee wouldn't accept her invitation. I didn't want to make a big deal out of it and ruin the day, but I wanted to make sure Mama knew Andee was my friend.

"I wish Andee would have come with us, she's a good friend and a lot of fun to be around, especially when there's not a whole lot to laugh about these days."

"Yes, I'm sure she is dear. Now, we're going to have our lunch in a park that is close by. I talked to Emily Anne this morning and she found a park that is near the home and she gave me directions. How does that sound?" Mama asked cheerfully, as she deftly changed subjects from Andee to possible lunch spots.

Aggravated with Mama for her obvious dismissal of my friendship with Andee, I responded, "Sure, that's fine with me, it really doesn't matter."

Our Erring Sisters by Carol Henwood

"It matters very much, Ella, I want our day to be comfortable and relaxed, and sitting in a hot car every Sunday, trying to enjoy our meal, isn't exactly ideal. Let's get going, dear."

The park was several miles north of the home away from the busiest part of Peachtree and any possibility that we would run into anyone that would recognize us. I read Emily Anne's expert directions out loud and we found the small park easily. It was a lovely area with many trees and lots of shade with picnic tables, benches and a playground. It was already ninety degrees outside and not a hint of a breeze.

"What a lovely spot and just perfect for our picnic," Mama exclaimed as she drove in and found a shady space to park, which was not difficult, since we were the only people there.

Mama was well prepared, as usual, bringing a tablecloth, cloth napkins, festive paper plates, and plastic forks, knives and spoons. I set the table as Mama took the food out of the cooler and picnic basket and set it on the picnic table. I poured us some sweet tea from a thermos, and we were ready to eat. We had the park all to ourselves, except for the birds flitting from tree to tree and singing as they fluttered above our heads, displaying their vivid feathers to our delight. The squirrels were industriously digging in the ground looking for hidden treasures and coming closer to our picnic table in hopes of finding a dropped morsel of food.

We made small talk about the inhospitable weather, Emily Anne's upcoming move to an apartment in Atlanta where she'll live and finish her final year of college, and Tarleton's summer and his excitement about beginning his senior year of high school. Finally, Mama got around to me.

I was starting on my second brownie when Mama carefully broached the subject of childbirth.

"Now, Ella, I know you will be extremely frightened when you go into labor, not knowing what to expect. I wish there was a way for me to be there with you, but it is not allowed for many reasons and we have to abide by the rules. Miss Mellete will place a call to us after you have given birth, I wish she would call us before the birth, but again, those are the rules. We cannot come down and see you while you are in the hospital, but will come within four or five days after and bring you back home. I am assured that you will be well cared for and given pain medication as soon as possible in order to make this already difficult situation less traumatic."

Once Mama had spoken her piece to me, she exhaled and her shoulders slumped.

"Do you have any questions you would like to ask me about the process of labor and delivery dear?" Mama reluctantly inquired.

Almost choking on the brownie at the mention of the subject, I flippantly answered, "No, nothing I can think of. When one of the girls comes back from the hospital after they've delivered, we get the entire picture, and I do mean everything, from the wonderful enema you get to the pubic shave, which to some is the worst part of it all. So I guess I'm as ready as I'll ever be," I declared with a forced smile and false bravado.

Embarrassed by the mention of the intimate details of the enema and the pubic shaving, Mama hemmed and hawed for a moment.

"Well, excellent, I suppose you have already packed a bag to take to the hospital by now, in the event you go might go before your due date."

"Yes, I did that yesterday, but I don't think I'll be going anywhere until September 3rd, or later. I go back to the clinic tomorrow, and I hope I see Dr. Reynolds again. I've had two different doctors the last two times, so Dr. Reynolds should be next. I sure do hope he is on call whenever I do go in, he is so kind and compassionate and easy to talk to. That reminds me, you've heard me talk about Bonnie, she is also a good friend," I stated emphatically, "she went into labor last night some time and is probably on her way to the hospital right now. Andee was going to check on her at the nurses' station when we left the home."

"Speaking of friends, I know you feel close to these girls right now, Ella as you are all in the same predicament, but after you leave, there will be no reason to continue contact with them. This is an unhappy part of your life that you will want to put behind you,

Our Erring Sisters by Carol Henwood

not prolong, and continued communication with them will only prohibit you from getting on with a new direction in life."

"Mama, please stop saying 'those girls' as if they're dirt under your feet. They're the only reason I haven't gone bat shit crazy since I've been here. They are not all low class white trash girls like you seem to think. Some of them are from fine families and some are from nothing, but they are the best people I've ever met. They're important to me and if I want to stay in touch with them for a while, that's my decision. I'm nineteen-years old and about to have a baby all alone, and 'those girls' as you call them, are my only support system."

"I don't approve of that gutter language you're using, you never spoke like that before you came here, and for your information Ella, your father and I have been nothing but supportive of you and you know it," Mama said as she got up and started packing up, not giving any ground.

I conceded for the moment and didn't pursue the conversation further. I was ready to get back to the home and see my friends. My worst fear was that my mother would ask about Lucas, and if I had heard anything from him. Fortunately for me, she didn't ask, thank goodness, I didn't want to get into that. Mama filled me in on the latest news from Desota, and her constant efforts to avoid our nosy neighbor Alice Babcock's probing questions about my whereabouts.

"Not to worry, I'll be back home and good as new within a few short weeks, armed with an iron clad story and I'll pretend it never happened and continue with my life," I said with just enough sarcasm to annoy my mother.

"I'll be more than happy to answer any questions that old battle ax has, and give her a piece of mind for sticking her big nose in where it doesn't belong. She'd better start paying attention to what mealy-mouthed Lila is up to, not me. I'm betting the studious bookworm that Mama and Daddy Babcock are so proud of is doing more than keeping her nose in a book this summer in Atlanta. The brainy, homely quiet ones are the first to rebel and go hog wild." I had no idea why I was taking my frustrations out on poor Lila. I

Our Erring Sisters by Carol Henwood

suppose I wanted to impress upon my mother that any girl could end up in this predicament. As we walked back to the car, a station wagon drove up and parked next to us. A young couple got out of the car and the man unloaded a stroller as the woman got out holding a tiny baby in her arms. She saw me and immediately smiled and I knew she was going to ask me when my baby was due and other small talk pregnant women share with each other. I didn't know how I was going to handle it. I looked at Mama and saw the wheels turning in her head, she probably had a story for this sort of encounter all ready to roll out, but I beat her to the punch.

The couple worked together to make sure the baby was in the stroller and safely secured. They turned to face us, proud parents ready to share their happy experience. I smiled as they approached, and looked down at the infant with tiny fingers and toes, sleeping soundly in the stroller, a baby girl dressed in a doll sized pink dress, several sizes too big for her and it made her appear even smaller.

"She is so adorable," I oozed, "how old is she?"

Bursting with pride, the father answered before the mother had a chance. "Two weeks old today. This is her first real outing, we know it's hot, but the park is mostly shade and we thought a little fresh air would be nice."

The young woman smiled and looked lovingly down at the baby.

"This is Anna, our daughter, I'm Leigh and this is my husband, Henry." This is the first time we've taken her anywhere besides the pediatrician," Leigh said with a laugh, and looking at my enormous belly, she said, "Looks like you're about to pop, you must be real close to delivery."

"Hi, I'm Elizabeth and this is my Mom, Della. Yes, I'm close, September 3rd or so. I'm pretty excited, too." I took a quick sidelong glance at Mama and she looked ashen.

"You and your husband will love being parents, it's so wonderful, better than we ever imagined," Henry added, naturally assuming I was a married lady.

166

Our Erring Sisters by Carol Henwood

Fiddling with her purse and looking all around, Mama said, "Elizabeth, we should get a move on dear." Looking down at the baby with a longing in her eyes that seared me to my very soul, she smiled at the young couple and said, "You have a precious baby and I know she is the delight of your life, enjoy every moment." Turning to me, she said, "Elizabeth, come on, sweetheart."

The rest of the drive back to the home was quiet and I knew my mother was trying to prepare something to say before she left me at the home, in the event I went into labor before next Sunday.

The sun was a large orange ball in the sky as we pulled down the driveway, both of us perspiring from the heat. We got out of the car and Mama walked around to my side. We always said our good-byes outside, it made it easier.

Looking out into the woods in front of the house where there is a clearing, sitting there on a spread out blanket was Sarabeth and a man and woman who must have been her parents, and a young man, her brother I guessed.

Mama was watching the scene in the woods and asked, "Do you know them, Ella? They look like a nice family."

"That's Sarabeth from Alabama, and I suppose those are her parents. I know she has a brother, so that must be him. Her baby's due around the same time as mine. She went to Auburn and teaches the pottery class here. I like her, she's a decent person."

"You're a good, decent person, too, Ella, don't forget that. I'll call you this week, and so will Daddy. Miss Mellete will contact us if you should go into labor. If not, I will be back next Sunday, and maybe we could have a picnic on the grounds, like Sarabeth and her parents." Her tender gaze lingered on me for a moment and as her hazel eyes glistened with tears, she hugged me tight, turned, and got in her car before I could even return the hug.

Chapter Twenty-One

I caught up with Andee once back inside the home and she filled me in on the events of the day while I was at the park.

"Nurse Jackson was really great and let me come in and sit with Bonnie for thirty minutes. They were timing her contractions to see if she should go to the hospital now or wait a while longer. Bonnie is a basket case and wants her mother to go to the hospital when she does, but I don't think that's gonna happen. It's not allowed, and they sure don't want to break any rules," Andee said mockingly.

"Have they gone to the hospital or not?" I anxiously asked.

"Not yet, but it should be pretty soon. Her contractions were about ten minutes apart, but not very strong. I swear, I think the nurses hold out as long as they can in hopes that another one of us will go into labor and they can take more than one to the hospital just so they don't have to come and go all the time, nice, caring angels that they are," Andee said with a sneer.

"Oh, come on, you know most of the nurses are good, except for Nurse Knight. She went into nursing just to take out her frustrations on unsuspecting victims since she is such an incredibly ugly, rodent looking creature, and it gives her a sense of power she never would have achieved anywhere else."

Shrugging her shoulders, Andee said, "I don't know, maybe you're right. How was the picnic?"

"It was nice for a change to be outside and not in the hot car burning up, although it was still hot, but kind of nice sitting at a picnic table. A little drama was thrown into the mix when this young couple with a brand new baby pulled up beside the car when we were packing up to leave. They got out of the car, unloaded a stroller and a baby, their faces bursting with pride, just waiting to show off the baby to the very pregnant me and Mama."

Our Erring Sisters by Carol Henwood

"Oops, awkward moment," Andee said.

"Yep, very awkward, but I managed to fake it nicely and make a clean get away before any probing questions were asked. I thought for a minute there that Mama was going to faint, worried what might come out of my mouth, but she managed to get through it. It broke my heart to see her looking at that baby, knowing she would never see her own grandchild. I'll be so glad when this charade is over."

Andee and I talked for a little longer and then went to the common room to watch television before our light Sunday supper.

Sarabeth was stretched out on one of the big, overstuffed chairs with her feet resting on the ottoman, Dedra was sitting at one of the tables looking at the latest *Seventeen Magazine* with Sheree and Divine, while Lacy, KC, Kylene, and several of the newer residents were wandering in and out of the room, sitting down and staring at the TV, no one talking. A heavy, uncomfortable silence permeated the room and surrounded us, it happened each time one of us went into labor and left the home for the hospital. Reality was always sobering, and their reality would soon be ours. Bonnie was everyone's favorite and we all knew she wanted her mother to be there with her when she gave birth, but we knew that was not going to be allowed.

I sat down next to Sarabeth who looked uncharacteristically glum.

"Was that your parents and brother with you today having a picnic?"

"Yes, it was. They drove from Montgomery just to have lunch with me, and brought my brother Peter with them so he could see me before he ships out next week for Vietnam."

"Vietnam?" I asked in shock.

"Yep, he was drafted and has been in boot camp for the last several months at Fort Rucker, and he just got his orders this week. I am so scared for him and my parents are sick with worry about it, as if they don't have worries enough already. Not a banner year in our house," Sarabeth said.

Our Erring Sisters by Carol Henwood

That was the most Sarabeth had ever said about her family. It must be particularly difficult time for them to have both of their children in unhappy and dangerous circumstances.

"I didn't know, Sarabeth, I'm so sorry; Vietnam," I said shaking my head. "I'm not even sure where it is, other than its half way 'round the world from here."

Sitting up and placing both hands on either side of her stomach, she sat very still for a minute.

"Are you okay?"

"I think so, just those pesky Braxton-Hicks contractions starting up again. They're pretty frequent now, whatever that means," she said with a laugh.

"We're both down to the last leg of this journey, and I've been having more of those Braxton-Hicks contractions myself," I whispered to her. "I guess we don't have to be concerned until they become painful."

After a supper of chicken salad, crackers and fruit, Andee, Sarabeth and I decided do take a walk, even though it was still like a sauna outside. We were bathed in sweat after the usual four laps, back and forth on the long driveway, which was one mile. We went inside when we finished our walk, and straight to the bulletin board in the hall to see what our new chores would be for upcoming week.

"Yay, dusting furniture is my job next week. Oh, the perks of being nine months pregnant," I said with glee. I had done everything from cooking meals to cleaning toilets and sundry other chores in between. The girls close to their due date where given any light duty Miss Mellete came up with.

"I'm back to kitchen duty next week," Andee moaned. "If you've been here as long as I have, you have at least three turns at every chore."

"I've got tough duty coming up, too," Sarabeth said. "Looks like I'll be watering all the house plants, I'm not sure if I can handle that," she said with a smile.

"Oh well, one day I'll be where you two are now," Andee said, resigned to her fate.

Our Erring Sisters by Carol Henwood

"Look at it this way Andee, it's almost September now, and you'll be officially in your ninth month, so cheer up," I told her as we walked down the hall toward our room.

Andee stopped in her tracks, turned to me and almost jumped up and down. "Your right, by the middle of September I'll be one of the chosen few."

"There you go, you have something to look forward to. Now, I've got to get out of these wet clothes that are sticking to me," I said as I started peeling off the clammy shirt and shorts before I got to the room.

I gathered my shower bucket loaded with the essentials – shampoo, soap, razor, along with my towel and washcloth. I couldn't wait to get into a cool shower and stand there and let the water wash over me. I had felt unusually tired for the last two days, why wouldn't I, carrying around all this extra weight. I stood there in the shower hoping the water would revive me, as well as relax me, because a good night's sleep was a thing of the past. I washed my hair, bathed myself, gazed at the ever widening stretch mark on my lower abdomen, and reluctantly turned the water off. I stepped out of the shower and went into a bathroom stall to relieve myself, as the pressure on my bladder was unrelenting. As usual, I didn't urinate much, but noticed a reddish, pink tinge on the toilet paper. Startled, I got up and looked in the toilet bowl where I saw more of a pink mucus-like substance. Was this the beginning of labor? I had heard that certain things would happen before actual labor started, one was losing the mucus plug, which I think I just had done. I stayed in the stall for a few more minutes and recalled all that I had been experiencing over the last several days; some lower back pain, but I didn't pay much attention to it, Braxton-Hicks contractions, no pain just the hardening of my abdomen for a few minutes then softening again. It was August 27th, less than a week from my predicted due date, and I hadn't even begun to prepare myself mentally or emotionally for the impending birth, and now it looked as if I may have run out of time. I came out of the bathroom stall trembling with the irrefutable knowledge that my baby was getting ready to be born, and I couldn't do anything to slow the process down. I decided not to say anything to Andee yet, because I hadn't experienced any painful contractions and I didn't want to get her excited or worried about me for nothing. I would just wait and see what happened in the next several hours, or days, before I said anything. I crossed the hall back into my room where Andee was studying for a history test for class tomorrow morning. I put curlers in my hair and sat under my hair dryer and read while I waited the thirty minutes for my hair to dry. We stuck to our usual Sunday night ritual of watching *Bonanza* with everyone, had a snack, and then went to bed. I was lying in bed, wide awake, my mind racing, trying to process everything that was happening to me. I remembered that the clinic schedule had been changed from Mondays to Tuesdays, so I would not be going into the clinic in the morning for a check up, but might be in the hospital instead. It was going to be a long night.

Chapter Twenty-Two

I must have fallen asleep sometime after 2:00 a.m. because that was the last time I looked at the clock. I had made it through the night without any new symptoms, not being awakened by painful contractions or something else, like my water breaking. Maybe all my fears of an impending birth had been premature, at least delayed, and I had been given a reprieve.

Andee and I got up and started our weekly routine, which consisted of breakfast, exercise, chores and whatever was on tap for each of us on Mondays.

Miss Mellete informed us at breakfast that Bonnie had not delivered her baby as of yet, but she should within the hour. She didn't even go to the hospital until midnight, and her mother was not allowed to be with her.

"I think that is about the cruelest thing I've ever heard. Poor Bonnie had to stay here until that sadistic Nurse Knight, a.k.a., 'bitch from hell,' decided that she was far enough along to go to the hospital, and she wouldn't let her mother come to the hospital, too, even though she lives in the same town. You'd think these people would try and make the experience less traumatic for us, but I guess that's not high on their priority list."

"You can give the home high marks for sticking to the policy. If they let one girl have her mother there, then they'll have to let everyone have their mothers there. I'm not so sure I would want to have my mother here. At this point, I don't really care anymore," I said with a shrug.

"So, Elizabeth, I hope you saved all your energy up for the tough job of dusting today. That should wear you out," Andee quipped, changing subjects nicely.

Our Erring Sisters by Carol Henwood

"That's the truth, I'll probably have to take an extra nap this afternoon I'll be so exhausted. Good luck on your history test this morning and I'll see you at lunch," I said as I went to get the feather duster, dusting rags and the Pledge. I walked outside to the large shed which was in the back yard behind the house, where all the cleaning supplies were kept. I sensed the slightest hint of autumn in the air, as I had earlier on my morning walk. It was 9:00 a.m., very pleasant outside, with a light breeze blowing through the trees, the leaves showing the first inkling of change from the green of summer to the many hues of fall. I could almost smell fall in the air. Fall was my favorite season; I loved the smells and the colors. Mama, on the other hand, considered fall a sad time of year because the leaves dried up and fell off the trees, leaving them naked and stark. Fall would be especially hard this year. It would be a time of birth, loss and sadness. This unspoken sadness would leave a black mark on my heart, and a pain to be endured but never spoken of.

I gathered my supplies and went back into the house to begin dusting the furniture in the main house. I felt good, even perky, not tired a bit even though I'd had very little sleep, so I forged ahead with gusto. As I worked my way through the house, I made sure I took my time and polished the wood to a shine. I was in the library, dusting the bookshelves when I had a sudden, sharp pain in my abdomen, at the same time my abdomen tightened up and stayed hard for several seconds, but it seemed longer. It hurt, the pain was bearable, but bad enough that I had to stop and hold on to a chair. I knew this was different from what I'd felt before, and very real. Just then Miss Mellete came into the library, passing through on her way to the dorms.

"Hello Elizabeth," she said stopping as she saw me grabbing the back of the chair and grimacing. "Are you alright, dear?"

"Oh, yes, just a little pain in my back, I'm fine, really," I lied.

"Well, you take it easy, dear, don't overexert yourself," she said as she patted me on my back and exited the room.

I looked at my watch and noted the time, so I would be able to tell the time between contractions if these were the real thing.

Our Erring Sisters by Carol Henwood

Approximately twenty minutes later I had another contraction that lasted around the same amount of time. Again, I noted the time, and decided I'd better start writing down the time, length and intensity of the contractions so I could give the nurse on duty all the details once I determined it was time to tell the nurse. I tried to concentrate on carrying out my work, realizing it was going to be a long day.

Lacy, Divine, and KC came through the library on their way to the classroom and stopped long enough to chat for a minute.

"How's it going, Elizabeth?" Lacy asked with a smirk. "I see you're on light duty this week like her Divineness here."

"Miss Mellete's given me some office work to do, so I get to sit on my big behind most of the morning," she said as she posed with her hands on her hips, smiling from ear to ear. "You look a little pasty, Elizabeth, are you sick?" Divine inquired with a look of concern.

"Just a little back pain, nothing more, I guess all those things have to start a couple of weeks before delivery. Other than that, I'm just peachy."

"You, too?" Divine asked. "I've been having some weird kind of cramps, too, but nothing else. I figured it's all this extra weight I'm carrying around. But you know, we're due around the same time so maybe we're closer to the big day than we think."

"Oh, that's just swell," KC chimed in. "All my best buddies will end up in the hospital at the same time. Who will I tell all my dirty little secrets to then?"

Lacy turned to KC and asked in a deadpan voice, "Oh, and what am I, chopped liver?"

"I can think of a lot of things you are, but chopped liver is not one of them," KC responded.

"Okay girls, enough sniping, I've got class to attend and office work to do. Elizabeth, hang in there girl. Let's go bitches," Divine said pushing the girls ahead and quickly moving on.

At lunch Miss Mellete announced that Bonnie had successfully delivered a baby boy weighing eight pounds, eight ounces, and both mother and baby are doing fine.

Our Erring Sisters by Carol Henwood

"Why is it Miss Mellete always says, 'mother and baby are doing fine,' when we know damn well Bonnie is anything but fine, she's probably comatose. The fact that she is physically fine is one thing, but her emotional state is another story entirely," Kylene said. We all silently nodded our heads in agreement and got up from the lunch table and walked our trays over to the drop off window and left the dining room and went our separate ways for the afternoon. I went back to my room and sat down at the typewriter to do some exercises in the typing manual. My speed and proficiency at typing had improved greatly during my stay here, increasing my chances at some sort of secretarial job in the fall. The contractions I had experienced earlier had stopped for the most part during lunch, but started up again as I was banging away on the typewriter. They felt more intense and were now fifteen minutes apart, lasting a minute or longer. I picked up my log and recorded the length and intensity of this round of contractions. I couldn't concentrate on typing any longer, so I decided to get up and go for a walk, even though it was a scorcher outside, but I needed to move around and I couldn't sit here and wait for the next wave to start.

In the hall I passed Sarabeth and asked her if pottery class was still on for this afternoon.

"Yes, I'm feeling a little puny today, but we need to finish staining our bowls, birds, vases, and everything else down there that's waiting for the finishing touches to be put on."

"You, too? Divine has been having some back pain, and I've got something going on. Wouldn't it be great if we all went into labor at the same time?" I excitedly said.

"I guess it's possible, at least we could keep each other company while in the hospital," Sarabeth replied with a sad smile.

For the rest of the afternoon and into the evening, I made entries into my log. I was becoming nervous, positive that I was in the early stages of labor. I didn't want to go to the nurses' station too early. I'd know when to take myself there. I was going to keep this to myself because I knew it would be all over the home by tonight and I didn't want all the drama. I decided to casually stroll down to the nurses' station to see who was on duty starting at 7:00

Our Erring Sisters by Carol Henwood

p.m. tonight. I stopped outside the door to check the schedule. Right now Nurse Jackson was on duty, I saw her and we spoke. I looked and my worst fears were realized. Nurse Knight was on in the seven to seven slot, replacing Nurse Robbins, my favorite, who had a family emergency. Just my luck. Well, the old hag had to take me to the hospital if I was in labor, but she could decide when in her own good time, and I felt sure she would keep me at the home as long as she could just for spite.

By supper time the pains were ten minutes apart, harder and lasting longer. I wasn't hungry, but needed to show up and pretend to eat. I would tell Andee what was going on, only when I absolutely had to. I didn't want to consider the fact that the end of my pregnancy and the birth of my child was so near. The dueling emotions of deep sadness and great happiness fought to get the upper hand in my fragile emotional state, and I didn't know which one was winning. These would be the last few hours I would have with my baby. Etched in my mind was the picture of Penny lying on the bed in the nurses' station, crying and holding on to her stomach, as if she was trying to stop the inevitable. There would be a monumental change in my life by this time tomorrow – I would not be one of the frightened and impatient pregnant girls anymore, who were my friends, my confidants, my companions in this unhappy journey. Tomorrow, after giving birth, I would slowly begin shedding my temporary identity as the phantom girl Elizabeth Nash, but for now, Ella Cane and Elizabeth Nash were having a baby.

Chapter Twenty-Three

It was getting closer to midnight and I had not been able to sleep a wink, contractions now coming every seven to eight minutes. I knew it was time to go see the nurse, I'd delayed the dreaded trip as long as I could. I got up, turned on my bedside light and went over to Andee's bed and shook her awake.

"Andee, Andee, wake up. I'm in labor and I'm going down to the nurses' station right now."

Shaking her head, and sitting up in her bed with her eyes still closed, she mumbled something incoherent, and laid back down. I felt another contraction starting to build and I sat down on Andee's bed, closed my eyes, held my breath and grabbed the sheets and wrapped them as tightly as I could around my hands, and rocked back and forth trying not to cry out.

After the contraction began to subside, I once again shook Andee, much harder this time. "Andee, please wake up, I'm in labor and I've got to go tell the nurse," I pleaded.

"What? Oh, my God, Elizabeth, when, when did it start?" she screamed at me, equally as frightened.

"Late yesterday, I've lost track, I just didn't want to go to the hospital too soon and be sent back home. I know first babies take a long time, so I waited, but I may have waited too long," I said with a slight sound of panic in my voice.

"Yesterday? Elizabeth, why didn't you tell me? I'll go with you to see the nurse and ..."

"No, no, you can't go, it's Nurse Knight, and she's made no secret of how she feels about you. I'll go by myself, you get my suitcase out and ready." Andee and I held on to each other tightly for a moment, and then I got up to leave. "I need to go now," I said and hurried out into the hall.

Our Erring Sisters by Carol Henwood

The hall was dimly lit and I walked as fast as I could without running. It was a strange feeling walking through the house at midnight, eerie really. The tranquility of the night was in stark contrast to my impending emergency.

Once I got to the station, no one was there. The light was on, so surely Nurse Knight was close by, and I even looked forward to seeing her. I sat down in the chair by the desk and waited. A few minutes later I heard someone coming from the area of the kitchen, I looked up and Nurse Knight walked in with a cup of coffee and a piece of chocolate pie on a plate.

Startled to see me, she gasped and almost spilled her coffee.

"What is it you want, Elizabeth?" she demanded to know, irritated that I had interrupted her midnight snack.

"I'm pretty sure I'm in active labor and I have been for a while. I think I should go to the hospital right now," I blurted out in one breath.

"What makes you so sure about that?" she asked with little concern as she sat down, placing her coffee and pie on the desk. She turned to the file cabinet and opened it up, looking for my file.

Casually she read my file as she took a bite of her pie and mumbled something to herself. I explained that I had kept a log, but left it in my room I was in such a hurry, but I could go back down and get it if she wanted to see it. Just then I felt another contraction building and brought my hands to my stomach and leaned over, squeezed my eyes closed and held my breath.

Nurse Knight just sat there and observed me, like I was a bug in a glass jar, and didn't make a move to offer any comfort, not even a simple touch to ease my mind and assure me it would be alright; she just sat and ate her pie. After the contraction had passed, I looked up and Nurse Knight opened up the locked drug cabinet and took out a bottle of pills. She poured one into her hand and held it out for me to take.

Our Erring Sisters by Carol Henwood

"Take this sleeping pill, and if you sleep through it, you're not in labor. If you still can't sleep, come back here and I'll check you."

"Don't you want to check me now? I'm having contractions about every seven minutes or so, and they're getting strong," I pleaded, alarmed at her casual manner.

"Not necessary. Do as I told you, and come back only if you cannot sleep and I'll check you then and make a decision. That's all, Elizabeth."

I started to protest, but knew it would get me nowhere. The cruelty of the woman was beyond belief. She appeared to take great pleasure in my pain and her control over the situation.

I rushed out and back down the hall to a water fountain, popped the pill and went back into my room where Andee was anxiously waiting. I related the exchange between Nurse Knight and myself and she was equally flabbergasted.

"We ought to make a formal complaint to the board of trustees, this isn't the first time this has happened, you know. I'm going to talk to Miss Mellete in the morning – wait a minute," Andee said fully awake and at her best. "Let's go wake Miss Mellete up right now! What if she still won't take you to the hospital, and you have your baby right here tonight? Miss Mellete should intervene and take you herself, then have that sadistic bitch fired for incompetence."

"Just hold on, Andee, let me see if this sleeping pill works. I'm starting to feel a little drowsy, maybe I will sleep right through them. If these are just mild contractions, I can't wait to see what else is in store for me," I slowly mumbled as I lay down on my bed, with Andee sitting next to me, rubbing my back.

One and a half hours later, I hadn't slept a wink and I was having contractions every five minutes.

"Let's go, Elizabeth, enough of this bullshit. We're going down there right now with your suitcase, and that bitch had better move like her ass is on fire getting a cab out here, or I'm gonna commandeer her car and take you to the hospital myself."

Our Erring Sisters by Carol Henwood

I knew I was in full blown labor now and I was petrified. Between contractions I was okay, just drugged from the sleeping pill. We walked briskly down the hall, Andee carrying my suitcase. As we turned the corner, we heard conversation and we saw both Divine and Sarabeth in the room; Divine on the bed and Sarabeth sitting in one of the chairs.

A worn out and disheveled Divine looked up from the bed and said, "I don't believe it! Look who else just rolled in, Sarabeth."

"Yes, me too," I sleepily replied. "Sarabeth, what about you?"

"Early stages, but I think Nurse Knight is calling a cab to come out just in case one or all of us have to go tonight, and she's really annoyed about it, too."

"Well, it's about time! Where is the angel of mercy, anyway?" Andee angrily asked.

I elbowed Andee, not wanting to make matters worse.

"She went to tell Miss Mellete she would be taking two or three to the hospital tonight. We wondered who the third one was," Sarabeth said smiling at me.

Andee ordered me to go lie down on the other bed by Divine.

"Elizabeth's contractions are five minutes apart, and that old bat gave her a sleeping pill, and told her if she fell asleep she wasn't in real labor, but if she couldn't sleep to come back and she'd check her and make a decision. Can you believe the nerve of that insensitive old crone?"

Just then Nurse Knight reappeared at the door, surprised and looking rattled at having three girls in labor on her watch.

"Andee, what are you doing here? Get back to your room right now," she ordered.

"How do you know I'm not going to have my baby right here and now on this floor? You sent Elizabeth back to her room two hours ago with a sleeping pill, and now she's having contractions less than five minutes apart, and you never even checked to see if she was in labor. You call yourself a nurse? "

Our Erring Sisters by Carol Henwood

I reached out and touched Andee's arm to get her to stop before she went too far, but she pushed my hand off, and continued.

"You're a cold, sadistic woman who's angry at the world because you never got invited to the prom, so you take your resentments out on others, particularly on girls like us who are alone and scared, and have no one here to take up for us except each other. Why don't you get out of the nursing profession and go into something better suited to your personality, possibly being the witch at Halloween carnivals every year, that's not much of a stretch for you," Andee concluded, breathing hard, red-faced and satisfied.

Nurse Knight stood glued to the floor, her mouth open and her face a sickly grayish color. No one had ever talked to her like that and she wasn't sure what to do.

"Get out of this office this minute young woman, I'll deal with you later," she scowled, not nearly as self-assured as she had been, realizing she may have a crises on her hands.

Andee came over to the bed where I was sitting and we hugged as she set my suitcase down on the floor beside the bed.

"Good luck, Elizabeth, I'll pray for that good-looking hunk Dr. Reynolds to be on call at the hospital tonight. I'll pray for you anyway, you're brave and I know you'll do great. We'll miss you at breakfast, girls," Andee said irreverently as she quickly hugged Divine and Sarabeth. She wished them luck, and left before her tough exterior gave way to the tears she held back, and the sadness she refused to show, as her three best friends were coming to the end of this odyssey they all had shared together, but a journey they now had to make on their own.

The cab driver did a double take as he saw two white, and one black, very pregnant teenage girls waddle out and squeeze into the back of his beat up old taxi cab. Nurse Knight instructed him to take us to Crawford Long Hospital and to go as fast as he could without getting stopped for speeding. Amidst occasional groans, moans and tears, we all managed to compare notes and talk a little on the way. We were sitting on towels, just in case somebody's water broke in the cab. I was fearful that it would be mine as I had very little time between contractions now.

182

Our Erring Sisters by Carol Henwood

"Don't hold your breath, Elizabeth, you're supposed to try and breathe through contractions, at least that's what my book about pregnancy says," Sarabeth told me as she held my hand every time I braced myself for the pain.

"Shouldn't we have had a class on childbirth or something, to get prepared for this?" I asked relieved after the last wave passed.

"You'd think so, but who am I to questions the logic of the Board, I guess they think making bowls and ceramic birds and things are more helpful, no offense, Sarabeth," Divine said.

"None taken, Divine. Pottery is something we can do with our hands to keep us busy and our minds diverted for an hour or so. Working with your hands is very therapeutic."

The black cab driver was nervously driving south on a practically deserted Peachtree Road, telling Nurse Knight she'd have to explain to the police what the emergency was if he was stopped for speeding. She was as rude and condescending to the cabbie as she was to us, telling him to be quiet and drive. We kept chatting about anything that popped into our heads, no matter how silly it was, just to keep our minds off the present situation. Our halting conversation took place between each other's contractions, which happened in sequence, me, Divine then Sarabeth.

We were in the downtown area in fifteen minutes, turning into the emergency entrance of the hospital on two wheels, and the cabbie slamming on the brakes so fast we were jostled all over the back seat. In spite of everything, we burst out laughing, feeling like we were in a slapstick comedy, waiting for the keystone cops to arrive.

Nurse Knight jumped out of the cab and hurried into the hospital, warning us to stay put, she was going in to expedite the admitting process. The cabbie, whose name we found out was Horace, opened our doors, and helped each one of us out of the cab as if we were arriving at a fancy ball. He was flustered and didn't know exactly what to do, so he told us to hold on while he went inside and came out with three wheelchairs and two nurses. We each sat down and were wheeled inside the emergency room where we were parked together against a far wall. We could see Nurse

Our Erring Sisters by Carol Henwood

Knight at the desk doing her best to intimidate the young admitting nurse, but to no avail. Horace stayed right beside us for fifteen minutes, telling us about his six children, all of them born at home except the youngest. Divine and I needed to be checked by a doctor real soon, and more importantly, have some kind of pain medicine. Sarabeth's labor pains had all but stopped, and she was worried the doctors would send her back to the home.

Finally Nurse Knight came over accompanied by two nurses who asked us for our names, and placed plastic bracelets on our arms, making sure our names and bracelets matched.

"Hello, ladies. I'm Nurse Ali Evans and this is Nurse Sophie Reese, and we're going to get you upstairs, checked out to see where you are in the process, and do what we can to make you as comfortable as possible," Nurse Evans said, which was music to my ears.

Nurse Knight marched over and positioned herself between the three of us and the two nurses, and began dictating to us how to act, what to do, and not to do while in the hospital. Nurse Reese suddenly turned to her and abruptly said, "We'll take over from here, these girls are in Crawford Long's care now. Good night," and with that, the elevator door opened and we were wheeled inside and away from the uncaring, glaring eyes of Nurse Knight. Before the door closed, we saw the kind, weathered face of Horace, our knight in shabby armor, who safely delivered us to the hospital in his broken down chariot, blowing kisses to us and mouthing the words "God speed."

The elevator door opened again, this time to reveal a beehive of activity on the maternity ward. Nurse and doctors, scurrying up and down the hallways, orderlies navigating gurneys carrying pre-and post-delivery women through the throng of bustling people, and finally, newborn babies bundled and wrapped in pink and blue blankets, looking like tiny, little sausages being lovingly moved to the nursery; this was organized chaos at its best. Divine, Sarabeth and I didn't even a chance to wish each other well, as we were whisked off to separate examining rooms. My pains were about three minutes apart now, and I wasn't sure if I could keep my composure any longer. I didn't want to scream, cry and carry on, the way I had always heard women did during childbirth, but I understood why they did now.

One of the nurses gave me a pelvic exam then quickly left the room. As one nurse was getting me hooked up to a baby monitor on one side, another nurse started an IV on my other arm. The door opened and Dr. Rhett Reynolds appeared with a kind, but concerned look on his handsome face, and I wanted to jump off the table and hug him.

"Dr. Reynolds, boy, am I glad to see you," I said through gritted teeth.

"I'm glad to see you too, Elizabeth, I just wish you had gotten here sooner. Nurse Evans tells me you're very close to delivering this baby. When did your labor start?"

"Late yesterday afternoon, I knew things had changed from earlier in the day. It wasn't too bad, so I waited until tonight to go to the nurse, and she gave me a sleeping pill and told me if I was in real labor I wouldn't be able to sleep, so here I am."

Looking as if he couldn't believe what he was hearing, Dr. Reynolds asked, "Did she give you an examination to see if you had dilated?"

"No, she said it wasn't necessary, just to come back if I couldn't sleep."

Dr. Reynold's look of disbelief turned to one of utter outrage. Aware that I was watching him, he smiled.

"Well, you're here now and that's the good news. The bad news is you should have been here much sooner, but I'll talk to the Board at the Parrish home at our next meeting, and insist on an evaluation of their nursing staff. Sounds like it's time for changes there."

"I'm going to examine you myself now, Elizabeth, and I apologize because I know Nurse Evans just did, but I need to see for myself where the baby is and how dilated your cervix is. I'll be as gentle as possible," he assured me, and he was.

Our Erring Sisters by Carol Henwood

Just as he was preparing to do the exam, I felt something warm and wet between my legs and anxiously cried out to him, "Something's happening to me, I think I'm bleeding,"

Dr. Reynolds quickly swung back around on his examining stool, and said everything was fine, that my water had finally broken and things would start happening rapidly now. I didn't know whether to laugh or cry.

He buzzed for a nurse to come back in and change my wet sheets and to call for an anesthesiologist to come and administer a drug to put me to sleep.

"I want you to relax, Elizabeth. You're not going to have to endure this any longer. You're going to take a nice, dreamy nap and when you wake up, it all will be over," Dr. Reynolds said to me as he held my hand and brushed damp strands of hair off my forehead.

There was a knock at the door and Dr. Reynolds introduced me to Dr. Sunkara, the wonderful man who would make the pain go away with his happy medicine.

"The Emmeriah Parrish girls are keeping us busy tonight. I know three of you came in together an hour ago, and now I understand from admitting that another one is on the way. Must be something Miss Mellete's putting in the water at the home," Dr. Sankara joked, trying to put me at ease.

He started another IV in my arm and told me to start counting backwards, slowly. "I don't know if I can do that, math is my worst subject in school," I said nervously, trying to make a joke of my own.

"Dr. Reynolds, all of the girls want to know if you're married, and if your eyelashes are real?" I asked, slurring my words, feeling queasy and lightheaded, but oh, so nice. Before he could answer, I was out cold, the image of his tender, compassionate face smiling down at me, holding my hand as I drifted off, feeling safe and pain free.

Chapter Twenty-Four

My eyes fluttered, opening and closing, as I tried my best to keep them open. I heard much chatter around me, and I felt hands gently lift and move me from one soft place to another. I finally managed to keep my eyes open long enough to see images of very busy people dressed in blue or green with stethoscopes hanging around their necks, and I wondered who was sick. Then I remembered and tried to sit up, only to realize it hurt to move and I was still heavily sedated.

"When will I have my baby?" I asked someone who was trying to put something underneath me on the bed.

"Good morning, Elizabeth. You are in the recovery room, sweetheart, and you have already delivered a beautiful baby boy. Everything went well, and you and the baby are doing just fine. You should lie still and try and sleep, and when you wake up, I bet you're going to be very hungry, so we will have the cafeteria send a tray up to you. How does that sound?"

I couldn't process everything the nurse had just told me, my mind was working at half speed. "I've had the baby? When?" I asked urgently.

"Early this morning at 2:05 a.m., August, 29th. You will stay here for an hour or so, and then we will move you to the ward to be with the other girls from Emmeriah Parrish."

I threw the sheets back and looked down at my stomach, which was no longer the size of two large watermelons, but was relatively flat and squishy, as I felt it for myself with both hands. I continued to examine my stomach, not sure I believed the nurse.

"So, it was a boy?" I asked as if I was inquiring about someone else other than me.

Our Erring Sisters by Carol Henwood

"Yes, he is a healthy baby boy. Someone from the nursery will come around when you are more alert and fill you in on the details, dear. Right now, you need to rest; you've worked very hard and had a busy night. Take advantage of this time and sleep now," the nurse said as she patted my hand. I took her advice, closed my eyes and allowed a soft sleep to carry me away.

I opened my eyes to find myself in a large room with five other beds, two of them occupied.

I was awake, but still feeling drowsy from the lingering affects of sedation. I looked around and saw Bonnie at the far end of the room, staring out of the window, and Divine was two beds down from me, snoring loudly. I needed to get up and go to the bathroom, my bladder was full and it was painful. I sat up and attempted to swing my legs over the side of the bed and get down. I stood up and realized how weak and unsteady I was. I tried to take a step toward the bathroom, but didn't have anything to hold on to, and I knew I couldn't make it by myself. I was very sore, in addition to being weak, so I scooted backwards and sat back down on the side of the bed.

"Ouch," I yelled as I sat down a little too hard.

Bonnie turned to see me sitting up and smiled. "Elizabeth, I'm been waiting for you to wake up. I heard you came in last night and delivered real early this morning. Little sore, huh? It takes a few days and a lot of sitz baths, but it will get better."

"A little sore is an understatement; I've really got to pee, but I don't think I can walk by myself."

Bonnie pushed back the sheet and easily got out of bed and walked over to me. "I can help you to the bathroom, I can get around pretty good now, and the nurses don't always come right away when you ring them."

"How are you doing, Bonnie?" I asked as she put her arm around my waist and helped me shuffle to the bathroom.

"Okay, I guess. This is my last day here, I leave in the morning to go back to the home for a couple of days, and then back to my real home," she said without a hint of enthusiasm.

Our Erring Sisters by Carol Henwood

Once I had taken care of my bathroom needs, Bonnie helped me get back in my bed, as the short trip had exhausted me. She sat on my bed and we talked about how quickly things had happened. A few days ago we were all lying in the sun in the back yard of Emmeriah Parrish, laughing, listening to music, and pretending to be average teenage girls, without a care in the world; that seemed like a life time ago. Fast forward a few days - here we are in the maternity ward of a hospital, having gone through labor, had our babies delivered and have only each other as visitors. We were isolated from the other mothers, those who had husbands and family members to share in the joy of their new arrivals. We were not able to share the joy of giving birth, or the anticipation of welcoming the new baby into our family, since these babies would bring joy and happiness to someone else's family.

Hesitantly, I asked Bonnie the question I had been pondering in my mind for the last week or so. "Bonnie, did you decide to see your baby? I know they tell us not to do it because it will be harder for us to give them up, but I haven't made my mind up yet. I just would like to see what's been causing the ruckus inside me for the last nine months. I know I probably shouldn't, but just one peek couldn't hurt, could it?"

"Could it hurt?" Yes, it hurts, but I've seen Beau, that's what I named him, and I feed him his bottles every feeding, too; I made that decision a long time ago. Once I leave here in the morning, I know that's the last time I'll see him, at least for a very long time. I can't tell you what to do, Elizabeth, but I think it would be harder not to see the baby you nourished and grew to love for nine months, at least it was for me. Neither choice is an easy one."

Just then a nurse came into the room and over to my bed. "It's time for your first sitz bath, Miss Elizabeth. Bonnie, go on back to your bed, your baby should be coming in for a feeding in a few minutes." Bonnie hugged me and whispered, "We'll talk later on," and she went back to her bed.

The nurse showed me how to take the hot sitz bath which would ease the pain from the episiotomy and stitches after the delivery. No wonder I was so sore! After soaking in the hot water

Our Erring Sisters by Carol Henwood

for fifteen minutes, the nurse gave me a pain pill, and I was helped back to my bed where a breakfast tray awaited. I ate voraciously and slept on and off for most of the day. When I woke up, it was after three o'clock in the afternoon, and I saw Divine sitting up in bed, eating, and Sarabeth asleep in the bed across from me.

I felt more rested and alert now, and it occurred to me that maybe I should call my parents. I thought Miss Mellete had probably called them already, but I wanted to talk to Mama myself, and let her know it was over and I was okay. I knew she would tell me not to see the baby, but I hadn't made my mind up about that yet, so I decided to wait for a few more hours to call.

I heard Divine's voice and realized she was talking to me. "Elizabeth, how are you doing, girl? You must have delivered that baby in a hurry once we got here. I had a big, fat, baby girl around 10:00 this morning and Sarabeth had to have a C-Section cause they found out the baby was in some kind of distress or something. So, she's really gonna be in a world of hurt for a while. I think she had a boy and he was okay, just a little small. How about you, what did you have?" she asked tenderly.

I thought to myself, we're talking about the gender of our babies as if we were discussing what color shoes we just bought. I guess detachment was the only way to deal with it right now. I hadn't figured it all out yet.

"I had a boy. I don't know anything about him yet, someone from the nursery is supposed to come see me today. I hope I haven't missed her while I was sleeping. I haven't decided if I'm going to see him yet or not. Are you going to see yours?" I asked eagerly.

"Yeah, I think so, might as well since we put all that work into getting 'um here, why not see what it was all for."

Just then a pleasant looking young woman wearing white pants and a print top featuring pink and blue baby shoes came into the room. "Good, you're both awake. I'm Angel Duncan from the nursery and I want to chat with both of you individually. Elizabeth, since you delivered first, I'll start with you before Divine." Angel lived up to her name, she had a sweet, nurturing nature and the face

Our Erring Sisters by Carol Henwood

of a cherub, blond, curly hair and a rosebud mouth, all she lacked was wings. I sat up as well as I could in my bed and was all ears.

"Okay then, Elizabeth. You delivered a healthy baby boy at 2:05 a.m. this morning, weighing six pounds, four ounces, and twenty inches long. He has been eating well since his arrival and all systems seem to be functioning normally. Now, are you planning on seeing the baby, and feeding him his bottles while you are in the hospital?" she asked gently.

The moment of truth had arrived for me. I didn't know what to say, so I asked Angel if I could think about it a little longer and tell her in the morning.

"Of course you can. It is entirely up to you. Some of the girls don't see their babies at all, some maybe once or twice, and some see them several times a day. Whatever you think is best for you. Just let the nurse that comes in tomorrow morning know what you have decided, there is no pressure." I was relieved I hadn't made a rash decision, but putting it off still didn't make it any easier.

I watched as Bonnie's baby boy was brought in and she fed him his bottle. Divine and I went over briefly to see him, but we didn't want to intrude on the precious time she had left with him.

I napped on and off until supper, then watched some television and was interrupted constantly by the nurses coming into take vital signs and check for excessive bleeding. I was offered a sleeping pill and a pain pill, accepted both and waited to fall into the arms of Morpheus where I could enjoy a deep sleep with no dreams. I was awakened to the sound of muffled cries somewhere in the room. I struggled to open my eyes as the soft whimpering continued. I discovered where the heartbreaking sobs were coming from; it was Bonnie. This was the morning she would be leaving the hospital alone, without her baby and the reality of the situation had settled in. I turned over, away from Bonnie, and put the pillow over my head. There was nothing I could do or say to help numb her pain. No one could.

The second day in the hospital was much the same as the first, in and out of sleep, the result of the heavy sedation during the delivery and the pain pills I was taking, not only for physical

Our Erring Sisters by Carol Henwood

discomfort, but emotional distress as well, but nothing could dull the heartache.

Divine's baby girl was brought in to her and she was a roly-poly bundle with a head full of black curly hair. While Divine and Bonnie were occupied and Sarabeth was still asleep, I decided to call my parents and was about to the dial the number when the telephone rang. It startled me and I must have jumped a foot, I wasn't expecting anyone to call me.

"Hello," I cautiously answered.

"Ella," Mama said and her voice was equally as cautious. "How are you doing, honey?"

"I was fixin' to call you and Daddy, but I assume Miss Mellete must have informed you that I went into labor and had the baby, so no surprises here. I'm doing fine, I guess, still sore and not fully awake yet, but other than that, I'm okay."

"Wonderful, that's good news, dear. Daddy and I heard from Miss Mettete early this morning after you had gone into the hospital, and we are so relieved that everything went well for you. I won't bother you with questions now, I just wanted to let you know how very grateful we are, and we cannot wait to get you back home with us for a while," Mama said, carefully choosing her words.

I asked a few questions about Tarleton and Emily Anne and other mundane small talk then there was an uncomfortable silence that followed.

"We will talk to Miss Mellete once you are back at the home and settle on the best day for us to come down and pick you up." Mama's voice took on a serious tone. "Ella, I hope you haven't seen the baby, because I do not think it would be advisable for you to do that."

"No, Mama, I haven't, but I also haven't come to a decision yet."

I did not have the will or strength to listen to my mother tell me all the reasons I shouldn't see my own child, I knew the reasons, but it was still my decision, right or wrong. I immediately changed subjects.

"I've got to hang up now, it's time for my sitz bath," I lied.

Our Erring Sisters by Carol Henwood

"Your what?"

"Sitz bath. I basically sit in a bowl of warm water for about fifteen minutes; it helps with the soreness and keeps the stitches clean." Embarrassed by the subject matter, Mama stammered momentarily. "Well, then you should go and take care of that, and Ella, please consider what I said. Your father and I are so happy this sad episode is coming to an end, and now you can get on with your life once again. We love you and will see you in a few days." We said good-bye and hung up.

After the conversation I thought I would get up and try and walk down to the nursery for a peek. I was still not walking very well, but the exercise might do me some good. I informed Divine I was venturing out on my own.

"You take it easy, girl, you're walking like some old lady," she said with a laugh.

"Pleeze, I could run circles around you right now," I said with false bravado as I started out.

I walked out of the door and followed the signs pointing to the nursery, shuffling along at a snail's pace. I moved closer to the wall and sort of slid along it as I trudged forward. I stopped and rested, not believing how weak I still was. When I saw how much further I had to go, I decided I'd better turn around.

"Elizabeth, do you need some help?"

Hearing a warm, familiar voice, I looked up and saw Dr. Reynolds coming my way. He was beside me quickly and took hold of my arm.

"Wherever it is you're heading, I don't think you're going to make it alone. I was on my way to see you right now. Would you like to go back to your room and try again later?" he asked with a smile.

"Yes, I think I'd better. I was on my way to the nursery, but I think I'll postpone the trip."

Dr. Reynolds put one of his arms around my waist and his other hand cupped my elbow as he guided me back down the hall to my bed. After I was off my feet and back in bed, I felt like I had run a marathon.

Our Erring Sisters by Carol Henwood

"I can't seem to completely wake up and I'm as a weak as a kitten. I'm sure I looked like an old lady dragging myself down the hall," I said with embarrassment.

He was standing at the foot of my bed reading my chart, and when he was finished he put it down and came around and stood next to me. "You were heavily sedated for the birth, in addition to the fact that you were walking around in active labor for most of Monday. Childbirth is a lot of work, and you will feel tired for a while yet. Are you in any pain, now?"

"No, it's better today, and I'm sure I'm no worse off than anyone else in here."

"Everyone's body reacts differently to sedation, and it just may take you a little longer to bounce back. Other than that, how are you doing?"

"I guess the good news is I survived," I joked. "I've been struggling with whether or not to see the baby. I had decided at first that I wouldn't, but now that I've had him, and he's right down the hall, I'm tempted. I know we are encouraged not to see them, it's easier if we don't, but I just don't know what …"

Sitting down on the bed next to me Dr. Reynolds took my hand in his. "Don't let the decision as to whether or not you see your baby take the focus off of you getting stronger and looking after yourself. When you leave Emmeriah Parrish, get back into the game, go out and enjoy yourself while you're young, have fun, and don't let this affect the rest of your life; your life is just beginning. You have made a good and honorable choice to give your baby up for adoption. Take joy and pride in your decision; let the rest of it go, Elizabeth," Dr. Reynolds said with as much love and concern as an old and trusted friend.

"Ella," I said, "that's my real name. Ella Louise Cane."

"Well, Ella Louise Cane, I've enjoyed our brief, but intimate friendship," he added with a wink and a smile, "and I wish the best of everything for you. I won't be back tomorrow for rounds, so that's why I came by today to see you. So, in the future, if you are in Atlanta and need to talk, give me a call and we can chat." Dr.

Our Erring Sisters by Carol Henwood

Reynolds leaned forward and very gently gave me a hug, and I hugged him back.

"Thank you for everything, and when I move to Atlanta in the next month or two, I may take you up on that offer," I said as my voice broke.

"I'll count on it. So long Ella Cane," and with that Dr. Reynolds left.

Nurse Robbins came in the door as Dr. Reynolds was leaving. They exchanged a few words and then she clapped her hands and squealed with joy.

"Look at my girls, all slim and gorgeous," she exclaimed as she came over and hugged and kissed each one of us.

"You girls caused Nurse Knight a passel of trouble the other night," she giggled.

"Good," we all three said in unison.

"I hope she gets her ugly ass fired and gets a job in a carnival, as if they'd hire somebody that mean and ugly," Divine said.

"I don't know nothing 'bout no carnival, but I do know Emmeriah Parrish Home won't be requiring her services any longer," Nurse Robbins said with her black face gleaming.

"She got fired?" I shrieked, almost jumping out of my bed.

"She sure did. The Board told her she was unfit to perform her duties and she needed to look for employment somewhere else."

"Well, there is justice in the world, after all," I stated with satisfaction.

"She had no business being in the nursing profession in the first place," Sarabeth said half awake. "You could tell she had no compassion for others, good riddance to her."

We visited with Nurse Robbins as she helped Bonnie gather her belongings as she was being discharged today. When she had everything together, we hugged Bonnie and said we'd see her back at the home, not knowing if she would even be there when we got back. Bonnie put on a brave face and said she would leave her name and number with Miss Mellete and that we should stay in touch; we said we would.

Our Erring Sisters by Carol Henwood

It was 9:00 p.m. and the night nurse came in to dole out meds. I had made my decision about whether or not to see my baby, and I asked the nurse if she would let the nursery know that I wanted to see him in the morning before I was discharged. She assured me she would take care of it. I took my pills and fell asleep, at peace with my decision.

Chapter Twenty-Five

I was awakened by the usual hospital sounds of gurneys, food carts and medical machines being pushed up and down the hallway, as well as nurses, doctors and cleaning people going in and out of rooms. I looked at the clock and saw it was a little before 7:00 a.m., and I was the only one awake yet. I sat up and discovered that I felt much better this morning, not as lethargic and sore. I got out of bed and walked to the bathroom with little difficulty, and decided to take a shower and get myself ready to meet my son. I knew that he would not remember having met me at three days old, but I still felt it was important to look my best. Ridiculous as it was, I wanted to look as pretty as I could when I held him for the first and last time.

The shower re-invigorated me, and after shampooing my hair and shaving my legs and underarms, I felt like a new woman. Since I didn't have any curlers, or a hair dryer, I simply would have to towel dry my hair and let it dry without styling, but at least it would be clean. Using foundation, blush, mascara and lipstick that I had packed, I looked in the bathroom mirror and was satisfied with the result, and I thought my baby boy would approve of his Mama.

After I had finished with my primping, I put on the pair of pants and blouse I had packed to wear back to the home from the hospital. The slacks were maternity pants, since I knew I wouldn't fit into anything else for a while, the blouse was one of my favorite pre-pregnancy blouses, and it fit pretty well. I packed my few belongings for the trip back to the home later on today, and after all of the activity, I was getting tired. I sat down on the bed, fully dressed and waited for my important visitor to arrive. I dozed off momentarily and was awakened by two nurses rolling three bassinets into the room. After making sure the baby's name and the mothers'

Our Erring Sisters by Carol Henwood

names matched, one of the nurses delicately handed Sarabeth her son, and then she reached down in the next bassinet and picked up another bundle wrapped in a blue blanket and blue knit cap on his head. She smiled at me and said, "Miss Nash, here you are."

She carefully placed the precious parcel in my unsure arms. "Just relax, you won't hurt him. He's already had his bottle, we weren't sure if you wanted to feed him or not, but he can stay with you for at least thirty minutes, then I'll come back for him. Are you okay?"

"Yes, yes, I'm fine," I answered quickly wanting the nurse to leave so we could begin our short visit. I stared at him in awe. His eyes were open, staring back, and I wondered if he knew I was his mother. I had heard an infant knows his own mother from others – who knows? I held him tightly in my arms at first, taking in every feature of his face. His skin was a nice, healthy color, completely unblemished and smooth, and his eyes were a dark blue, but I knew all babies' eyes are blue when born. I removed his little hat to find a shock of fine, black hair, and I laughed out loud. I was both exhilarated and enchanted to know that I had given life to this flawless little person. I unfolded the soft, blue blanket he was encased in, and his delicate arms and legs popped up and began moving around, happy to be free. I examined each hand, all ten fingers and toes, his front, his back and his miniature penis, just to make sure everything looked as it should. It did. Once I was satisfied he was perfect, I wrapped him back up and nestled him in my arms again. I rocked him gently and began talking quietly to him, and he cooed back as if he understood every word I said. I looked at him closely and tried to memorize every feature, and commit it to my permanent memory bank. I had an overwhelming sense of peace holding him in my arms, a contentment in knowing that my decision was the right one, even though my love for him was already filling my heart. I wanted to take him home with me, but my choice was to surrender him. This perfect little person should have every opportunity to be with a family who could love him and give him everything that I couldn't, a man and woman who were not able to have children of their own, and had been waiting

Our Erring Sisters by Carol Henwood

for him. As much as I wanted to be angry at my parents, I accepted the fact that they were right. I was happy that I had decided to see the baby Lucas and I had made, and I was beginning to take pride and joy in my decision, as Dr. Reynolds suggested I should; there was no other way. I relished every remaining second we had together, and I think he did too, as he never once closed his eyes, but watched me as I observed him. Maybe he was aware this was our only time together, and he wanted to remember me, too. I softly kissed his forehead and held him on my shoulder, inhaling the intoxicating scent that only babies have, that clean, pure smell of innocence. When the nurse came back into the room for him, I kissed him on both cheeks and told him I would always love him, and maybe one day we could meet again. I reluctantly handed my son back to the nurse and pushed the overwhelming sadness and anguish of the moment down deep in my soul where it would remain for thirty-seven years.

I left the Emmeriah Parrish Home with mixed emotions, happy to be leaving and going back home as myself, Ella Cane, but sad that I was leaving behind the girls I had become so close to and bonded with in this surreal and unimaginable situation. I would never forget them, whether or not we ever talked, or saw each other again, their faces and stories would remain with me forever. We shared a unique experience, one that played a large part in shaping who we would become, but from our pain sprang new life, and therefore hope. The phantom girls would wait patiently for the light of day and a new openness to emerge where understanding and forgiveness would be asked for, and gladly given.

The End

Epilogue

It was the Monday before Thanksgiving and being the organized woman that I am, I want to have everything done ahead of time so I can enjoy the day along with everyone else. I arrived at the crowded grocery store, found a parking space that required some walking, made sure I had my extensive list in hand, and opened the car door to be met by a brisk wind. The grocery store wasn't as crazy as I had expected it might be. I have been in the midst of bumper to bumper shopping cart jams on previous holidays, but everyone was good natured and seemed to enjoy the hustle and bustle of it all. Going up and down the aisle in a leisurely but purposeful manner, I managed to stay focused and was having success in finding everything I had on my list, and more. The turkey was the last thing to buy and I headed in the direction of the large freezer which was overflowing with frozen turkeys of all sizes. It was there, while contemplating which bird would be coming home with me, that I received a call on my cell phone that would force me to acknowledge my past and face an uncertain future.

The call was a surprise, although I had expected it would come someday. After all, I had put the wheels in motion that precipitated the call, but had not considered the impact it would have on me upon answering the call and hearing the words, "I have found your son and he would like to meet you."

Standing there as frozen as the turkeys I had just been inspecting, I was unable to gather my thoughts and respond to the lady on the other end of the line.   The soft spoken, soothing voice of Marnie St. John from the Reunion Connection continued.

"He will be faxing his consent form to me shortly and would like to speak to you this afternoon, in about an hour, if at all possible."

200

Our Erring Sisters by Carol Henwood

"One hour?" I asked in an incredulous voice. "I don't know if I can be ready in an hour." All of a sudden the hidden memories from almost four decades ago were staring me in the face and demanding attention.

"Take your time and decide what is best for your, Ella," Marnie said in her calm, reassuring voice. "This call does not have to happen today, or at all; you've waited almost forty years so a day or two shouldn't make any difference. If you want to go forward with it today, let me know and I will give you your son's name and number. He sounds like a nice young man."

A flood of questions came pouring out of my mouth. "Where does he live, is he married, does he have children?"

"I'm sorry, Ella, but I cannot answer any of those questions until I receive his consent form. That will give you some time to decide on your next move. Go ahead and finish your shopping and get back to me when you are ready. Take care and enjoy your Thanksgiving, if I don't hear from you before then."

I was now impatient to get out of the grocery store, go home and get in touch with my husband Stuart, to tell him of the call. I quickly chose a turkey without the usual scrutiny, found a check-out line with only one person ahead of me, paid for the groceries and was on the way home, my head spinning.

Stuart had been supportive of my search, albeit a bit skeptical. He has always been supportive of me in any endeavor I have undertaken, and tries to guide me around hazardous obstacles. Most of the time I listen and follow his level headed, no nonsense advice, but not always; learning the hard way seems to be my way. Stuart is a decent and moral man, one who lives a principled life, and I know I am blessed to have had him in my life, lo these many years. I believe God put Stuart in my life to help me maneuver through the many mine fields I have wandered into, and barely escaped, avoiding complete destruction. He is a forgiving man, and I believe I am his burden to bear. He is a prince among men and I love him very much.

Confronting my past and newly found child would mean resurrecting the memory of another teenage girl, the one I became

Our Erring Sisters by Carol Henwood

for my confinement in the Emmeriah Parrish Home for Unwed Mothers. One Elizabeth Nash, the other me, the girl I became for a brief time, who gave birth, surrendered her child and quietly vanished. The ephemeral life I had lived as a sort of phantom girl could finally be put to rest and the possibility of meeting the child I had relinquished all those years ago was a reason for Thanksgiving.

Carol Henwood is a native Southerner born and raised in the north Georgia town of Rome. Having been brought up in the innocence of the 1950's and the turbulence of the 1960's, the subjects she writes about are drawn from her experiences and observations growing up in the changing South. She hopes her stories will make you laugh out loud, bring a tear to your eye, and even make you look for her next book.

CPSIA information can be obtained at www.ICGtesting.com
Printed in the USA
LVOW08s1031131214

418676LV00006B/877/P